Knife Party at the Hotel Europa

Also by Mark Anthony Jarman

Fiction
My White Planet
19 Knives
New Orleans Is Sinking
Salvage King, Ya!
Dancing Nightly in the Tavern

Poetry
Killing the Swan

Non-Fiction
Ireland's Eye: Travels

KNIFE PARTY

at the

HOTEL EUROPA

Mark Anthony Jarman

GOOSE LANE

Edited by Bethany Gibson.
Endpaper map: Matthus Merian, *Roma*, 1641
(Wikimedia Commons, Geographicus Fine Antique Maps).
Cover design and page design by Chris Tompkins.
Cover Illustration by Chris Tompkins.
Printed in Canada.
10 9 8 7 6 5 4 3 2 1

Library and Archives Canada Cataloguing in Publication

Jarman, Mark Anthony, 1955-, author
Knife party at the Hotel Europa / Mark Anthony Jarman.
Short stories.

Issued in print and electronic formats.
ISBN 978-0-86492-918-1 (bound). — ISBN 978-0-86492-740-8 (epub).
— ISBN 978-0-86492-830-6 (mobi)
I. Title.

PS8569.A6K66 2015   C813'.54   C2014-906847-6
C2014-906848-4

Goose Lane Editions acknowledges the generous support of the Canada Council for
the Arts, the Government of Canada through the Canada Book Fund (CBF), and the
Government of New Brunswick through the Department of Tourism, Heritage and Culture.

Goose Lane Editions
500 Beaverbrook Court, Suite 330
Fredericton, New Brunswick
CANADA E3B 5X4
www.gooselane.com

Contents

The Dark
Brain of Prayer

A fellow of mediocre talent will remain a mediocrity, whether he travels or not; but one of superior talent (which without impiety I cannot deny that I possess) will go to seed if he always remains in the same place.

—Wolfgang Amadeus Mozart

A slender hoop with seven charms hangs from a brass nail in my hotel room; Natasha the slender Russian librarian brought me these charms from Mexico, where she stayed at a cancer clinic, hoping to find a homeopathic alternative to surgery, hoping for a miracle inside her body, inside her uterus. How much did that trip cost her in American dollars and the quack clinic did nothing, despite her hopes, despite her prayers, despite her many charms.

"I know you will scoff," Natasha said, hesitating to tell me she was going to a costly Mexican clinic. And she was right, at least about my judgmental side. I did scoff, just as she feared. Natasha knew me too well.

•

Seven tiny figures of tin: a goat, an arm, a leg, a tooth, a foot, a fish, and a veined heart with a dagger stuck through it. *Milagritos*, they are called, little miracles. At a shrine you pin them to a statue of a saint or the Virgin, one of the many Mexican Virgins, and pray for help. Our Lady of Perpetual Help, Our Lady for those who have no one with, Our Lady for those who want whiter teeth, Our Lady for those who went straight to video.

For years Natasha was my shrine. Her many, many charms. She always meant well.

In Rome a woman sips her drink and says of my weightless metal charms, "Yes, we are adept at mixing the pagan with the Catholic." She lives in San Miguel de Allende and is touring Italy with Father Silas's art group. My elderly aunt has known Father Silas for decades; they chat and walk by the river.

By the river in Canada my wife asked, "Why didn't you tell me Natasha had cancer? That changes things," she said. "Something like that transcends petty differences."

Well, I thought you hated talk of cancer and hated her. And how to casually start that sentence, that information?

Everyone around me seems to have cancer; I'm a new age Typhoid Mary, wandering Canada's incoherent weather and at my neck a tasteful bell warning others of my danger.

In Rome's anvil weather I worried about her cancer and my future cancer and wore a damp white T-shirt, wet the shirt under a tap and walked into Rome's heat, and sometimes a T-shirt over my head to protect my burnt scalp; I looked Arab, Moorish, I was turning Turk. If under Pompeii's wild sun I did not receive a catalyst toward skin cancer, then I will never kindle its benediction, its retaliation, its charm, its curse.

In Rome an older Roma woman cursed me when twice I refused to give her money. Deep crow's feet at her kohl eyes, or as they say here, *zampe di gallina*, hen's feet. The woman guarded a set of steps leading from a broad piazza up to a park. Everyone was necking in the park. I went up the steps and said no to the woman and I came down the steps and I said no to her again. When I said no the second time the woman aimed a bony finger, made her most impressive evil eye and uttered in a horrible voice, "Today, you die!"

Her scary evil-eye curse might have been more impressive if it came true (I didn't die) or if she was a teensy bit more specific, e.g., *Today you will pay too many euros for a shiny Hohner chromatic harmonica! And your beloved will dump you and you will rake leaves in stunned sadness, in furious cursing disbelief.*

My picture was in the newspaper in Canada and Natasha saw the photo. I had invented a combination bicycle and lawn mower, a bright orange frame with neat welds on the forks. Look at those welds, almost invisible! I was by the river in bare feet for one photo.

"It was odd," Natasha said. "Your feet were so *familiar*. I hadn't realized how well I knew them." Her words pleased me. To hold her foot again, to be at the foot of God, our *secret* gods.

I remember her feet in the river shallows that hot humid day, how many years ago now. They slip past. Natasha was running on the north side past the shuttered mill, and by the sandbars and green rushes she stripped and dipped her beautiful secret body in the river to cool down her bare skin. Men in trucks stared and uttered quiet remarks to each other.

•

Natasha emailed when things were good, when we were still possible. *Miss you and can't wait to see you! xoxo. PS I'm going to a baseball game tonight with Jack & Jill.*

These three are such good friends. And they are *my* friends too. It's good to see everyone take such good care of each other, friends smiling at the sunny ball game. But Jack and Jill fall down the hill, Jill decides to leave poor Jack, Jill moves away to a far city, and then the tearful Jack takes up with my Intended and I am out in the cold. Turn right at the desert, teeth gnashing, and keep going for forty days and forty nights.

Then in that desert I heard Cat Power singing about Major Tom drifting out in space, *Tom's a-cold* in a spooky car ad with Cat Power. Amazing, I must tell Natasha! No. I forgot. That I'm not speaking to Natasha *ever*.

But who else to tell? I have to confess to someone. The bomb doors wish to open; it is their nature to want to be used.

In Italy I went to see the bombed ruins of Monte Cassino, where my uncle fought SS paratroopers in the valley below the blasted abbey. Dropping the bombs did not help matters, the heaped rubble from the bombs made the fight more difficult.

My aunt lives by the Spanish Steps. She has arranged that I join Father Silas's art group while I'm here. With Father Silas we walk crowded stone lanes, Father Silas limping slightly and using a cane as he shows me the sights.

My aunt says, "It's all changed, I'm afraid of the gypsies, I'm afraid to ride the bus. They let in anyone, Albanians, Bulgarians, Romanians, welcome, welcome! We'll pay your medical bills." Father Silas looks bemused.

My aunt says, "Do they think Italy is a landing strip? Any

trash can float here, anyone can cross the border. The crime!" She turns to me. "Do you have this much crime where you live?"

Before I can answer, my aunt holds her hand as if she has a knife, stabs at Father Silas's torso and warns me, "They will kill you for ten euro." My aunt looks tense, as if expecting a physical blow.

"I think we're supposed to call them Roma now," says Father Silas. "Madonna said so."

"Roma, ha. To me they are gypsies. You know what Hitler did to the gypsies. Well." She leaves the thought unfinished.

Gypsies in Italy are accused of being professional pickpockets, unrepentant thieves, false cripples, confidence artists. Italians don't like gypsies in their country, but Italians don't like me either, they are tired of me and all the other sunburnt tourists, tired of drunken frat boys and fedora hipsters descending on Rome in cheap flights, the Italians are weary of everyone.

Father Silas is kind to show me around the city he loves, but he has a bad knee or hip and at times has to give me directions and wait on a bench; he waits for me to come back and tell him what I saw; he details a serpentine route in the walls so I will be surprised by the view of each startling piazza. He loves Rome but can't see it freely; I have a bad knee from skiing and this is one of my fears, to no longer walk.

You're not supposed to use the term *gypsies* (which comes originally from the word *Egyptian*), but in a city called Roma can you call them Roma? Or Romani? Or Bohemians? My aunt says the Italians call them *zingari*.

In Ireland there are wanderers once known as tinkers, with horses and caravans, mending tin pots and pans, the equivalent of eastern European gypsies. Irish people seem able to spot travelling folk simply by their look, refusing them service in a public house or hotel, but genetic tests show their genes to be the same as most of the citizenry, they are Irish and not Roma. Father Silas calls them travellers, but my cousin in Dublin calls them knackers. It gets confusing.

One gypsy woman in Rome was more specific in her words to me. She said, "You. There is something you are trying to forget."

I'm trying to forget Natasha inside a Midwest gas station; she was picking up cold milk and I was outside pumping gas into her beat-up car and watching her chat and laugh with the woman at the cash. I loved to watch the way Natasha moves and smiles and listens, yes, I love her so much, I think of her for hours on end and she does not think of me and she does not write or call. She transforms me into a child: *it's not fair!*

Resentment builds with each day of no messages, no word from her. Do you know the venom that can build from a Tuesday to a Sunday? Is that venom for takeout or here? Six days × twenty-four hours = 144 hours of pure venom (Rome wasn't built in a day, ha ha ha). If an Irish traveller dies, they burn his caravan; no other traveller will use a dead man's caravan.

One day in Canada my stalwart fridge dies, howls its last day in the house, compressor *agonistes*. The noisy creature dies, but comes back to life on the day of the new fridge's arranged delivery, the day they will come cart the old one to the knocking yard. The freezer is suddenly solid and roaring, a bon vivant, now the juice tins are frozen hard and our ale and bitter chilled again. Is it a miracle, another *milagrito*? Pilgrims come to my door and bow and pray and pin charms at this new shrine, this fridge by the roadside.

Keep me, the machine begs. Don't let them take me away.

What to do? Like my old cat near the end: do I give it one
more chance to live? Like with Natasha. Do I give up too easily?
No, I think I hang on too long. I want it all. You must make a
decision.

"Does that cat scratch?" the delivery man asks. "Because I
had a kitten that scratched my daughter and I tied it in a bag
and put it under the ice."

Okay, I will keep the old fridge.

I live in hope that someone will make me forget Natasha, forget
that mental intimacy we had, the way she could read my mind,
sitting through a horrible play or a band with winsome steel
guitar, could give me a glance or a tiny conspiratorial smile
and we both *knew*. But who can make me forget? No one, it
seems. Now I hear a song by Howlin' Wolf: old and grey, no
place to go.

Raking these wet black leaves in a yard so far from the white-
hot Roman sun; this can't be the same world. By a river and by
a river. I rake and think too much: why do such fiascos always
happen in late fall so that I face another winter alone, feeling
old and cold, feeling already *dead*.

This black mood passes, I recover my senses, but at that
juncture it seemed logical, correct; at the time I kept thinking
of death, understood its quiet attraction. I thought, Just bury
me quietly like a cat or dog in the corner of the yard under
the skunky leaves, under my butternut tree by the shed with
the ants.

Or wait — maybe a big New Orleans brass band and an
Irish wake.

Write on my tombstone that I can't make up my mind, write
that I am murdered by night-riders, by mumblers and nitpickers,

by fellow travellers and Roman gods, by cold staring statues, by Hermes, by Natasha chatting at a gas station. Write that, like everyone else, I am murdered by love, that I am nibbled to death by ducks, brought low by normal events.

In this state of suburban bathos I wish to see my dead parents again; the dead world courts me, invites me into its haloed bosom, its final mysterious orgasm. It is my choice, up to me: lie down dead inside a cold lonely graveyard or go back and live another summer, running around Rome eating and drinking too much wine. And Rome is so beautiful, so warm, such amazing food — squid ink linguini, fried chickpea fritters, sliced spleen sliders — Rome's raucous life and appetites!

Yet this choice, to snuff myself or not, is not obvious, my mind not right, as Lowell said. I am seized by dread autumn spirits, I myself am hell, said Lowell, said Milton, said Roman and Greek poets before any of us breathed and suckled at wolves and mothers.

I must be nobler, be better than this. I must lift myself, steer my mind free of this base muck. I am not in Stalingrad, not encircled, not about to die. I must simply get through some time and then get through some more time. Though this seems impossible in the middle of the ill season, this dead season: can't I just hibernate like a bear and come out when it's over? Make it go faster.

I'm not always this morose. Have I said how much I loved my rooftop terrace in Rome? I found joy just washing shirts in a sink and hanging them in the hot sun, Italy's fireball sun burning my head, the sun killing me, a fire hanging over a desert. My damp T-shirt's cooling effect didn't last — soak the shirt at every fountain and the cool feeling on my skin lasts a few minutes and then the shirt is dry, water vanished from the shirt.

"Everything is temporary," I said to an Iraqi woman at the market, then she vanished, proving me right.

I must get back to those small thrills. I grow giddy at Roman markets when I find the right food, the right words, find I have exact change. The store a chore for some, but for me it's a minor buzz to hunt and gather in a foreign city.

I love the vast outdoor market arrayed under a shaky tin roof, a roof sheltering slopes of apples, olives, pears, peaches, greens, and heaps of strawberries with a striking Italian woman at the top. She looks like a buxom cinema idol, Gina Lollobrigida posing at the top of the pyramid of peppers and tomatoes and strawberries, but this is not a studio and she is not a salaried movie star and she will grow old and cold toiling one winter at the outdoor market on Via Andrea Doria.

And across from her, that bread with the brown crust — *pane di lariano* — should I buy that? Or ask for the gleaming eggshell loaf?

But they are so impatient, don't ask any questions, hurry, hurry, fumble a few words or just point and pay for your loaf or vino or green bottles of Peroni and Moretti or frothy wheat beer. I am so happy in Italy to just cope, but the Iraqi woman is depressed about the future; she won't go out for a meal.

"I'll never see my mother again," she weeps before she disappears, "I can't go back to Iraq, I can't pay my rent here, no one will hire me, I have no prospects, I am homeless, my life is hopeless."

There are times I feel I have no home, that this is a tough part of my life, but I am aware that I am very lucky compared to this young woman exiled from Iraq by a fool's war. And look at that homeless man who mumbles past me on the street, truly lost while I have a key to a room with towels and a terrace and

Egyptian pearls and seven hundred euro hidden in an envelope under the bed. I bought running shoes for the Iraqi woman, I took her past the buskers and bought her fruit and coffee beans. I think of Joni Mitchell's song about the clarinet player playing for free while she shops for jewels.

Every day a metropolis of jewel-light and gold awaits us — every day candle-flame cafés and tanned faces and blurred dancers and yellow cobblestone lanes below and a celestial alley of blue stars above — and ceiling frescoes where we lift our pious gaze to indoor skies of pale robin's-egg blue behind frothy pink clouds and Ecce Homo, Christ crowned with thorns.

A few from Father Silas's art group meet for drinks on my tiny rooftop terrace and tiny Tamika says with some regret, "I fly back so soon to Philly." A wallflower, Tamika has not made friends here among the drunken college crowd. I saw her in bright white sneakers walking the Coliseum on her own, like my son doing the same in his lonely schoolyard, and for this she has become my hero. On her own she has grown to love Rome, to learn more about Rome than the others in the group.

"Back to reality."

"Give my best to reality," says Ray-Ray. He was born in Nigeria, now lives in a satellite suburb past Pearson airport, but has flown to Rome all the way from China. "I hate reality, man. Are you hungry? You must eat. *That* is reality, my friend." At a modest flame Ray-Ray makes us a quick dish of fish and rice and I am impressed. Initially I had been suspicious of him, a smiling con man with maxed-out credit cards, but this gesture makes me like him.

I will fly home someday, but I've spent my sense of home; by being so serious I've made my life frivolous.

•

Sunday morning sun ripples on the river and healthy joggers stride proudly under trees where, just moments before, drunks staggered in the dark and purged and bellowed like elephants. A strange change of guard, but the exact same turf.

The women take off their business suits or loose dresses and run. Some runners are shy and hide themselves in big sweat-pants; more athletic parties don teensy sport bras and black shorts that cleave to the inside of pelvis and buttocks and make sufficient data available to any interested eyes.

In Indonesia's Aceh province, to promote strict moral val-ues, the police are handing out loose dresses to women and confiscating tight trousers. I will try to be loose, I will try to be tight, I will try to be a saint from now on (riding on the back of saints or pinned under sinners). No more cheating on the rituals, the concert wristbands.

The wrist I need, the world I need, the world I want to love. There is beauty in clouds, a world above, and my beautiful one lives in cloudland. On the plane to Rome I stared at cloudland and thought of her wrist, those blue veins I kiss in the skin, beautiful thing. Moonlight in the bedroom, a delicate vase, her derrière and legs in moonlit strips and sheets beautiful as a pension.

Natasha and I used to joke about cloudland as our secret place, we thought we had made it up, some ideal world where we could have oodles of free time without fear or guilt or hurting someone else, some locale free of complications. Then I learned that the Greeks of old had the same name and idea, my idea was an easy Xerox and cloudland was not ours. On the plane to Italy I stared at cloudland for centuries.

•

Italia; what a word, what a pretty cracked world. Wasn't Christopher Columbus Italian? The day he found America — it was trying to hide, like Natasha's cancer, but he found its shores. Go back, go back to Spain, to Italia, go back to childhood, to cloudhood. Go back to the wind blowing off the sea for centuries down dolomite passes and rivers, fly back to floral meadows and mountain chained to mountain like slaves and Centurions killed in lines in valleys and beaches, buried with murdered martyrs and whores and Popes and pretenders and partisans in the heat and dust of tainted town squares.

My tainted life, my travels: vaguely free to travel to Italy, Ireland, Death Valley, to ski distant peaks on a whim, mobile, but always a trade-off, no stable home life, no one to depend on. Perhaps because no one can depend on me?

My wife sends me a newsy email from home, what was home.

> All the boys are working, Calvin got a haircut for his job, and I bought that house by the church. His hair looks good short, but no one recognizes him. The house is more than I wanted to pay, but I think it will be okay. Nice hardwood. As you say, if I run into problems, I can just sell. I didn't think it would happen this fast. Calvin's hair or a house. Still kind of in shock and not really breathing yet, but by the time you get this, it will probably be better. I deposited that cheque, hope that's okay. I paid $300 for the brakes. I know it's my car now, but you can use it when you're back. The dog is fine, say hi to the green parrots.

My father was happy to stay home; my mother wanted to go out; I seem to have inherited a healthy portion of both tendencies, inherited two masters.

My son is so polite to me on the phone. "Please hold on."

He looks like me, but I feel like a stranger. I have fixed his bike, want him to have a working bike, to be mobile like me. Trying to think of him, be a good father. At school he is flunking math. I was terrible at math. How can I help?

He says, "No, I have no need for a bike."

"Want to go skiing with me next time? I hear there's a great mountain in Newfoundland."

"Yes," he agrees with some gusto, which makes me happy.

I tamp loose French Mariage tea into a silver tea-ball and am reminded of my polite father tamping cherry tobacco into a pipe. In this new kingdom I am a weak lord and the radio plays marches to our Dear Tyrant; the tapeworms are kicking in, demanding a tithe.

Chinese men killed their friend playing a drunken joke, he was passed out, they inserted an eel into his rectum. This part troubles me, I am not that familiar with my friends' rectums even when intoxicated. The eel damaged the man's intestines and he had internal bleeding and died. A prank. Like Natasha and me, what seemed a good idea at the time.

Her large eyes when she listens. The horizon widens, but I want it to shrink. There is that odd piano again. Did you know I can see through matter, through concrete? But I can't change the ending of the story. Natasha and I ate fresh bread and taut blueberries, but I'm sure she's forgotten.

In Italy the evening shades darken, rich. Elephants climb the Alps, a piano sounds. Here are fishbones in stone and the brook where the priests of Cybele washed the image of the goddess.

Come stai? How are you?

Bene, grazie.

Night. Like stealing a kiss, like stealing a drink straight from the chill milk bottle.

Once I asked Natasha if she would put me in her mouth while she peed sitting on the toilet, just to see what that was like.

"Let's try it," she said happily. She said she liked my imagination, Natasha was always agreeable, yes, always splendid. She said yes, but ultimately she said no. I am dense, but I can see that our life is severed, over. I was a servant trying foolishly to serve two masters, trying to keep a home calmly intact while pursuing her like a relentless dog. Who now will admire my ineptitude, my talent for irritation? I will never forgive her for making me consider forgiveness.

Below the towering Vatican walls stand my more modest walls and my clay pots and pink geraniums and flowering trellis vines. The many flowers on my terrace belong to the *residenza,* belong to a tall older man, but I care for them since the automated sprinklers are not working. I don't want the flowers on the terrace to die on my watch.

Natasha liked the flowers I grew every summer and she emails that she is growing black-eyed Susans on her balcony in my honour. One winter she dreamt she came to visit me in a house in the woods, a house surrounded by my flowers. Is she dreaming and waking in stone mountains and swimming glacial waters right now? She visits a valley of firs so far from Italy and so far from me. She loves her summer river in the Kootenays, the flat rock at the river's edge that catches the sun, warming her long limbs like a cat on the stone ledges.

I climb into the gondola that hangs on a string over the Alps, climb away from the plain to ski, or I climb into my kayak in Canada to separate myself from shore, separate from her, paddle waves for hours to forget her, my shorts sodden from waves washing over the low kayak, river water keeping me cool for hours in the heat, like my damp T-shirts in Rome's redolent furnace.

South of Sorrento and Naples and Pompeii a bus moves like a gypsy down the coast, light on striated cliffs and walls, villages viewed from the sea, villages glued like nests to dizzy cliffs. Does the rain fall on you like doubt? Does volcanic ash freeze your world? Light hits the sand and I am kicking diamonds at my feet.

Rome's art groups and sick golden art and all these gilt frames, all these rows of gold rectangles, are too much to take: is that what drove po-mo painters to those pizza-tinted abstracts and rusting I-beam installations? I'm such a sucker for surf guitar. I came, I saw, I went away, I want to come back, *vorrei un biglietto di ritorno. Ritorno*: that sounds so nice.

Once Natasha and I played in that lucky movie where things go well, lit perfectly, our backstory made perfect sense. Natasha made me laugh as we walked by the water, as we spied bald eagles and mottled ospreys, she made me happy in ways I can never explain to her or others. Like sunrays catching far bridges, pleasing stone balustrades lit in late sunlight and river water the colour of gold pilsner and mysterious green shadows lurking beneath the curve of mossy stone arches.

Then Natasha moved to Vancouver for work. One fall day we stood chatting and laughing in Vancouver in a Mexican bar. Come visit, she had said on the phone. It was a galaxy diminished, I knew she had met someone else in this city — well, had met Jack, who I knew too well, but I was trying to be an adult, and the visit was lovely in its way, in her way. It seemed fine. We were laughing when her cell rang.

"Where are you?" he asked suspiciously. I could hear his voice from the small phone.

She panicked, not wanting to wreck things with her brand new bozo.

"I'll be home in five minutes," she yelped to the phone and she ran to the exit sign, vanished. There was no warning and I was a TV left at the curb. I knew of Jack, knew this was a possibility, but what had been manageable as a mature conversation was now animal, mineral, visceral, sickening.

After that my hotel room seemed haunted by my ecclesia, my drear congregation, I was afraid and had to have all the lamps lit, no sleep, thinking and creeping room to room slow as a monster. From a Mexican clinic to this fake Mexican bar in Vancouver and then to nowhere really, to a bill slipped under the door.

The big country was no longer big enough for my bile. After she abandoned me in the fake bar, anger became my giant country. To cross that anger became my choice, I paid my way across, the same way I paid money for six hours of growing hatred on the plane, fleeing her face, fleeing her western side of the country, her side of the argument. On the plane I could not shut down my mind, I could not stop dwelling on her provincial cruelty mile by mile in that seat, in that bland tunnel.

What is the antidote to your own mind, to poison filling your ear? Trapped in the seat I purchased (*fly the unfriendly womb*), the seat I chose from among all the seats without thought, without knowing how bad the trip would be, when it was still going to be the best visit ever. It changed so quickly.

"Come visit anyway," Natasha said when I expressed my reservations, now that Jack was in the picture.

"It won't be the same. Maybe I should cancel."

"No, come visit!" she insisted. Her voice always so nice. "It won't be the same as we expected," Natasha said, "but it will be good."

And it was fine at first, but then her exit from the Mexican place like a physical blow, I was staggered at the bar. Can I please crawl out your window? Why did I listen, why did I travel? I should have stayed home.

I had thought she was a home. I lost my first home and then lost this home and had no home to go back to (*the goddess Athena cast an obscuring mist over the familiar landmarks; he did not know his way home*). I was an experiment that failed badly, an explorer so far from cheer and my former state, too far gone. Maybe I'll go to Rome.

In the Baltimore airport I began to come apart, a subtle disintegration, or was it Buffalo or Winnipeg, some modernist metal-and-glass outpost of vertigo and tears, another gypsy way-station in the chartered tunnels that worm their way through the false wall of the time zones, and the English ballad "Matty Groves" echoing in my jealous head: *and how do you like my feather bed and how you like my sheets and how do you like my lady gay who lies in your arms asleep?*

But what do I want from my lady gay? Do I want her to beg me to come back, claim it was a huge error, can you ever forgive me? Maybe I do want to hear those words, but it's moot, she will not say that. I know this and I hate this knowledge. She made her choice the way I chose a seat on a plane, the way I dispose of my faithful howling fridge.

Time passes, as one hears it will. Days crash into nights and trembling ghost-jets criss-cross over my head, leaving white glowing contrails in the sky, jets playing a giant game of X's and O's. I am blunted, a former expert, I stared into the abyss and the abyss tried to sell me life insurance. I am living in cool Canada, but one ordinary day I flash back to Italy, I swear I'm in a sun-washed crosswalk outside my hotel in a vision of warm Roman colours and spinning tires and spooky statues with empty eyes staring overhead.

Why the hallucinatory flashback a year or two later? I'm in Canada and I'm in Rome at a crowded gelato shop spooning out crazy colours, not a memory but a palpable feeling that I'm walking noisy streets, I can see and smell Via Candia this moment in the heat and din of scooters and skirts and the Mouth of Truth, which bites off the hands of liars; and which side of the street has shade to protect my roasting head and where will my black shoes stroll in Rome today? What is the catalyst for these delayed Italian flashbacks?

The very next day I am inside my house, but I am also prowling Trastevere's twisting lanes, exploring dim chapels and brew pubs and swallowing the sun-warm juice of blood oranges. What is the trigger in my head? I am standing in a room in Canada, but I swear I'm across the sea in bright Italy. A flashing sun and an odd sensation; something mysterious transports me twice and I walk in more than one place.

So odd to have lived where those odd gods live, those hungry, ravenous ghosts. Noisy troubled Italy troubles me in its absence, Italy so crazy and corrupt and cryptic, so loudly lewd and warm and violent — nimble cutpurses and thieves trotting our roof tiles, and who are these three dead gypsies who could not swim? Three limp bodies laid on heavy blankets on the beach under the cliffs, dead wanderers at a way-station, wandering no more. These travellers tried to eat the world, but the world ate them, left them nameless, purse-less.

•

Somalis and Afghans jump off vessels and in the p
other over turf, Italians in the prosperous north loo
those in the hardscrabble south, and I look down on the dead
bodies at the bottom of the cliff.

The waitress says in all seriousness, "Can I beverage you?"
Can I forgive her? I can't forget Natasha. Nor can I forget
Napoli's nipples and slim limbs and cocaine murders or Rome's
nine hundred churches and beautiful clothes and faces in the
Metro.

And what was the name of the wind darkening the sea, and
what names have those gaunt churches hidden in the dark brain
of unanswered prayers and humans falling from high cliffs and a
woman attacks the Pope and a man bloodies the prime minister
and an enforcer shoots a mayor in a seaside town — what an odd
place is Italy — yes, yes, I'll be back in Italy just as soon as I can.

Maybe I can travel using points, fly into Rome in the off-
season, say September or October, when Italy's poised boot is
sweetly breezy and the peninsula's marble-fountain piazzas are
less crowded with cameras and pilgrims roped in line to view
the endless miles of framed faces and silent statues in sorrow
and moonlight.

I lack the money now, my euros are gone, but I hope to go back
to Italy in the fall and have it to myself. I have years on me, but
like a child I am greedy. I want Italy to be all mine. You see
that I am all ego, that I lack the brains God gave a goose. Like
a child, what I see I want all to myself, whether it is a laneway
of ospreys or a giant country viewed from a plane or Natasha's
small anxious face praying for a miracle at the Mexican clinic.

•

When times were best Natasha lay on my bed, lingering, without guilt, without the usual rush to rise and dress. The zipper on her jeans is so tiny, only two or three teeth, such a short journey, more of an off-and-on switch than a zipper. Someone sewed it there, but really, what is the point?

In Ireland swans lazed outside the hotel in a dark river of stone bridges and past that a good pub. I took photos of her stretched out, as if I needed proof it was real, couldn't believe Natasha was there with me in the same room. In the photos she looks at a bedside book, languorous, topless, in cute red panties, an arm over her eyes to stay anonymous, though I can sense she likes having her picture taken.

Natasha holds a smile for the camera; women seem to know how to hold a smile in a way I cannot. In photos I am caught moving between expressions, smile faltering in slow motion. In slow motion I touched the small of her back, the curve of her hip — how I admired the pronounced shape of her hips, those parenthesis shapes, those commas in my life, commas in the middle of an unspoken sentence. Then she vanished before the end. Natasha's phone rings and she flees from me.

"There is something you are trying to forget," teases the gypsy woman in Rome. I am a kohl-eyed raccoon at the stream washing a cube of sugar: where did the sweetness go?

I dwell on affliction, on bloodstream messengers. What is the message? That it is hard to meet someone new. I'm thinking tonight of my blue eyes. Nothing compares to you. The jukebox plays the same loyal tunes and my skin rebels, my skin breaks out: a wet horseshoe-shaped constellation on the flesh of my palm, and rows of red dots on the skin above my wrist, like an addict's route map.

Are we travelling in the horse latitudes or in an ancient country or empire or home no longer on any map? Travellers travel to find the crooked self, travellers worry the edges of roseate maps, the map's muddy skein and dark brain filia, the lost borders and routes and lost colours and no idea what they tread upon.

Italy, Italy, Italy, all the glittering kingdoms shaken and mixed in my head, the long love song and boot and heel into the sea, the north, the south, the mountain kingdoms and wooden fleets resting under the cliffs, men and women draped in corvid clothes shrugging off the stunning heat to gather grain and grapes and olives. Marc Antony lying with Cleopatra (*we have used our throats in Egypt*), Caesar stabbed in the back, *Il Duce* hung like a side of meat at the outdoor market, crack Nazi paratroopers hiding in the rubble of the Hitler Line, young Canadians and Poles killed trying to climb bombed slopes and cliffs, the living forced to strip ammunition from the limp bodies of dead friends. Barbarians milling at the bronze riveted gate, armies on the azure beach, so many invasions, so many lost fleets, so many prayers to the wind. It all makes me want peace. I'm waiting for peace in our time.

Che ore sono?
What is the time.
Time to move on, time to forgive? No, not quite yet.

I wait a year, or is it two, and then I do meet someone new. She is brainy and pretty and funny and she lived once in Rome. The new life where she drops in for Russian tea in my kitchen in Canada. It seems very good.

But a slight complication, a speedy psycho blocking my driveway who says you don't know who you're fucking with this time, who says I will break your face, I will fuck you up if I find that anything is going on with you and my girlfriend.

His crewcut, his contorted face close to mine.

You have the wrong idea, I say, though really he doesn't.

Unaccustomed as I am to public speaking, unaccustomed as I am to getting my mouth smashed.

I'll fuck you up, he says over and over.

Yes, I think you've made that clear, I say.

Now I see why people carry a gun. Why is nothing ever simple? Should I keep a crowbar handy? She flees in her car and he follows.

That was an eventful tea party, I say by email. Are you all right?

It's not the same after that. He has robbed us of the best part, the early part. Or maybe not. Maybe that'll be our moment, our birth. This is my new life. What is best about us may be what dooms us.

We met in winter, in winter downtown we walk an icy sidewalk after a good dinner, holding each other, holding a Styrofoam takeout container. Then the black pickup truck prowling King Street. How many hours has he been up and down King and Queen looking for us? He shuts off the engine, leaving his black truck blocking the middle of the street, and walks to us. Is he going to break my mouth, as promised? I stand there, strangely calm.

"I'm not a lunatic," he says to me.

"The body's not even cold," he says to her, "and here you are with him. I love you," he says to her in a trembling voice.

I watch and think, I've had my heart broken, I don't want to visit the same on someone else. A game of musical chairs, musical torture. But I stay.

"This is stalking," she says, her voice rising.

"No it isn't," he says.

Stands a boxer in a clearing, or stands a boxer lacking a clearing. He will not move on. This world is glazed in ice. Is there ever such ice in Italy? The river closes, the river opens again in spring.

We met in winter and we survive winter and love is back: darling darling darling, when love comes back to town trailing its bridal train of verve and stomach aches and complications and sweetness. After two years of a form of solitude. Unaccustomed as I am. The lawyer wants to know if she should keep representing me, my wife's lawyer wants copies of my last three tax returns. All rise.

My new sweetheart has anxiety attacks at three a.m.

"Good night, have a good sleep," I say.

"Sleep," she says, "is something I can't control."

She lies awake and worries about her bank statement, ballooning mortgage payments, power bills she is afraid to open, her dead father's car, her line of credit, the future — she says she has always been suspicious of happiness, she says I am too guarded. At three a.m. she decides she must break it off with me.

Guarded? I am no more guarded than the average paranoid person. I walk out to check my mailbox, and her ex who is not a lunatic drives past my house. The next day she phones me, says she misses me. She loves my smell! Clings to my neck and sniffs. She reads upstairs in my bed while I work downstairs and it is pleasant to know that she is up there in my bed. Can this work? Can doubt or love be measured by a machine?

The word *haven*, her scarlet sofa overlooking the river trees and her fireplace burning all winter, months of fire, and her musical voice when she comes (the *second* one is *always* more intense, she says, as if all know this). Her private school idioms in my ear, her dead parents' hardcovers lining the shelves, her costly see-through French bra!

She dreams I carry her through her neighbourhood in Trastevere with one arm. If only she will read to me above the Tiber and I can rest my head in her lap (*Lady, shall I lie in your lap? I mean my head in your lap*). Would she recognize my naked feet? That she has doubts brings my own doubts, and the doubts have many children.

Why her suspicion of our happiness? Happiness is all I think about. Is my concern with my own happiness egotistical, self-centred? Is happiness a dead end or is it the only worthy pursuit? She lived in Rome, was engaged, an Italian fiancé, she showered on a sunny rooftop terrace, a view of church domes as water ran her lovely skin. Like me, she was giddy on a cinematic rooftop. Love's octane octaves in my head again, madly in love.

But how much is madly? What portion? I want to know to the exact decimal point.

No, I don't, I never want to know that math, to dissect that division.

She sleeps beside me in a car to Sackville and I stare at her peaceful face. I want that peace, a haven. But it all makes me wonder, can love be both madness and a haven? Does temporary love burn brightest? A bright dewy chemical bursting in the blood, a world of pepper and gunpowder sparks, my chemical romance, my doomed petrol emotion.

Climb above the world in a plane and on a steep mountain in the Rockies ride a chairlift strung dizzyingly high above a lunar crater of peaks. The conifers are tall as rockets, yet their sharp tips are far below my boots. My son shut his eyes on the chair, hates heights, which was news to me. The chair is a Poma lift, but I thought it said *Roma* and wondered if it was named after gypsies or the city. My eyes are bad, I'm a one-eyed knave.

The lifties who help us on the chairlift are all nomads from New Zealand or Australia; the sunburnt lifties work and ski winter in western Canada, then the lifties jet down under to a second winter, and then the antipodal gypsies jet back to Canada to carve more powder, gypsies craving snowy slopes, shunning summer, gypsies chasing the thin air of permanent winter.

I go to glacial mountains of peaceful snow and carving my first turns on the ski hill I find I can finally forgive the Russian librarian and her seven charms: the goat, the tooth, the dagger to the heart.

I forgive everyone as we ski up and down all morning, up and down and stop in the lodge to devour hard crusts and cold butter and wild-smelling jam with scalding honeyed tea, and above the clouds and peaks (cloudland!) the old world has vanished and this other kingdom seems stunningly great.

We leave a world happily to come up here and at the end of the day are happy to strip the snow-pants and hard boots to drive back down and embrace the lost world, the world below our feet, the gas pedal, the car moving past a herd of mangy mountain goats licking salt from the mountain road and a tour-bus driver honking at the animals, the car driving down to plates and glasses and a pub's stone fireplace, to the many cozy worlds by the rivers that never cease running, the Kicking Horse River, the Bow, the St. John, the Liffey, the Thames, the Tiber.

Ci vediamo, I think of those absent or shunned. We'll see each other.

•

Partway up the Goat's Eye chairlift I see a big raven swoop down-hill. The high sun pins the raven's exact shadow on the bright snow just ahead of a snowboarder racing below my chairlift vantage point. The raven's shadow, all wings and curved Roman beak, races at the same speed as the young woman's board, moves just ahead of her like a future, and from above I watch the race and wonder if the snowboarder is puzzled by the shadow-shape she pursues, this jerky slide show projected on the snow, this raven's perfect black shape flitting in her path as she surfs white moguls and leans into pockets of untouched powder just inside the magic-lantern blur of steep evergreens.

Why didn't you say she had cancer, my wife asked before break-ing off contact at Easter. Sometimes my ex needs an ex break. A black shadow on an X-ray and this black shadow marrying the perfect white ski hill. Is it real? Do we need to pay attention?

Once I saw two small bears outside a Bengali blues club in Rome, and at first I didn't notice their slim silver chains and I wondered if bears were loose in the city like dogs. And by the Vatican I saw a girl tiny as a crow with iridescent red fairy wings attached to her back and a silver plane shaped like a sunlit cross crossing a world, rounded clouds in the distance like broccoli going slightly brown (my doc asks that I eat more broccoli). And the Pope in bright white and gold robes addressing the multitudes in St. Peter's Square. Or the woman in the rooftop shower who meets my eye and says, *You're funny*.

These are moments my reptilian brain becomes confused as to what is real and what is a vivid dream, what you can talk about or keep to yourself, what is prayer and what is miracle.

•

Twice now I thought myself dead, but clearly I am not dead, I am back on the crowded merry-go-round (*you are merry, my lord*), I am back in love when I thought it would not happen again, I am back on rental skis thinking that life can never be predicted and people you haven't yet met are full of beautiful surprises and I am very glad I am not dead.

I ride up the mountain as the light fades, ride past a lone tree decorated with beads and bras of all colours, a tradition to toss an item from the chairlift as you glide above the tree, and now whisky-jacks and ravens investigate the bright lingerie. I am elevated to great heights and stellar views of the top of the world and ski down as swiftly as I can and say thanks getting on the Angel Express and the Australian lifties so far from home reply, "No worries, mate."

The lifties lift us up, take our worries. My son learns to ski faster and faster with each run, he has a goggle tan and zinc on his nose and we ascend and slam down Viking Ridge and slalom Boundary Bowl and brash sunlight glows on distant snowy peaks à la Lawren Harris's luminous oil on canvas and none of it real estate, none of it for sale. I can see so far into the next province, the next world, peak upon peak in lovely washed blues.

On fat demo skis I am a loose cannon in the loose powder of the Continental Divide and I feel free, I bounce gleefully from one mogul to another, using the curves of the downhill slope, not battling the bathtub moguls but letting the bowls and sidewalls steer my way. I want to quit my job and be a ski bum, roar downhill as fast as possible (*this is so great*), ski faster than I ever dared as a kid, my speed a calculated touch past the edge of control. Speed equals danger, speed equals release, speed equals forgiveness.

•

When the light goes flat later in the day it is hard to pick your turns, you quickly lose confidence, and your eyes ache to know. In a high-altitude whiteout my sister felt an odd form of vertigo, unable to tell up from down, but most hours on the mountain are so bright (*this is so fucking great*). I will try to not be suspicious of happiness, of the sun, of a life of tin charms and little miracles, *milagritos*, a life cobbled from fragments I have handy. We'll work it out, we'll see each other, *ci vediamo*, no worries, mate, as the lifties say.

Our gondola hangs by a thread over the gorge, my winter ascension, lifted in my secret Shangri-La. Natasha was splendid and my new love is splendid and today's skiing is splendid and the world on high is splendid: is there a better word to end on?

Butterfly on a Mountain

They are ill discoverers that think there is no land,
when they can see nothing but sea.

— Francis Bacon

The law, in its majestic equality, forbids the rich
as well as the poor to sleep under bridges,
to beg in the streets, and to steal bread.

— Anatole France

Perhaps there is no station waiting, no mouth. In lovely Roman streets a young woman begs for coins among drunken pub crawlers and Bengali men hawking red roses. A child and a young man wait nearby, all three faces handsome, but unhappy, a troubled trifecta, their cursed aura palpable, an urban detail you take in, like the dimensions of a roomy Gothic doorway.

My cousin Eve and I have seen this trio in the street before, the way the young man glares at the woman: clearly their situation is *her* fault, saddling him with a child and no prospects in a joyless city. The child plays with a toy and the young man pretends to ignore them both. The young woman's hair is longer than Eve's and she wears a long skirt mirrored with silver threads and platelets, looking medieval amidst the tourist shorts and singlets.

Eve studies the three, says, "I wonder if they are Roma."

"How on earth can you tell?"

"Well, they may be *zingari*, gypsies, or they may be Croatian, or Tunisian, or they may be from Iraq or Afghanistan. Who knows these days."

The locals complain, *merda*, too many gypsies and too many illegals coming on boats from every direction, more every day! It wasn't like this in the old days, they say. And last week a stowaway fell from the sky, crushed on city pavement, the poor guy, his head broken open after he dropped out of a DC-9's wheel well. As they say, sin is geographical. The stowaway wanted this city, and he had such an amazing view of Rome's river and steeples and temples until the wondrous diorama rose up to kill him.

The young man crosses the road and straddles someone else's parked motorcycle, his body bent forward and his hands wide on the grips to pretend that the powerful motorcycle is his own hard machine, and on this machine he is far away from everyone, zooming freely up some fine valley in a soft leather jacket, wind in his stubbled face and a fat roll of euro notes in his pocket, a dream valley with no begging for a stranger's pennies and no child glancing sideways to gauge his surly moods.

He hunches over someone else's motorcycle and the young woman approaches merry drunken tourists for coins. Tour groups follow a flag-holder down narrow cobblestones that shake with tour buses; a bus kneels at a hotel door like a camel, a hydraulic trick. In the undeclared war, the winners are winning, but you know money is there, money walking past in wallets and purses.

"Let's go," Eve says.

I can't move from the suggestion of menace. I feel I can read these three like watching actors work a lit stage: she is trying hard, but such streets are not paved with gold, no one will hire him, and in the script the young man blames the young woman, in the script the brooding young man will take it out on the young woman.

In Rome, goldfinches; and goldfinches zip by my house in Canada. When I left Canada wobbly tulips were trying to straighten up under goldfinches flying in crab-apple blossoms and flooding rivers withdrew to let fiddleheads open their tight furls.

My maple tree was starting to fill out and throw down shade on my lawn, but this Canadian season could not be called summer — winter still looms, too huge a recent memory, like an army departed in the night, raw gashes left on salty ground, grass boulevards in ruins and chunks of ice and straw and flotsam caught high in the river's muddy trees where the water rose into the upper branches.

That stunning crashing freshet and river ice seems only hours ago, I can't forget it, an icy spectre that was just there. But stumble from a plane and Italy is already furnace-hot, no ice in this murky chocolate river and horses dreaming in the shade and heat addling my brain.

"Hotter each day," warns my cousin Eve.

I am not made for it, my thermostat very different than the Italians'. Why is it that I can reconcile myself to winters of thirty below and blizzards that would cripple and maim many Romans, but I can't take this simple southern heat? After high school I worked on a paving crew, we created our own hellish climate laying down boiling asphalt, but I don't recall this degree of heat.

The Quebec stewardess told me to not fight it. Give yourself over to the heat, she said, but I worry my brain is shrinking and bubbling in its bowl of bone.

Eve gazes around the empty piazza with her movie star sunglasses, looks north as if she might glimpse the Alps seething with snowy vapours just past the old city gate. The crowds in Rome will get much worse in a few weeks. Eve prefers the north of Italy, Milan, Bergamo, Venice, *Italia Settentrionale*. I only know the south, often seen as wilder, trashier, savage, dangerous. Rome is a pivot, a door. I try to stop staring at her. Her face, her body in a silk blouse, her hand, eyes; how many genes do we share?

"Do you miss the mountains?" she asks. As a teen, Eve raced the downhill event, was a fast skier where I was a coward.

She knows that spring skiing is an annual compulsion, my pilgrim destination, my religious service in the contorted peaks. But not this year, the peaks are too far away and I have no money left for my pilgrimage. Last spring in Canada I saw an orange butterfly high on a snowy mountain.

"How on earth did it get there?"

Eve smiles widely as I try to convey my amazement at the sight.

"Did the butterfly ride up on the gondola?"

"That's just what I wondered."

In Canada the puzzling butterfly fluttered the chalet's snowy sundeck, a butterfly lighting on the boards under our massive ski boots. How did the tiny creature survive, map its way to such a cold altitude, flying in snow above the treeline? In a nearby hanging valley a lordly black bear once chased me, tried to kill me, and now a butterfly pursues me.

Why did the bear want to kill me? What did I ever do to the bear? His strange loves, no existential ennui for him! Our chemical moods: the bear wants me, I want Eve, and the butterfly wants satori on the mountaintop. What primal urge drew the butterfly to this lost world in the sky?

When skiing I forget that I am connected to the rest of the world, I am separated, elevated, changed, cupped in some odd land in the sky. I skied Tod Mountain years ago — new owners changed the resort's name because in German *Tod* means death (welcome to Death Mountain) — and the chairlift carried us through clouds and above, clouds now a floor under us, an escalator piercing the clouds. A brighter higher world out of time, mythic, exhilarating.

I rise up a mountain and a stowaway sees the city for the first time as he falls from the plane, as his head hits the street, as his head breaks on a city. Now all our grandparents are dead and my parents dead and I am separated from my wife and children and this café in Rome seems a separate world from Canada. I left my father's house decades ago, fell into the city; my mother and father are dead so there are walls between us, but I still see them, I still dream of my mother and father.

The butterfly opened and closed its wings, flew a few feet, but hurried back to us; I worried our great ski boots might crush the creature after it had moved like a genius so far across the planet and climbed to us on these windy hiemal heights. Guttural ravens I am used to at this altitude, white ptarmigans exploding out of a snowbank hiding spot, demented jays begging for snacks. But never a butterfly, especially when winter is still with us. How many million movements of the creature's wings carried it from Mexico to this mountaintop?

That same day my worn ski boots, also orange, fell to pieces,

I'd skied on them so long, frugal decades in the same boots, that the aged plastic simply gave out and trailed debris on the slope and I kept skiing hard down the mountain, bent over staring ahead, thighs hurting and my poles barely ticking the deep moguls, I didn't even notice the debris. My eyes were bloodshot, almost snow-blind from the bouncing light, so my sister lent me dark glasses, clunky rectangles that looked like they came from Ray Charles. I skied all day in a white crater ringed with teeth in a kind of ecstasy, a king of ecstasy.

Eve worries, frets about the future, worries about her teeth and future dental bills and insomnia. I don't worry — I just want to touch her and I'm not allowed. In the hotel I saw her open suitcase, beautiful French bras on top.

Eve's father used to tell an old family story, they were living near Lincoln, Nebraska, and a tornado tore up their house and blew out all the windows. In the basement a heavy oak bureau fell on her little sister, and Eve, a skinny teen, lifted the piece of furniture and rescued the smaller girl. Eve tried later to lift the weight and she could not budge the mass of oak even an inch.

And more recently an addict boyfriend, when Eve refused to see him, dumped a load of farm manure into her white convertible. Or was it into a Jacuzzi on a cedar deck? The private girls' school in the Swiss Alps is a long way from Nebraska and her old lives in Tornado Alley.

I ask Eve, "Do you believe in an afterlife?"

"I have to," Eve replies. "This one ain't working out at the moment."

She surprises me. My eye and mind are clearly imperfect: everyone seems fine to me and yet they are *not* fine, not jim-dandy. I remember hearing from my mother that Eve was involved with an addict, painkillers from an old injury, a car accident, and then he wouldn't stop the pills; I'm sure any addict has a few unlovely secrets. She couldn't shake him, his weird love, she'd resolve to not see him again, they'd break up and get back over and over.

This pattern doesn't seem true of her, but can you ever know anyone or even hope to know your own secrets? It's a world of secrets. Once in a while we are given a glimpse behind the faces held up for us in a room, but such glimpses are rare.

Eve harbours doubts about the men she chooses, men with manure and front-end loaders. Does anyone get along? Are we all on the rocks? Is it even possible anymore, to get along for any length of time, or is that talent lost to most of us, a vanished skill? My grandfather the dowser could find water with a branch, but I can't do it. Of late Eve has turned to Jung for answers, but I don't know if that's going to fly. The heart is part diplomat and part vandal.

Summer washes us in warm water, what is Hecuba to me? Part of me remains winter, always winter. I suppose I must go home sometime, when I am out of money and drinks and sofas to crash on.

On the other side of the gloaming river Eve and I walk hills and piazzas, haughty statues gazing as Mars rises over a gold church and precisely painted house. Rome is piled upon Rome, a field of broken crockery, a ruined kitchen. I follow Eve through demented crowds of hipsters and party girls sampling dipso concoctions that taste of fried bread and marigolds, bands on the river barges playing fuzzed-out meteor storms, bands on the river playing bits of accidents muted as cough syrup.

•

When Eve raced in the mountains she was fearless, on the ski team she liked the speedy downhill event and I was afraid that I'd die in the icy gates, die head-down in a tuck and zooming like hell, hoping your edges held as you flew up and down and the steep turns got greasier.

And if you skid off the course at high speed through the B-nets and hit a tree? I had a teammate who died that way. He was alive on the hill of pines and lifted in a chopper to the city hospital; we heard he was okay, but the blow altered something in his head, a brick dislodged, a hole opened somewhere in the brain. The next race I thought about that more, I preferred some measure of control.

Travel can be that balance between control and letting go. In Rome odd bits of memory surface from the ski team days: motel rooms, rising early with files and wax and my mother's old iron to warm the wax, and what wax to choose for the weird weather and conditions on the mountain high above this motel. We were kicked out of one motel in Jasper for working on our skis in the room. The course has teeth and everyone else on the team so confident, bullish, wanting to win the race and I didn't want to be on the team. Eve loved racing and I hated it.

I had zero confidence as a downhill racer, preferring the longer curves of giant slalom, leaning in and tagging the gates in rhythm (don't catch your head in the gate), elbow almost on the ground and feeling your body swing like a perfect pendulum, the constant scraping sound, legs trembling and a rooster tail of snow behind when you're in the groove and not skidding into the trees. Giant slalom is fast but forgiving.

•

Eve stops and kisses me by the subway stairs; I am Canadian, so used to being part of someone else's empire. Narrow steps lead us down to a cellar's brick arches and blue electric light where a band stops and a drummer crashes snare and toms and the audience applauds wildly.

"No!" moans my cousin, holding her head. "Don't applaud."

"Why not?"

"You don't want to encourage drum solos."

We keep moving fountain to fountain, as I once hoped to do with Natasha. I'll sleep when I die, I feel wonderful staying up all night in Rome. My mother a night owl watching Merv Griffin, David Frost, me a night owl and Eve a night owl too — is such a thing genetic? A magnetic magic night, lights alive like glowing coals in the bottom of a river and in two café chairs my hand on her leg seems a very good idea, that shore seems possible. All of my body is keyed up, aware of the next body, the leg, waiting for a dispatch from the border.

"On the corner, those three again."

Who? Oh yes. The medieval young woman begging for coins, the young man and child; hell, I'm in a decent mood; maybe they'll be all right. Is the sky lighter? For some in Rome the night has too few hours, for other wanderers the night has far too many. Is the gap my fault? *Come and give the fiddler a dram.*

In sunrise's tireless light my cousin and I cross back to our side of the river, cross the river to read graffiti on a wall: *You Are Entering Free Prati.* The words sprayed in English, not Italian, which puzzles us. A black shamrock is sprayed on the same wall: does this signify a lost tribe of the Irish?

"*Il trifoglio,*" says my cousin, "the three-part leaf, *Nuovo Politica,* more of a fascist symbol than to do with leprechauns. Fascism still has its appeal here. As does Mr. Mussolini."

Another wall has a tag, *Difendi Roma, Salva l'Europa*. Defend Rome against outsiders at the borders, at the gates, from those falling from the sky like errant tightrope walkers. Those with money retreat behind walls and gates; what was ancient fortress becomes fortress once more.

"Wall-building must be a profitable profession here. Rome is all walls."

Look this way a wall and look that way a wall and the Vatican walls loom behind us like a wide brown mountain around the old German Pope and down that side street I see spray-painted walls and locked gates linking more walls, more crooked graffiti and no greenery to soften the sunlit streetscape, few trees to shade the bourdon tone of traffic. But at times I glimpse lush plants and lewd blossoms past the walls, private gardens hiding in the block's interiors.

I'll never know interior Italy, the sedate green courtyards, only the chaotic exteriors and the jail of language, of not knowing the lovely language. So many curious tourists and camera eyes in these public spaces, but Italy is private, Italy is walled off.

Eve comes to see my high room and terrace and I am nervous with her in my room, I wonder about us. I show her my tiny bathroom with its screened window, the small square mesh like a confessional in the sky. Five storeys high, a fortress tower with an open terrace with vines and flowers and a vast white umbrella to shade us from the drugging sun, the stabbing light: Eve likes all of it.

"You're very tidy." I can tell she is surprised.

When drinking I can be reckless, my life is messy, as if in a car crash that takes many years to unfold, but my room is clean.

Dark-skinned children play inside the next walled garden under fruit trees. Are they apricots or tiny oranges? From five storeys above I can't be sure. She leans forward and her taut calf seems to represent something.

"The orphans," I remark to my cousin Eve.

They might just be daycare kids, but I enjoy thinking of them as my orphans. Nuns in white habits drift out to check on them occasionally.

Curious about these gardens and walls below, we walk the nearest streets until we find a locked gate and a brass sign affixed to the wall beside the locked gate: *Istituto San Giuseppe Della Montagne*, which I believe means St. Joseph of the Mountain. My mysterious neighbour!

Their compound and treed garden has a wary, guarded look, perhaps an old rectory or nunnery (the pure *hortus conclusus*), high walls with broken glass cemented into the top to belay trespassers (*forgive us our trespasses*), and inside the high walls fruit lies on the ground.

Who was it who built the first wall? Was it a wise God expelling a puzzled couple from the garden? Such a loss to him, and over a fig, *fico*, a trifle.

A view of gardens during the day, but at night my neighbourhood below behaves strangely. At street level are arched gates and palm trees and high walls a dun sand colour, so in evening's diffused light I no longer see Rome's riverine blocks, I gaze over a dim desert crossroads, an Algerian outpost, the sand and palm trees of a Moroccan fortress and Eve in my bed; we wait for a caravan of camels to cross under the next streetlamp, Bedouins whispering past in silk robes. Night alters the urban world under my flowered terrace, night reboots the look. I dream I find gold coins on the ground and I'm picking them up, but no one else seems to see them.

In the morning Eve pulls black tights over her pale legs and takes me to a giant street market, a vast display of vendors and wares under a roof of tin sheeting that stretches for blocks. Is this cornucopia world possible? Can the Pope, with all his treasures, ever say that: *She pulled on her tights and took me to the market.* Why would I want to change anything, be anyone else? I have it far better than Pope Rat, yet I am fascinated that a Pope is right over there with his gold, perhaps peeking out his window at my flowery terrace, gazing at our gardens.

We walk streets spilling with ripe fruit and herbs and oils, we take from the gnarled trees and vines and mustard valleys, we drop nets into schools of fish the colour of wriggling fire, haul sea bass and sea urchins and Jerusalem artichokes under this tin roof for all to gaze and taste, stall by stall, the way my Irish grandmother shopped every day in her Usher's Island neighbourhood beside the River Liffey.

Flayed plane trees rise in crooked columns, but they disappear beyond the market's tin heavens. Broad tree trunks rise in this interior, but our eyes cannot follow them all the way up, the tin roof interrupts, we cannot see the branches and foliage that blossom above the roof. It's a form of separation — a strangely discombobulating effect, like huge elms growing inside your bedroom, like kindred city blocks cleaved by a stone wall or railroad embankment, the natural lines interrupted.

I see the young woman in her long dress begging down the street, but today I don't see the unhappy young man with her. I buy two loaves of bread, they seem attractive to my eye, and each heavy as a baby. In the market they are all selling; what am

I selling? The bone-green air between tree trunks, the green shadows between trunks: who owns that property? I feel that Eve owns that grainy air, right now I feel Eve owns any part of the world where my eye strays.

My cousin's eager green eyes, her lovely jaw; am I allowed to touch her leg today? I offer one market loaf to the young woman begging and she looks at me suspiciously, says no, she refuses my loaf of bread. By the purple Christ what addled engineer designed the divisions in our heads?

The loaf is very heavy and almost yellow inside, corn perhaps. At the hotel I show the loaf to Angelo the hotel owner, proud of my acquisition, its heft and weight.

The old owner holds the loaf and shakes his head, then points at the paving stones.

A honeymoon couple falls into the hotel's tiny mirrored lobby, a funhouse chamber, but they are not having fun, they are very upset. A unregistered taxi driver swindled them, nabbed them at the airport, forced on them a long tour of Rome that they did not want (*yes you must see the Coliseum, and Garibaldi's statue and the fountains*) and then he demanded a king's ransom before they could get out of his taxi, charged them five times what I paid for my taxi ride with the Quebec stewardess and pilot. At the airport the Quebec stewardess saved me from just such a crooked cabbie.

"We tried to get him to stop the tour, just take us to the hotel! Please stop."

This is the couple's honeymoon, and so much beauty and romance in Rome, such stunning sights, but their first moments in Italy sullied. And they paid the ridiculous amount just to be free of the driver. They came to this shore and he knew they had money on their bodies.

Monique, the French woman who runs the hotel desk, is jubilantly indignant, phones the local *polizia*.

The policeman says, "What can we do if they are stupid." And it's true, at times we must seem like morons to the Italians.

"What!" the French woman cries out. "They are not stupid! They are from somewhere else and don't expect to be treated this way. They were like prisoners. You are the stupid one, you are an imbecile!"

Monique hangs up and says to me, "That's the problem with Italy. They think it's funny to trick people, they love the *beffa*, their tricks, they think it proves that they are so clever and you are so dumb. They think they are so clever. I hope someone drops a big bomb on that policeman's head and then we'll see who is smart or dumb!"

The French woman at the front desk has lived in Rome for decades, she is married to the hotel owner, but she has not taken to Italians. Their bread, Monique says. It just does not compare.

An older British couple arrives at the hotel via Hong Kong, jet-lagged but very jovial, their annual European grand tour. The man is retired, an expert on archeology who at lunch must share his bullish expertise on details of Italian life.

"Don't order that! Try the tripe, try the Sicilian horsemeat! No, not beer, order wine. Live like the Italians!" he shouts as if I have a hearing aid. "That's what I say!"

With age they have started to look like each other, but he is loud and bearded and she is quiet and non-bearded, so I can keep them apart. He keeps using the word *criteria*, he loves coming to Rome, lives for his annual visit, and his joviality and erudite history lessons soon irritate and depress me.

Shouldn't I feel gladly *connected* to other humans? Aren't we the same basic components? Shouldn't we all hold hands and dance in a circle? Why am I so happy to distance myself, to just walk away from the ski team? We are all kin, idiots or not, and this truth makes me bitter.

When I was a child it was a keen blow to realize that others have their thoughts, that others also have this private radio in them. This was an epiphany the opposite of religious conversion, this was a letdown, a violation of some implied contract. My mother said I was such a sweet child, so how did my bitter side triumph? Orwell wanted his tea as bitter as possible, but to add honey is not a crime.

"We're turning in for a ten-minute power nap," the retired archeology expert bellows in the sunny atrium. "Helps greatly with jet lag," he says. "I highly recommend it."

A full day later I see him rheumy and blinking in hallway light, forked beard askew, a King Lear of the long corridor.

"Been sightseeing?" I ask, dreading more Italian expertise.

"Well sir, I've been exactly nowhere. We fell asleep! What bloody time is it?"

"Almost five p.m."

"Well what day is it?"

The expert and his spouse lay down their heads for a few minutes after our lunch in the atrium and woke up the next afternoon with no idea of the day. Twenty-eight hours of sleep like bears in a cave. Yes, I can see that such a power nap might help greatly with jet lag.

The twenty-eight-hour-power-nap couple argue at an adjacent table.

She says, "This is about more than a parking space."

"No," he says, "it's all about a parking space."

In polluted Rome I am one of many millions and don't enjoy that feeling. I only need a few people, maybe just one, but some lean into doubt the way others lean into faith.

My cousin Eve says she must get back to Switzerland's fresh air, she must cross the mountains that divide the old cantons, the honeymoon is over.

I spend time with Eve, but it's like visiting another country. I can't really know Italy, can't really know Eve. We change so quickly. Once alive with ardour and fever and whatever is the opposite of due diligence. Now we will float back to our possessions, their lovely burden. I kiss her at the taxi, but I'm not really allowed, she turns slightly, is no longer comfortable.

In the garden oranges or apricots lie wasted on the ground; no one touches the fruit. In the garden the Pope's nuns come out to look at the orphans, nuns like Bedouins in their flowing white habits, covered wholly in this heat.

Nuns covered wholly in Rome, and on Canada's snowy mountains women ski in bikinis, almost naked; the temperature not yet warm enough, but they want to ski in bikinis, they want to ski naked. The Ray Charles sunglasses borrowed from my sister were so dark, altering the world, the sunglasses made the women's bare skin look purple, ghoulish, the colour of zinc lotion applied to a nose to prevent sunburn and skin cancer.

In Canada we skied all day in a celestial crater ringed with teeth, up and down we went on the blinding snow in a pleasing rhythm, a whole crowd in sunglasses and zinc noses. My new ski boots were so hard they hurt my ankles. It is hard to walk in new boots, hard to tromp up the chalet stairs, trying to dig for coins for a hot chocolate.

Everyone walking past has money, but no one begs for spare change on a ski hill. There are no walls on a ski hill. Perhaps the troubled trio could make the journey from Rome to Canada's far mountains. All three could fit on a stolen motorcycle speeding north out of Rome past the northern gate and city walls and turn the wheel into glorious foreign valleys and this move may stay his hand from her cheek. But what are the chances? So many travellers and refugees at sea and stowaways falling from the wheel well as light snow falls from the sky, all of us believing riches are waiting if we find the right shore.

No one asks for money while you wear ski boots, an unstated rule. My old orange boots — I'd skied on them so long they fell to bits. The new boots are so inflexible, and I like flexibility, but hard boots are needed to hold me tight in the quick turns in the ziggurat mountains.

Is it luck that you find yourself on one side of a wall or the other? People sit outside in goggles and jackets and they spread their lunch at cedar picnic tables, eating and drinking and sharing sandwiches with joyful smiles. This is the way it should be for everyone. The chairlift moving station to station, the sky so high above the mountains, and wind always touching our faces in the strange hanging valley we dreamt of so long ago.

Knife Party

Mistakes are part of the dues
that one pays for a full life.

—Sophia Loren

My wife is from Florida and is moving out of my house on the cold Canadian river while I stay in Italy. She takes the frisky dog down to the freezing river and hits a ball into the water with a tennis racket. The moving van comes and the moving van goes. The river moves and the faithful dog swims to retrieve the ball again and again, the dog floating in a state of grace.

Our train speeds into the side of an Italian mountain and we have no eyesight, we knife noisily into black tunnels and then shoot out again, our new eyes viewing the patient volcano and ancient sea.

Our noisy engine halts iron wheels at seaside towns where families alight with beach towels and fashionable sunglasses and sunburns that still have hours to flare into ripeness.

We have entered the Mezzogiorno, land of the midday sun, so close to Africa. The train's exit doors have small windows, but they do not open and the cars are furnace hot. Tough kids from the exurbs stand near the exit doors in an alcove with no seating. They hail from the illegal neighbourhoods built up the sides of the volcano, the *zona rossa*. If the volcano erupts again their homes in the red zone will be wiped out. Ray-Ray and Eve are thirsty, are looking for a bar car; some trains have bar cars and some do not.

The ancient train moves into light and out. In the confines of a dark tunnel something incredibly fractious and noisy grinds against our traincar and the tunnel walls that hug us. The high windows are open to roaring air, open to relieve the hellish heat, so much noise already, but this new clamour makes all the passengers flinch and panic, metal debris bouncing and crashing and wrenching our heat-stroke dreams. What hammers are hitting the curved bell of our train?

In the darkened alcove sketchy teenagers are moving shadows and I see a lithe shadow leap to kick a window in the train's exit door. In the heat the teens demand a breeze. When the train is in a tunnel they attack the door's sealed window, thinking no one sees them in the blackness.

One kid swings nimbly on a high chrome bar, a true acrobat who, with both feet, hits the window hard, a human battering ram, and more fragments of glass and metal frame break away in the dark to clatter and bounce along the outer skin of the rocketing train.

We burst out of the tunnel and they stop smashing the window to pose casually in mad light. In the next tunnel the kicking starts again.

Wives look to their husbands: will you do something? Each Italian husband shrugs. *Polizia* ride many trains, but

I don't see them today. Where is the stoic conductor I like so much?

The Italian teens try to look cool in huge mirrored aviator shades, but their childlike faces are so thin and the aviator glasses so large — the effect is of Clownish Boy rather than Top Gun Pilot or Corrupt Saigon Major. I should wait, but I react primitively at times like this; I know they carry knives, but I'd like to trash *them* the way they trash their own train, our train, see how they like it. But I know we'll all be elsewhere soon if we just sit and do nothing.

Don't engage, my wife used to say to me, and it's good advice.

So why do I walk to the alcove and stand beside the cretins? My move was not well thought out. There are more of them in the hormonal antechamber than I realized and sullen girls lean in the mix. I wish my cousin Eve and Ray-Ray were here beside me, I wish I was a more confident vigilante man with amazing eye-hand coordination and hidden weapons. Those in the group look to each other for guidance in child-thug matters, but no one steps forward to test my skill set, my tennis elbow. Uncertain moments hang, served to us like writs.

The unruly gang (am I way too ruly?) clambers off at the next stop, shoving each other out the doors with high masculine spirits.

Ah, youth; how I hate them.

The damaged doors opened for the rabble, but now the doors won't close. Now our arthritic train cannot move. The stoic conductor examines the damaged doors, tries to heal them in the heat. He wears a dark blue uniform of thick cloth but seems unaffected by the southern climate, while sweat falls from my sleeves. Father Silas gave our group a talk that men in Italy do not wear shorts, that shorts are for children only. The conductor and another Italian man work to coax the doors to close.

On the station platform I see my pretty cousin Eve and Tamika talking with the gang that smashed the doors. No sign of Ray-Ray, but that is par for the course, he disappears for hours, days. Why are Eve and Tamika on the platform? For pancakes and syrup? Did they jump off at the wrong stop? Why do people think turquoise track suits are a good look?

I leap from the carriage just as the afflicted doors finally close and the train and stoic conductor shunt away without me. The suburban station sign and walls are crowded with Day-Glo graffiti faithfully imitating American-style tags, going for a *Fort Apache the Bronx* look. A new empire paints over an old empire and the rebels all agree on hairdos.

"Hey!" calls Eve. "We met these Italian guys at the beach this afternoon. Really. This is Giorgio and Pepino and Santino and I don't know all of them yet. They invited us to a party. Want to come with?"

Tamika is not sure. "Maybe I'll go back to the hotel." Tamika is wise and she is shy; we both try to avoid crowds. "The next train won't be long." Tamika has some stick of polish for her white sneakers and they glow like lamps as she moves away in the sun.

"Well, then *you* come with me." Eve drags me by the arm. "Please!"

Eve is visiting from Switzerland, where she teaches at a private school. I have no desire to go to this party, but I worry about Eve going alone. She likes to move, likes to jog and dance, is enthused by the world, where I am reticent, hesitant.

My cousin says, "We can buy beer right here at the station." Eve is betting that cold beer will appeal to me, she is canny.

"You will come?" says Santino from the beach. "It's a very nice apartment for real in a very nice freaking party. Yes, you may also enjoy it."

•

In a line we pass the military base and pass rows of monochrome flats, a line of pedestrians in a drab herniated Italy, walking to a party and party to an Italy that has little to do with tourist brochures and silk suits and Bernini's genius marble limbs and asses.

We walk inland, away from the sea, around a dun hill and heartbroken canal (oh what gummy toxic sludge dumped at these banks?) and a cluster of Chinese factories and a military base with dark green tanks, World War Two vintage tanks like hunched guardians either side of the gate. A fat bee accompanies us for a few moments, some kind of Mother Nature fugue I enjoy, then the rotund bee rejects us for greener pastures. Odd to think of all the centuries of history here, but to a local bee an empire means little, does not alter its minutes.

Outside we can hear the party before finding stairs like a ladder into a crowd, a crowd spilling into a dim hall from the main rooms. In the living room leans a pole lamp with blue light bulbs, so we all look reasonably unhealthy, and every surface crammed with glasses, ashtrays, vats of red wine, cloudy ouzo, grappa, tins of German lager, and green bottles of Italian beer.

Past the pink sofa hides an invisible but loud stereo: the Jesus and Mary Chain ply distorted fuzz-box ditties. Are Jesus and Mary Chain still churning out discs? I liked them when I was younger; funny to hear them buzzing in this other world. A circle is smoking dope and a young woman is coughing up a lung. The fuming joint finds its way to us. Of course I feel nothing at first, and nothing will come of nothing.

A man flashes a glassine envelope of coke to the young woman. He's a neighbour, we are told by Pepino or Santino — Eve can tell them apart. The neighbour lives across the hall, a party crasher attracted by the crowd, the women. The neighbour is not invited, he is not welcome, he does not carry himself well.

"*Come stai?*" asks the person who is Pepino or Santino.

"You are from America?" asks the other.

"I'm not from America," I say.

"Yes, you are."

"No, Canada."

"Ah, Canada. That's much better culture."

"*Bene.*"

"So, Mister Canada," asks a third man, "do you like Napoli?"

"*Sì*, Mister Italy, *certo*, very much, *molto simpatico*, it's amazing."

"Mister Canada calls me Mister Italy. Ha ha ha."

Eve laughs with them.

The unwelcome neighbour offers coke on his wrist to Eve and the younger woman, he says, "My coke is very fine. Just think, all the way from Ecuador to Napoli and to your pretty nose. Think of that. I bring it here in crates of bananas."

"Don't listen to his big talk," says Mister Italy. "He doesn't bring it here."

"You should watch your fat mouth," says the neighbour.

"Bananas!" says my cousin. "Bananas have big hairy spiders! I hate spiders!"

Eve gets mad if I laugh about her spider phobia, my cousin very serious about this fear, as if spiders are hiding now in the small amount of coke. I wonder if I might sample some of that man's product. We are sweating and I drink cold beer I bought at the train station. The party-crasher neighbour with the coke is after the women. Like me.

Mister Italy tells the neighbour he should leave the party. Mister Italy turns away, the unwelcome neighbour sucker-punches Mister Italy, and the young man drops, holding his slim face.

"Get out!" shout Santino and the others. They insult the neighbour, slap him, push him out the door to go back to his apartment. Eve looks at the table as if there might be spiders there.

"That cake," she asks me. "Is that icing or mould? It looks like mould."

"I'm going with icing," I say and try some.

"I can't believe you ate that."

"I'm more pleasant when I eat."

In the corner a bearded young man rocks in the fetal position, arms hugging his knees while three women look bored. They are all younger than me, the new norm; now I am always the oldest person present as music plays loudly and wild ones turn this way and that, shouting into songs and bright conversations.

I'm happy when I eat. Did I say that already? I'm losing my mind. I don't want to be the guy with his fly open or food stains decorating a shirt-front, but I suspect it is in my future like a train approaching and not long before it arrives at the station.

A stoned woman walks past with a half-open blouse, the curves of two breasts much revealed. Rare once to see even a lady's bare ankle. Blouses fling open and life goes on. A startling blue vein runs down one breast to disappear into her blouse. Bright as a streak of blue paint or a cobalt serpent and she is so happy to make public the blood pulsing in her vein.

My high school girlfriend worried about veins on her high school breasts. Your breasts are beautiful, I tried to reassure her, but she worried about a tiny vein. And this Italian girl so happy to show the bright paint of her breast, a giant vein moving blood like a map inside her omniscient breast, a scaffolding in there holding up the 3D model. Blood is red as wine so why is a vein blue? Why am I blue? I wish to be canny, captivating: is that too much to ask?

The neighbour motors back from his apartment carrying a staple gun, the neighbour crosses the hall, crosses the room, and puts the staple gun to Mister Italy's thigh, driving in a heavy-duty staple. Mister Italy leaps, tears springing out of his eyes, Mister Italy flees the room yelling and cursing.

"I'm worried about him," says Eve.

"Is he all right?" says the stoned woman. "Does he even know his way?"

"To what?" I ask.

The stoned woman disappears down the hall of muffled echoes. Later she comes back to the pink sofa and says to my cousin, "Don't worry."

Good advice. I try to not study her sea-blue vein, though I find it fascinating and would pay money to look carefully and touch it, but I do not believe she would be interested in such an examination.

The neighbour wanders off to the kitchen, still wielding the staple gun; everyone in the kitchen is shouting normally. The party in the living room rages around me, roller coaster voices, the droning fuzz-tone of the Jesus and Mary Chain picking up speed and slowing to a halt.

The stoned young woman with the cobalt vein on her breast dances jerkily in the living room, blouse coming completely asunder, her skin taking in the air, the last button free, no longer intimate with eyelet. I assume Cobalt Girl is aware of her blouse and breasts out there like vivid menus, though who knows. Above her neck hovers her very own brain, choreographing her dance in conjunction with our music and shouting.

My cousin pins her mouth to my ear. I enjoy Eve's mouth at my ear.

"What?" I whisper into her warm hair.

"Have you not noticed?" My cousin directs my gaze with her eyes.

This young woman's brown nipples are extremely thin and long, like tiny twigs, where a bird might perch. Now, would milk squirt a greater distance from such narrow nipples? A question of physics, pressure. And my cousin's nipples so tiny and pale pink glimpsed once in a hotel room, in repressed memory. Forget that image.

Cobalt Girl dances with Santino, dances with elbows close to her waist, hands and wrists outward as she shimmies, almost the Twist. I would like to start a new dance craze. Do the Mashed Potato. Do the Staple Gun, do the Lazy Lawyer, do the Dee-vor-cee dividing his assets and shekels.

Santino grins at me, Santino whispers in her ear and they dance some more and then they stop.

"You must watch, my new friends," says Santino. "In an American movie we saw a dancer do this."

The other, is his name Pepini? Penino? My brain is not to be relied on. Where is my drink.

Santino takes one paper match and with a pen-knife slices the middle of the match so that there is a narrow opening. Cobalt Girl takes the match from Santino and carefully places the opening of the one match to her breast so that the match grips her long nipple. Santino hands her another such match and then she lights them both, pointing each head up and away from her skin. Cobalt Girl dances proudly in front of us, shifting her hips and smiling at her party trick.

She says something in Italian.

"Do you see this in Canada?" Santino translates.

"No."

"No, I thought not. Not in Canada, eh."

Is that an Italian "eh" or a Canadian "eh"?

The stoned woman dances and moves her head side to side, she's seen this sultry style of dancing on videos, she moves so that her hair swings, like a star on celluloid. I worry about the small flames hurting the skin of her breasts, but instead the burning matches cause her swinging hair to catch fire, perhaps a tad too much flammable hairspray or some weird gel.

Eve points a finger like a gun, says, "That isn't good."

Santino looks from us to Cobalt Girl, stops grinning and calmly throws his drink on her, so I pour the remainder of my beer over her burning hair. Others add their drinks. It is as if we are allowed to urinate on her. Cobalt Girl is crying, tears and drinks tracking down over her bare breasts and snuffed black matches, Cobalt Girl runs to the bathroom, hair smouldering like a volcano. It's kind of sexy. Where is the volcano, I mean the washroom? Where am I?

Sometimes when travelling I must look about and remind myself where I am, what new kingdom I gaze at. I like that feeling of being momentarily lost, of a brief gap, of having different eyes, new eyes upon gnarled trees and brightest scooter. I am near Naples on a scratchy pink couch and I am prying open a cold beer that is warm. Sometimes I feel like that dead Roman rat I saw beneath the trees. Sometimes I feel like a chocolate bar with too many bite marks. Sometimes I feel the world is a very beautiful white T-shirt.

Another giant joint makes the rounds, strong and harsh behind my teeth. I feel instantly stoned or re-stoned, I'm not sure of the order, not used to this quality. Eve says that Mister Italy is back. By the door a teenager from the train is showing Santino and Mister Italy a knife with a beautiful handle the shade of dark honey, as if an ancient scorpion might be trapped there in amber. They admire the lovely knife.

The woman with hair so recently on fire is laughing again, though her hair looks frizzily fucked up: she moves room to room laughing, smoking up from a tiny bag of weed.

She says to me in Italian, "After that ordeal I am very thirsty, tell me, do you have *birra*?"

"Yes," I say. "I'm happy to share."

"That's good you are happy with me." Cobalt Girl smiles, puts on a porkpie hat, just an old-fashioned girl who likes the traditional drugs. It may simply be the fine dope, but her laughing makes me laugh, I like her.

I'm not happy (especially about Natasha), but I know I can be happy again. I know it is there, but what port of call, what passport, what bright map on my wall, what coast and sea? I know a port exists, know it is close. When I find it I will write a book called *Duct Tape for the Soul* and it will sell gazillions.

"Thank you for the *birra*."

"*Prego. De nada.*" Or is that Spanish? I get the words mixed up, think I'm in Spain. Pliny was in Spain. I wonder if Cobalt Girl was with the group kicking out the train window. She mimes tossing beer on her hair. *Sì, sì.* She mimes a moonwalk. Michael Jackson! Yes! I get it now. His hair caught fire too!

The kitchen group fights as if one pulsating organism. *Perché vendichi su di me l'offesa che ti ha fatto un altro?* Why are you taking revenge on me for someone else's offence? It sounds too Sicilian for words. Why are they all so fucking loud?

The white doorway pours noise into the living room; young males run out and males run into the kitchen talking in tongues, raucous Italian voices producing a rapid clatter of words, like a rock beach rolling in brisk surf.

Mamma mia, che rabbia mi fai! How you enrage me!

Mi trattengo dal dire quello che penso solo per buona educa zione. I refrain from saying what I think only because of my good upbringing.

Santino has a silver pen, or is it the knife? What is he saying to Mister Italy?

Hands waving. To give a lesson!

In the kitchen they shove each other, Naples's surly suburban dancers pushing and fighting, two sides, three sides, one room of the party becoming a minor brawl. A young woman says something and is knocked over and kicked by the older neighbour and she crawls the floor like a shouting crocodile. Maybe this is normal (the word *normative* pops into my head from Sociology 100, hi Professor Gee), I can't tell as there is so much noise in Italy, so much life, so many scooter horns beeping threats and throats calling out *la dolce vita*, vim and vengeance.

During the day they shout at me at the grocery cashier, at the café, in the street, from the kitchen; it's a hectoring country, it's almost comic to be shouted at so much. Someone shouts *dargli una lezione*, give him a lesson, a leg for a leg. Which leg do they mean? Mister Italy's leg? Staple Gun Guy the neighbour's leg?

I start to stand up, but the stoned woman laughs and pulls me down into her lap and smoky smell. She says her name is Maria and she's friendly and warm, she's Italian! From this odd perspective I have a sideways view of the crowded kitchen.

Santino bends low, his face looking sleepy as he swings his arm in a resigned arc that ends with a knife driven into the neighbour's thigh. Blood gushes immediately at the base of the knife, as if Santino struck an oil well, and in the room a general hiss of understanding and pity and then more voices, more shouting, more gesturing. His leg, his blood-splattered denim, blood falls from him, blood on the floor.

I stand up too fast and feel pressure in my brow; my brain is collapsing, back to the baboon, back to the apes. Maria props me up as Santino runs out of the crowd like a hunched assassin. Mister Italy and others follow him out the door in a more assured manner. Staple Gun Guy looks at his liquid leg. The knife is gone from his leg. Who removed the knife?

Maybe the assailant thought a jab to the leg was not dangerous, but how the blood wells, how it pours from the man, blood born in the kitchen, he can't stop the blood freed from tiny culverts and tunnels. The neighbour's blood is dark, but glistens. Blood polka dots around the kitchen, dots the size of coins, red coins painting the canvas so quickly. Maria the stoned woman stares at Staple Gun Guy. It's like opera. How can there be so much blood draining from one cut? The eye can't understand the image it seizes (*I smote him thus*).

The neighbour looks down at his leg, nature staring back. No more chronic for you, no more nose candy. A young woman holds a tea towel to the gushing leg. "It won't stop!" she cries.

The knife must have met an artery, severed an artery, we meet in a rented room of blood, blood so scarlet on their white floor and dark rug and a trail as he heads to the door, to another country. Don't move, they say, but the neighbour wishes to go home with his staple gun. It's my party and I'll die if I want to.

He passes by and my cousin Eve stares as if a monster is walking past on a moor (*amore!*). The monster passes the armchair the shape and colour of an ancient tombstone and the coffee table with my bottles and the small baggie of cocaine under the blue light bulb. Eve took a first-aid course, says he shouldn't walk if he's bleeding like that, he should really stay still.

The neighbour makes it to the door, but falls in the hall like a Doric column. He has bled out. Now the kitchen empties, groups pushing and shoving, not to fight, but to exit. Partygoers nimbly leap his body and flee like goats down the long hall. An older woman opens her apartment door to peer out at the raucous stampede, the mad stomping hurdle race. Spying blood and a body, the woman dials her small silver phone, whispers, Madonna save us.

A few linger in the living room; either they didn't do it or they live here; until this second I hadn't thought of someone living here. A home. It was just a party. One well-dressed man stops, calmly checks the body on the stained carpet.

"*E morto,*" he states as if saying the weather is inclement.

Maria the stoned woman takes the staple gun and leaves.

Eve says, "Let's go. They called the police."

"What about an ambulance?"

"The *polizia* will handle it. We have to leave."

"My beer."

"Forget your fucking beer!"

I grab the tiny bag of coke and step over the stained carpet and body in the liminal doorway. Why did I ever walk up this narrow hall? *Morto*, blood flees a human so quickly and all of us drain the rooms so quickly and down the crowded stairs, slim bodies draped in black suits and pants, knees and arms moving jerkily in black-crow angles against sharp white stucco, stucco where you cut your elbow and bleed if you touch the wall.

•

On the street we run past the World War Two tanks again, run like pale ghosts past the same Chinese factory and radioactive canal water and a distant figure throwing something, a tiny splash in the silver canal, perhaps a stolen phone or the knife from the neighbour's leg.

Eve and I turn a corner and there are two policemen standing in pretty leather boots and jodhpurs.

Oh fuck, I think. We attempt to impersonate people walking calmly, but how? I have forgotten the details of calm, I should have taken notes during a calm time knowing this would happen down the line.

One policeman hugs a middle-aged woman who is crying non-stop, she can't stop. The policeman holds up a device for her to breathe into. Is it a puffer to help her breathe or to measure alcohol in her system? No idea. The policeman tells her to stop struggling or she can be charged. She grips the policeman's face in her hands, chants something into his face. He asks her to stop, but she won't remove her hands from his face.

My cousin whispers a rough translation: "I'm putting my fifty-year-old hands in your face if I feel like it. You're half my age, you little fucking dick."

Perhaps, as I've told my cousin and Tamika, I'm invisible. The police don't care about us as they are busy loosening her hands from his face. Men in soccer shirts outside a social club watch my cousin and me come up the sidewalk. Word cannot have spread of the nearby party.

"*Scusi*," says my cousin. "Train? *Treno? Stazione?*" Her Italian is better than mine.

They point down the boulevard toward the sea. "*Gira a sinistra.*"

"Left," I say. I know that sinister means left and enjoy that word, *sinistra*. The left hand is unlucky.

"*Grazie,*" says my cousin, "*grazie.*"

"First you come drink with us," the man says.

"Sorry, we must go."

"No. One drink! To life! One drink!"

"*Numero di telefono?*" another asks hopefully.

"No, no," says my pretty cousin, "in Italy I have no phone."

"*Andate a piedi?*"

"*Sì*, we're walking."

"A nice walk," says one and grabs her backside. "If that was my wife…"

"That's my ass!" I yell. Why did I say that?

"Fuck off," she yells.

"To life!" they yell. We're way down the block, I think that's what they yell.

We're running, we run blocks to the train station and I'm gasping; I can ride a clunker bike all day, but I'm not used to running. The station ticket window is empty, no one is in charge, which is fine by me. I've been travelling on an expired pass that also allows me into art galleries and museums around Naples. I'll pay a fine, I'm just glad to be on board. Now if the train will just move. I can't sit. *Move, move.*

I don't care where the train goes, I just don't want to be around if the *polizia* are looking for witnesses or a scapegoat for the knifing, don't want to be a person of interest. Father Silas's art school is not officially recognized in Italy. *Move!*

My cousin asks, "Are we supposed to carry our passports? Mine's at the hotel."

"Any blood on us?"

"No one knows we were there."

We check our clothes for blood splatters anyway, our hands.

"Check the bottom of my shoes."

Did we walk in blood? And that blood-sodden tea towel.

"Maybe the guy's okay."

"I'd say he was pretty well gone." Gone west. We sit for what seems like humming hours, then our train betrays that buzzy feeling just before movement begins, that pre-coital imminence, and we sail forward in a silent sway of deliverance.

I remember a funeral for a good friend on the west coast, a lively giant of a man, very well liked. I've never heard so many people say, *He was my best friend*. I was getting jealous. At the open coffin funeral we sat in solemn pews waiting for the sad service to start and instead the Steppenwolf song "Born to be Wild" roared to life, loud as hell.

Everyone in the funeral chapel laughed; he would have liked that, he laughed a lot. But I saw his big face blank in the coffin and his combed beard and thought, Yes, he is spent, he is dead, he is missing from his own face. Some force that was him no longer there (Elvis has left the apartment building). Maybe that's why we have open casket funerals or a wake with the body right in your parlour, so you *know*, really feel the knowledge physically and don't wait for him to show up at your door or expect to see your old friend for a pint in Swans pub. *E morto*. You must know.

Our night train will swallow us, will travel all the way to Sorrento. The swallows return. Now, is that Sorrento or Capistrano? A leg with a knife severing a major artery. No more stoned young women for the neighbour with the staple gun. Come back. The dead hand, like the men on the crowded subway in Rome leaving their hand low to grope women, *mortua manus*. See the wonders of the ancient world!

"Did you even see who stabbed him?"

I decide to lie. "No, no, I just saw legs and a blade swinging." And all that blood that should stay inside.

"I just want to be back at the hotel. Be back home."

·"We'll be back soon enough."

She looks so forlorn, whereas I feel immense relief that the train is shunting us away. I show my cousin the stolen baggie.

"You took that from the dead guy? Why?" She looks around the train. "Are you fucking crazy?"

"I had some years ago and really liked it, but I could never afford it."

"Fuck! What if we get stopped?"

"I'll get rid of it."

·"They'd see you tossing it."

My Irish cousins have an expression when something is of little use: like throwing water on a dead rat. I realize it's my birthday and I missed it wandering this beautiful rat's nest on a bay. My birthday present.

"I don't know. It was sitting there. I wanted to try some again. I'll hide it in my sock."

We'll be okay. The familiar train will deliver us back to chapels and chipped frescoes and Fabergé eggs and our whining art group. The aged conductor always so calm in the heat and sweat of day and the ennui of night. Our conductor possesses natural dignity. He does not bring up the idea of tickets. I am glad he runs the train. His childhood bride waits at home; this

I am sure of. She is plumper than when they met at the dance and the world was shot in black and white.

The calm conductor and his bride make me think about marriage. Marriage is success, marriage is failure, marriage is music, a ride, marriage is a train with windows. Every room is a train with windows, every office and every head is a train with windows, everything in the world is a train with windows.

The question is, Do you kick out the windows or do you sit politely and hope for the uniformed conductor? Does our conductor live with his wife in smouldering Naples or far out on the flank of the famous volcano? Does Maria the stoned Cobalt Woman live on the volcano? She was nice to me and then ran.

A man very near answers his phone: "*Pronto?!*" His voice sounds so hopeful in my ear, rising sharply at the end of the fast word: *pron-TO!!* But his phone will not agree to work.

"I'm on the train," he shouts. "I might lose you."

The dead man went pale as we lost him, as we watched, no more phone calls for him. In the mountain tunnels this time no one kicks out the glass. There is no one Italy, there is a vast collection of Italys, but this Italy tonight is sombre, in black, this Italy is sixteen coaches long, our train moving beside the sea, our train on top of the rolling sea.

Dories on painters drift, reach the end of the rope, pale boats wobbling between stars under water, submerged light the shape of lost milky amphoras, yachts and white moving lights on water and light under the sea and then I see the spotlights touching the church and City Hall, where I bought a handsome watch from a flea market table.

Ah, I recognize where we are now. Next stop. I'm becoming an old hand, an expert.

"*Prossima fermata*," I say very slowly to my cousin, my best singsong Italian accent, drawing out the pleasing words as I try them on. "Next stop is ours. How are you doing?"

"Rock and roll," she says weakly.

"*Pronto!*" calls the man. He is having such problems with the tunnels. "Can you hear me now? Now can you hear me?"

When he finishes his conversation he says *Ciao* musically five or six times, then looks at the phone: *did I say it too many times or was it just right?*

We stop and start with the train's moves, lean into each other, her head fitting under my jaw. I like my cousin's warm form against me.

The room is warm and Eve lies on my hotel bed stripped down to a T-shirt and small white panties. She says, "You don't need to sleep on the floor because of me. But I'm afraid to be in my room alone. You still have the dead guy's dope?"

"You don't want that now."

Her clean leg by my eye. She says we can share the bed. The unstabbed skin of my cousin's fine thigh leading my eye up to her hips and her secrets, where I want to touch, tension vibrating in the air like silver wires, I will explode if I don't touch, but I don't touch her. *Mortua manus*, the dead hand. She is worried, jittery, but there is no knife in her leg. The night air is sweet and light golden on cobbles below.

"At the topless beach today I was so happy," Eve whispers as she moves into sleep. "I met those Italian boys. We'll pray for him. In a real church. Promise? That one with the amazing Caravaggio that just pops. The other paintings, no. That Caravaggio is the one. Promise?"

Yes, I promise. She is drifting off in my bed and I stay on the sea-coloured tiles the Croatian woman cleans every morning. In my head for some reason an old Blondie tune, "Fade Away and Radiate." Those NYC junkies, the Chelsea crowd, how did they hang on through all the shit like this? Does Eve mean the Caravaggio with the boy bitten by the lizard or the crucifixion (some noteworthy, but not Christ) or the man on the horse or the daughter breastfeeding her father who is starving behind bars? My cousin's face looked so pale reflected in the train window in the tunnels, our train inside a dark mountain, something pushed into a body. Tomorrow we'll pray for everyone. I promise.

Later that week I discover that my party souvenir is gone, my baggie with the dead man's cocaine is gone. Maybe Naples is also gone, buried once again by the volcano.

Could Eve have taken the baggie? She is, as the police say, a person of interest. Certainly not clean-living Tamika with her bright white shoes or the train conductor who loves his wife so. The pretty Croatian woman who cleans my room? Or did I consume all of the dead man's cocaine during a deranged night and also consume the memory? That has happened before.

Around this same time Father Silas misplaces his fat envelope full of so many euro notes (cash is king at Italian hotel desks) and now our group is bereft, now we are bankrupt. Is our dauphin getting dotty or were the euros nicked by the rooftop cat-burglar who plucked an American's Rolex and Nikon camera from an open third-floor window? Knaves and harridans and coal-burners and a slim hand coming into your room.

Our director wears a houndstooth jacket draped on his shoulders like a cape, hoping for that continental *La Dolce Vita* matador look. How will we survive now that our leader has lost all our money? How to pay for meals at Francesco's café, for so many nights at the hotel? How will we get home? Perhaps our future holds a giant dine-and-dash with luggage. Can we sneak our backpacks past the vigilant French woman who never leaves the front desk?

And what happens after you feel the sly knife penetrate your thigh and you expire in a kitchen across the hall from your home? Can you bring your staple gun to heaven? His daughter was there at the party, saw her father die. I don't know how I missed that, but my cousin insists this is true (*no lie, GI*). In the hall the weeping daughter held her father in her arms as we left the party, as he left the country, as the father vanished into the afterlife.

The stoned girl with the cobalt vein and volcanic hair: I threw my drink on her to help her, did we have some strange chemistry? Maria! How do you solve a problem like Maria? So many things you will never know, so many naked legs you will never touch. But if any of us make it to heaven, I hope these matters will seem less important.

Some nights Eve can't sleep and takes tiny blue pills; my pretty cousin says she remembers the knife and can't sleep. Like me she remembers waiting on a train and willing the monster to move. But time passes and we forget. I love time. Time gives me everything, time cracks me up, time kills me.

Hospital Island
(Wild Thing)

I would have made a good Pope.

—Richard Nixon

The afternoon sun hides a thief in my eye. My cousin Eve hides so little as she sunbathes on my rooftop terrace, hides almost nothing as we read the newspapers or work together on a crossword. She loves gazing at newsprint; I believe if Eve owned a moped here in Rome she'd happily read a rattling paper while buzzing Rome's boulevards. When was the last time I drove!

Eve and I fled like thieves back to Rome via high-speed train, the trip seemed only minutes, cool air and blue seats on the train to Rome and no one in the car talking, a train so much quieter than the old train circling the volcano. In Rome I can't believe how comforting it is to be back in our same rooms, the hotel a refuge; we hide inside and lie away the day, eyes shut, but Eve can't sleep after the knifing at the party, Eve can't stop thinking about the knife in the Italian man's thigh and why so much blood, she can't stop thinking.

"How does one just go to sleep? It's as if I've never learned."

Yet I sleep soundly, a genius of sleep, which my wife resented greatly. I sleep like a groggy winter bear; what is wrong with me?

I say, "Can't you think about something else, try to not worry?"

Eve looks at me for a moment as if I am a complete moron, but does not say that. She says, "That's like saying, *Why is the sky blue?*" That it is part of her makeup to worry. Her tiny sleeping pills are bitter on the roof of her mouth.

"It's not the best sleep," she says, "but it's better than none." A green lizard peeks out from a hole in the wall as we start in on a bottle of ferocious red wine.

My mouth tastes of mufflers and conflict (*Rome throat*, says Eve of the exhaust clouds and particulates in the air we breathe, she says it's like smoking a pack of cigarettes, that only Bulgaria is worse), but the moped riders look so beautiful, sleek executives and office workers in silk suits and fluttering dresses and sharp winkle-picker shoes coming at you in formation, a phalanx of Valkyries balanced on tiny toy wheels.

They killed St. Valentine on February 14th outside the Flaminian Gate during the reign of Claudius the Goth. Valentine's skull was crowned with birds and flowers, he gave eyesight to the blind, hope to the bland. They beat him with clubs and stoned him and later severed his head at the gate; they took their time. Christian couples came to the city gate, young couples he had secretly married, they came and left gifts for this martyr as he died slowly for his true faith. Or this saintly man did not exist and was invented by Chaucer, or he worked for a chocolate lobby group, like the Easter Bunny. The Church is no longer exactly sure.

But the riders look so beautiful. My admiration for Roman drivers grows and grows. Local drivers seemed crazed at first, but now I see their staggering talent; cars and scooters fly from all sides like jets in a dogfight, but I have yet to witness an accident. Lanes and lines mean little and at each red light hordes of scooters wobble past rows of stopped cars and assemble ahead of their bumpers, a dozen scooters across the real estate of two tiny lanes, scooters ready to roar away at the green. Drivers share such little space without border wars, without crashing, though I did see a woman fly off a moped on a corner by the open-air market, her moving cry the exact pitch of the engine she was leaving behind. The ambulances park right on our street so she was in good hands.

"Look at this photo," says Eve. "Before the war, the German company Hohner gave Pope Pius XI a chromatic harmonica covered with jewels."

Eve passes me her book with its colour photo: a gorgeous harmonica with fluttery brass reeds and a gold casing encrusted with jewels and ivory. We both glance over at the imposing Vatican wall; is the harmonica still *there*?

"Can we ask the Pope for a look?"

"The current pontiff doesn't seem very approachable. He is not simpatico, he is not, how do the Italians say it, not *papabile*. They need to clean house."

Eve doesn't like this German Pope, she says his raccoon eyes speak of bad vibes and red-hatted cardinals stabbing each other in the back, Eve says you could hang pork chops from both his ears and the dogs still wouldn't play with him. She wants a new Pope, she says. "You'd make a better Pope than this Nazi goof."

The green lizard glows in the wall and we punish the bottle of red. Eve becomes more and more certain that I can be the first Canadian Pope. (I wonder, can we count Louis Riel as a Pope of Assiniboia?)

"Yes, the votes are being counted," says Eve, "now I can see the white smoke from the chimney, they've decided!"

What odds would British bookies give on a foreign tourist becoming the new Pope? Slim to none. But I am not the worst candidate. Once I was an altar boy serving First Fridays at dawn, I know my way around the rosary beads and confessional and Stations of the Cross, I know some Latin, the Credo and the Confiteor, and as a child I left room for my guardian angel to sit beside me at my school desk and I left room for my guardian angel alongside me in my tiny childhood bed.

"Listen," says Eve. "The Pope is Catholic and you are Catholic, or were once; the Pope has a cool apartment in Rome, you have a cool apartment in Rome; the Pope does not golf, you do not golf; the Pope does not ride a noisy Vespa, you do not ride a noisy Vespa; the Pope likes 'Wild Thing' by the Troggs, you like 'Wild Thing' by the Troggs."

I can see no flaw in this logic. I am made in God's image while this Pope's raccoon eyes speak of secrets and bad vibes and Machiavellian rooms of red-hatted cardinals. How would I look in a scarlet cassock and beanie cap? My first act will be to free the Pope's butler from his Vatican jail cell and he will kiss my mobster holy-man ring out of gratitude. I'll have a butler! *Ditat Deus*, God enriches.

As a child I wanted to be a priest and I envisioned my guardian angel as blond and slim and kindly, not unlike the Quebec stewardess who helped me with the taxi, not unlike Natasha, who was kind until the moment she left me. Has that childhood religious vision affected my expectations of real women later in life, of those I make room for in my bed?

I say, "I always assumed my guardian angel was blond. But Jesus was Middle Eastern; would he not be dark-haired?"

"How many angels are there in total?" Eve asks. "Does the Pope know? Do all the angels sleep together in a dorm and have pillow fights?"

There are gaps in dogma, but I love the look and colours of Rome, its lovely hues stuck in my eye, shades of crimson and cinnamon, salmon and sienna, charcoal and blood, black brick touching blond brick touching walls of ashen stone, ochre clay and yellow plaster and tile in startling nebula swirls and slabs of veined green marble.

I could live here, where cobblestones lift around the bases of ancient trees and that bridge over the river dates from before Christ. Once they loaded plague victims on barges to float them out of the city to the sea. Laundry on the next building slaps in the breeze, a nautical effect, linen and blouses like mizzen skysails and royal staysails and flying jibs, as if the tenements will also weigh anchor and slip into the Tiber to drift downriver to Ostia and the sea.

"Chin-chin," says Eve in a toast, "to a Canuck Pope."

Voices drift to us in perfect clarity.

"Tom Hanks just walked right by!"

Tom Hanks is filming some Dan Brown crap in a nearby piazza.

"On the set he made a sour face when someone blew a take, but he just seems so nice!"

Maybe Tom can help me, he's got connections, he's got juice, he knows where the bodies are buried. But what if Tom Hanks also wants to be Pope? Maybe that is his real reason to be in

Rome, and this execrable movie is a foxy diversion. Tom has
boatloads of money: why doesn't he try making a good movie
instead of a bad one?

Eve tells me of past Popes, reads a list of how many Popes
were murdered and how many Popes were murderers. This is
not a happy story. Constantine II: murdered. Stephen VII:
strangled in prison. John X: strangled in prison. John XI: died
in prison. Benedict VI: strangled in prison.

"Is Pope Joan on the list? What was the life expectancy?
This sounds a dangerous job."

"But you'd be famous. The first Canuck Pope."

"Louis Riel had a similar idea and I seem to remember that
led to Mr. Riel hanging on the end of a rope in Regina."

Fame to me does not seem a good thing. Fame seems like
some form of dementia or Alzheimer's where everyone knows
you but you don't know them.

Pope John XIV was killed by a certain Francone, then the
newly installed Pope Francone was himself murdered and Pope
Gelasius was set upon with stones and arrows. Pope Gelato was
destroyed by diabetes and Pope George Ringo lost his record deal.

Italian newspapers drift soft as Kleenex outside every station of the Metro. I look at each page for a news article, but
the nervous suburb under the distant volcano seems to have
absorbed the bloody knifing without comment. They expect
it of Napoli.

Eve puts aside the book, says, "See that cloud? It looks like
a penis."

I wouldn't have thought that. "Very like a penis."

The clouds are there, but the rain is holding off.

"Or a killer whale."

She says, "I want to see the fresco *The Liberation of Saint*

Peter from Prison. I saw the *David* long ago and it looked so lonely."

Eve is scholarly, better at languages and accents than I am; she can mimic any passing tourist voice (*how much is that in real money?*) and she comfortably teaches in French and Italian at her school in the Alps. She skis mountain frontiers and she appreciates fine food more than I can, has made a point to educate herself in French and Italian cooking, likes meat rare where I want it charred black, makes a tasty piece of salmon. When a meal arrives she admires the bright vegetable colours, meals so pretty we don't want to disturb the plates.

"Wait," she says, "wait. The eye must eat before the stomach."

We are deep in a city of millions, but songbirds flit the nearby boughs and a green parrot balances at the tip of the tree; it makes me happy to spy the fabled green parrot in the tree, my eyes, my tree, my parrot's weird chirping as goldfinches zip behind Eve in lines of yellow light, swift radiant birds leaving the imprint of a sunlit laser show on my eyeballs, wild birds asking nothing of me, selling nothing, possessing nothing but beauty and song.

On the sunny terrace above the shaded warehouses my cousin reads to me from her book of Roman history; she knows I am obsessed by Pliny the Elder and she feeds my obsession: here is Pliny battling in northern swamps, Pliny fighting barbarian tribes on horseback, Pliny beating up the Franks, Hungarians, Vandals, Pliny smoking blunts and tossing deadly javelins from horseback.

Pliny rides and our green lizard glows in the wall. The next bottle of wine is reminiscent of cabbage and sardines so we decide it must be way good. My bookish cousin Eve looks nice in that female-who-isn't-yours sort of way: dark glasses, pigtails, capri pants, Chinese slippers.

St. Valentine is the patron saint of beekeepers and travellers, so I feel close to him (does it really matter whether Valentine existed?). I'm not a beekeeper, but bees seem to like me and I'm a traveller. Pliny travelled the far edges of his Roman world, but he came back to the centre of empire to die under the volcano, asphyxiated near Pompeii, or did Pliny suffer a stroke? The volcanic cloud rose through green sky, a ghost tree hanging over beautiful villas until the shape collapsed and crashed in ash and heavy stones to crush the beautiful villas. I can't stop thinking of Pliny and his last deadly moments in Pompeii, sky gone black as a room with no light, his small apocalypse in the same town as the knife party where the unwanted neighbour fell in the hallway and we ran like spooked goats.

During the day I worry about Eve's pale skin in Italy's powerful sun. My cousin doesn't worry, no, she thrives on sun and heat in scanty summer outfits. Others limp back to their rooms exhausted from our exalted tasks in the world of art and red-faced from our master the sun, but she seems unfazed, Eve thrives.

As the sun fades behind walls I quietly play my new chromatic harmonica, silver flashing as pink Roman stone turns dark, and I gaze at her form, a thief hiding in my eye.

On my rooftop terrace Eve says, "You know you have to get over her. Dwelling on it is not going to magically change things." Eve enjoys lecturing me about my lost Natasha, my girl from the north country. Eve has brought beautiful tart berries from the street market to our rooftop, she passes me a cold lemon drink and reads an André Gide aphorism from her endless heap of used paperbacks: *To be utterly happy, you must refrain from comparing this moment with other moments in the past.*

Yes, but how to *not* compare? How to stop the built-in comparison machinery in your head?

"Well sir, that's another problem," says Eve.

Archimedes worked out problems in the sand. They killed Archimedes in 212 BC as he was drawing his circles in the sand, his colony invaded.

Wait, Archimedes said reasonably as crazed Romans attacked him with swords, wait until I finish my math problem, my circles in the sand.

We must all deal with our problems, the zestless bottled water, the border wars over armrests in dark cinemas, the lost yellow-cake uranium, we must forgive the recalcitrant lawn mower.

But did the Roman soldiers wait for Archimedes to solve his crisis of the lawn mower? No. They put Archimedes to the sword, soldiers invaded the colony, invaded his body. I suppose that is a sort of solution to a problem. Or the problem is swiftly made a lot less relevant.

I am aware of my need to get past this niggling crippling memory, to put to the sword this rash abandonment by Natasha. Don't be a stick in the mud, they say, get out more. LBJ said to me once on his ranch in Texas, "Son, don't let dead cats stand on your porch."

I do thank you, *sage* advice, got it, I hear where you're coming from, I must stop.

But then I realize — I *am* getting out! I'm out skiing the snowy Alps and walking dusty excavations in Pompeii (the fine grit of Pompeii's ruins ruining Father Silas's camera), I'm out for wild-boar sausage in Naples and good craic in Dubrovnik and dear dirty Dublin (though I loathe the techno maelstrom of Temple Bar) and I stroll sandy strands on Dingle Bay and cheer on pig races in West Cork, I'm drinking wheat beer under the street in Manchester (tiny stellar jukebox hung on the wall), sangria in Madrid, mariachi music in Mexico, I'm up in planes and I'm jumping out of planes, I'm violating Mayan airspace, I'm moving like an illegal crack-block through the high-stepping June Taylor Dancers, I even snowboarded sand dunes just outside Dubai and man oh man the sand hurts way more than snow when you wipe. No dead cowboy can accuse me of letting dead cats stand on my porch.

Yet my moves and trips don't seem to count in my own head, my jittery journeys on the Adriatic or Irish Sea don't seem *authentic*. I am cowed, I am more awed by any stranger's matrix of travel, real trips with tidy storylines and clear beginnings and madrigal endings and pettifoggers and riot-police Plexiglas and fine hotels in latitudes of lassitude. Why do my own journeys not impress me, why do I have no faith in my blurry couch-surfing pilgrimages to see graves and relatives and breweries and the haughty swans of Sligo. Why do I have no faith in my own life?

The knifing in Napoli may have given me some gruesome perspective. This perspective changes moment to moment, but right now I think I'm weirdly better about Natasha.

It is good to at least *once* be in a relationship with this kind of depth and fervour, to know it, but not to the point of leaping from a bridge. After Natasha abandoned me in a hotel I hit a point where I understood why people leap from bridges, I was on the bridge and fully understood the attraction, but I did not leap from the bridge. I am resilient, I will bounce back, I will be the Superball driven into the pavement and bouncing clear over the roof of my childhood home.

It's a bit of a surprise, but Rome's rouge walls and running water spigots seem familiar and pleasing after Naples's grey hulks and volcanic dust and volcanic drugs and jackal bedlam and mountains of aromatic refuse and a knife steering its formal way through the air of a kitchen party and a man lying like meat in the hall.

I knew that Rome had a pleasant complexion, but until I left and came back I didn't know that I'd taken it in my head this way, that I was returning to a place that seems an old friend, an open city that seems warm and broad and green — so oddly comforting to be held in Rome's glowing walls again.

As I walk Rome it seems almost a home, as if I know it well and have spent some bright worthy part of my life here, which may not be true, but is a fine feeling since I seem to have lost my sense of home and I don't know if I'll have it back.

In Rome we live inside the beautiful sun; in Rome we live where the ambulances start. The ambulances park on the street below and race away to help the unfortunates, a pleasing musical quality to their sirens, almost mariachi. Where we live in Rome is not far from the river, a nineteenth-century district that Benito Mussolini expanded while feeling expansive, before things went bad in the twentieth century and they hung Benito and his mistress Claretta by the heels in Milan, the way the mob cornered Cola di Rienzo with all their sharp knives on the high steps, on the monumental steps leading up to the gods envious of our blades and opinions.

So many blades and invasions — I can't keep track — so much meat and so many martyrs and monsters and gargoyles and gods and I study Eve's face transfixed listening to a woman's high lovely voice singing music of such formality and grief, *And thou true God gave thy only son.* And Croatian daughters on hands and knees scrubbing halls to earn pennies.

Il Signore sia con voi. The Lord be with you.

E con il tuo spirito. And with your spirit.

These Italian church refrains still familiar from childhood Sundays, bells pealing and Sunday memories turning over like those venerable Pontiac Laurentians with straight-six engines that run forever. In Regina the new country hanged Riel by the neck and stole his modest church bell, took it east to Ontario.

Eve hovers near another varnished painting, cracked faces and black shadows, the stone church cool and quiet, mysterious as a suicide on a bridge, and all that sunshine just outside — just a dark chapel bent under endless stone light.

Studying the Immortals makes me feel so very mortal, staring up at shadowy paintings and marble faces speaking of sorrow, staring at the work of murderous turbulent geniuses, at tapestries and crazily amazing ceilings, frescoes in colours like faint laughter from within planets, and angels and saints flying up into the sun, flying from sin and guilt, and collections of gilt Byzantine icons, gorgeous metallic paintings of the Madonna in starry blue robes with a tiny child and sober aquiline faces, faces bent into long cubist angles.

These devout Byzantine faces make me want to jump up and tear across an ancient map to know Istanbul's eastern empires and all the Virgin Mary's collection of custard-yellow halos and cobalt gowns.

Pliny the Elder tore around the ancient papyrus maps. I have an image of Pliny when he was much younger, as if I am there on the deck of his wooden boat, part of his crew and Pliny my captain cutting the waves in a speedy Arab felucca, firkins lashed down and sharp sails snapping and swinging around my sunburnt face.

I hang my white shirts in the sun near a lazaretto, the hospital island named after the beggar Lazarus, the island where they sent plague victims on open barges to the sea and I wonder, how does Eve's skin feel and smell, and what is it to cradle her limbs on a high Irish hill and feel her shirt, feel her shadow move over me like a cloud on gold grass.

Mr. Tom Hanks has been zero help in my campaign to be Pope, I must now consider Tom Hanks an adversary. Memo: no more causes. Unlike me, Tom has the money to run a real campaign. And he is well liked. He may well be the next Pope instead of me, Tom waving from the balcony. Tell me, is luck a thing you manufacture, like a set of tires?

In my hotel room late at night I can't stop listening to Cat Power's troubled cover of "Moonshiner," listen over and over to her lament, *if drinking do not kill me*. Her voice, ghostly slow, seems to accrue more distant meaning and weight than the song's plain words should ever be able to convey. It's a spooky puzzle and I keep trying to figure it out, at two a.m. the matter seems of utmost importance.

Eve downloads music on her laptop; she is a student of Italian opera, but she also likes drone blues and alt-country. Her strange authority.

Eve says she can't stop thinking of the art we've seen, like so much chocolate, too many treasures for one spot. We whisper to each other in the gallery: how was it all collected here in one spot, how many robbed and murdered in its superb suspect provenance?

Eve says, "The big thieves hang the little thieves."

The groaning galleries and museums are too much to take in at once, we stagger as if eating too much, it's staggering. But that rich swag is why we are here.

Our sheets and shirts spread on the bright terrace as we taste apples from Afghanistan and dates from the Euphrates and sip sharp juice from blood oranges. It's so lovely to eat outside with a view of this fabled city. Mangoes and blood oranges, mangoes her new favourite and Eve waves a tiny knife to demonstrate how to peel the lovely skin.

She smiles widely. "Remember we saw that huge fish jump in the Tiber? What timing, just as we walked up. Two or three feet, and fat!"

She seems bright today. Is sleep coming easier at night? Will we ever be reconciled with the knife at the party, will the mind forget the body twitching in the hall and the dead man's poor daughter weeping? All those body parts worked as a perfect machine until the introduction of the knife into the sensitive wires under the surface. We escaped to the silent train and the town's closed shutters.

"What is Italian for blood oranges? I should know," Eve says.

Later she remembers and emails an answer: *Arancia sanguigna. Ci vediamo presto! xxx*

See you soon. In Gaspé the laundry lines so noisy flapping in the winds off the sea, but in Rome her sheets are silent in sun and heat, no noise or fanfare as moisture exits the cotton, cloth dry in moments.

"Are you peckish? I have some smoked salmon and honeydew apples. We'll have a bite and then go wander."

When wandering I enjoy happy accidents, enjoy my mind's momentary lapses and I forget where I am. I wandered through Piazza Cavour the other afternoon and found a huge bruised palace fronted by groves of shaggy palm trees, tropical palm trees and erotic statues on stone plinths, this otherworldly palace decorated like a Cuban wedding cake — such long stripes of ornate balcony and porticos and fluttering doves and steroid blossoms pushed toward me from every meaty tree in the piazza. I stand in Rome and walk someone else's fever dream of Latin America. What a dream, what a bewitching chimera city, where they beat the shit out of the patron saint of lovers, beat him with clubs and separated him from his head.

In this concussed city Eve cooks a beautiful omelette of market eggs and goat cheese, in my tiny kitchen she chops spinach and green onion and layers a thin membrane of smoked salmon within the eggs. She wields a sharp knife. Does my cousin wish to kill me, leave me twitching in the hall? No, she slices her creation so neatly, half for her mouth and half for mine, and on the terrace her tender omelette melts on our tongue, the best I have ever tasted.

Later we will walk fountain to fountain, drift palace to palace, painting to painting, but first we eat and drink at our small table on my sunny terrace. Tomorrow we will travel to Cannaregio to dangle our legs in a canal, sit at a canal drinking beautiful chalices of frosty white beer and eating tiny *cicchetti* from the bartender with the shaven skull at Birreria Zanon. I travel so large a world, but my favourite is the tiny world we create when two people are kind to each other.

The Petrified Florist

Eve lies on the sunlit terrace of vines and blossoms, sated after
the meal, Eve is listening to Lambchop and that band's strange
sly songs make her remember the terrazzo stairs climbing past
tall windows, circular stairs, each step of stone underfoot worn
over decades to the curve of a wave. The stairs a coil around a
lift the size of a phone booth, but for Eve the lift does not exist.
Iron Italian bells fill the air outside with harmonic notes and
scales and tiny birds flutter like moths in marble landings on
the way up to the room.

Eve wonders, is that the hour that is best? Do you prefer
the daylight stairs, the heightened possibilities and beautiful
moments *before* the knock and his door opens?

Or is it *after*? She thinks of those sweet seconds afterward, two warm bodies close, a dreamy drift, almost unconscious, yet both keenly aware of Townes or Portishead's perfect sway, perfect singers and songs and the best possible state to hear such minor-key melodies, their lost voices travelling over her and his breathing soft as a song along recent skin. Was *after* the best?

In his room the wooden blinds allow slats of muted light, light the exact colour and slender shape of ice cubes, and Italian bells report their carillon music from another country and there is time to doze before you remember the stairs leading back down and the other decent lives the stairs lead to, to what follows, to *after* after.

How to choose? Eve basks in the Roman sun and tries to not think. To choose is like a radio springing free songs from ridgeback hilltops and stark city towers or to choose is like erasing a recording. Which hour and light do you prefer and which life is best? There is a kingdom on this side of the mountains and a separate kingdom on that side of the mountains.

To choose does not seem possible. Eve senses it is not in the cards to feel contentment in either country for more than short stretches, more than a few steps on the marble stairs. Before and after are both so fine in the exact moment, but one is destined to destroy the other. In fact, in the end, most of us are left with neither.

Pompeii Über Alles

Every morning war is declared afresh.

— Marcel Proust

In the modest Pompeii hotel the patrician couple from Berlin
makes plain their demands.

Where is orange juice! Where is marmalade!

And Pico the portly Italian waiter hurries with their items as
if balancing a head on his swaying platter. I didn't even know our
little hotel had OJ and marmalade; it is news to me that we can
demand such items. I like juice and marmalade with breakfast,
but I accepted the piquant dishes Pico brought to my table.

These loud visitors from Berlin are all confidence, they are
the new Americans, but I am weary of these confident ones.
Give me a shy person any day. Some days I awake to almond

croissants and sweet honeyed tea, but perhaps I deserve more bitter food and drink with my secret bitterness, my private culture of complaint.

The marmalade trapped inside a tiny white dish triggers a lost memory of my Irish mother buying oranges to make her famous marmalade. Thick rinds hanging in their bitter world, and jars of crabapple jelly with gleaming lids. When, in that long series of concessions to age and Alzheimer's, did my mother stop jarring fruit, stop baking soft Yorkshire pudding for my father? It seems shadowy eons ago, their decades of life after World War Two. By describing it, by singing about it, the Kinks destroyed my parents' postwar world.

The couple from Berlin shuns their warm croissants, *take them away*, they insist, making a minor scene, they want to put their teeth to hard biscotti from a factory. Pico stares at the rejected plate, a hurt look as he tiptoes back to the kitchen with the untouched crescents. A gentle mountain of a man with sore feet. The Berliners puzzle Pico. I like Pico. Why do they boss him so?

I know not all Germans are as loud and demanding as this couple. Many years ago I fell in love with a thoughtful woman from East Germany, a devoted cyclist; she lived on a farm near Dresden, and we met cycling in the west of Ireland, near Dingle. Growing up in the German Democratic Republic she learned Russian as a second language; she had little say in the matter. When sledgehammers thumped into the Berlin Wall, her school switched from Russian to English, the language of the new overlords. She had little say in the matter.

In O'Flaherty's, my favourite pub in the world, we chatted and drank pint after black pint, her red-tint hair reminding me of the German actress in *Run Lola Run*. She was on holiday from a job in a hospital; she showed me a photo of her posing with a medical skeleton; she loved County Kerry's mossy walls and monks' stone beehive huts, she loved Ireland's minuscule fields and did not demand marmalade.

For hours we spoke shyly and listened to live trad music, close enough to touch the fiddler and accordion at the next table, brushing each other, not wanting to part, and the next day we cycled to the end of the peninsula; the next day in the rain we strolled a seaside strand and dried our wet clothes in Kruger's pub as we ate sandwiches the old woman made for us, no one else there but the two of us and our bicycles and the walls and a view of stone islands surging in the sea, our own misty world and the talk between the talk.

Where is that misty world gone, our magic talk, its memory itching me like a butterfly.

Let me know if you come to Prague or Dresden, it's very close to where I live.

To make extra money the red-haired German woman sold rabbits from her small farm; she said her brother killed the rabbits with a small pistol. We said goodbye at a bus in Limerick and so I hate Limerick, sick rainclouds and gangsters and dealers shooting each other and electric blue light on the graves and I wonder if I will ever see her again.

Travelling last Christmas I sat on a plane beside another woman, a woman escaping Berlin's bleak Nordic winter, a professor of German language and history. A strong accent, but really Helga's English was flawless. There is some complication with the washroom at the back, so the professor strolls up front to the sacred blue seats to use the first-class loo.

"No, I'm sorry, that's reserved," insists the male Air Canada steward.

"Reserved?"

"Yes, we do ask that you please go back to your seat. We do ask."

"And they are reserved for who? The super elite? A superior race? And their asses are so different?"

Helga's glasses have big red frames and she peers out quizzically, her head tilted sideways, her thick blond hair cut short around her face.

"And the toilet is gold? You are worried I will steal it?"

Helga's accent becomes more Teutonic with her rising ire, but the steward stands firm, turns back Helga, turns all of us back, the elite passengers undisturbed in their comfy blue coffins, civilization and golden toilets saved from our ministrations, our mithering.

Helga returns to her seat fuming.

"He will see," she mutters, opening a German textbook. "That little eunuch, he will see."

They have us in their narrow slum, in their metal snakeskin. My bike seat — is it making me a eunuch?

"Will you be all right?" I ask Helga. "Can you wait?"

"I will wait, *ja*."

Helga waits. Our plane bounces a few times off the tarmac and turns hard to a brake-wrenching stop. We used to applaud, but no more. The crew poses by the exit trying hard to smile: *Thanks have a nice day bye now thanks bye now.* Three hundred times, give or take, one for each bitchy passenger. The crew must hate this part, although it means they are free until the next faceless batch lines up.

Thanks bye now thanks bye now thanks.

Helga approaches the exit and I am just behind her, our line moving inches at a time.

Have a nice day, the steward says.

I will, the German professor says.

Professor Helga lifts up her skirt and squats to pee in the open galley area by the cockpit, passengers and uniformed crew paralyzed in a coiffured tableau. Her pent-up pee bubbles and tumbles to the edge of the plane's mats and metal plates. We have not viewed this inflight movie before.

Gootbye! Helga calls out with her Berlin accent and a satisfied smile, Helga trotting into the tunnel and airport chambers and halls and electric-eye exits to the exultant world of a thousand free washrooms without gatekeepers or even doors. Just walk right in!

Not everyone saw Helga hoist her skirt and hunker down to pee by the stewards' galley; most passengers had filed off the plane. How many stunned citizens actually saw Helga pee? Passengers, flight crew — perhaps ten of us total, a chosen few spreading into city and suburb, telling our story downtown over drinks or later at home, tearing into Loblaws jerk chicken at the kitchen nook. "Hey kids, guess what Daddy saw today?!"

This anecdote of aeromarine conflict will be replicated in taxis with broken shocks and monster homes dizzy with Christmas lights, in sundry hotels and solemn Maple Leaf Lounges, the German prof's succinct revenge play, voicemail from those in the sardine tin, her direct and fluid art.

Most people will bluster of rebellion and revenge, but Professor Helga quietly envisioned an option and followed through. She was not loud. Her act could be an art installation at the Tate in London or that Berlin gallery in Kochstrass

— what a place, what a gallery! First a Nazi bomb shelter, then a dungeon of a prison, then a warehouse storing bananas, then an S&M fetish club, and now an underground art gallery; could such an odd yet strangely logical metamorphosis take place in any metropolis but Berlin?

In sun-drenched Pompeii women wash windows and sweep steps while men stand trading insults in musical rhythms, fundamentally superior to any brand of insult in North America. While playing hockey, a forward might utter, Fuck you, and on defence I might reply, No, fuck *you*. We lack imagination, are afraid of words.

Here one man calls out, "I have more lead in my clock than you, Mister Fish Eggs."

"You?" laughs the other. "You are nothing but an old saliva-spitter with a chest full of coughs and testicles that go down to your knees."

"You were raised on whore's milk and you wear your donkey idiocy like a mantle."

"Stop it, you old fools," the women mutter as they clean windows and steps.

The men all have good hair, big hair, no matter the age. Why is that? The locals are very friendly to me, though I still worry someone one night might knife me, it's always morose stabbing season in jittery Campania.

Ciao! Buongiorno, signore. Everyone knows everyone. Skipping the sweaty train, I walk to the ruins, pack riding my sweaty back, excavations open at my feet, dead conversations with that woman from East Germany on a loop in my head.

•

In Pompeii's roofless ruins I think of Dresden's firestorm palaces and Berlin flattened to the cellars by the Red Army and my mother and father hiding from Berlin's bombers in formation above them in London's Blitz; one city's love letter to another, so many fine cities unroofed and what is gained but smoke and enmity. As they say in Italy of their gangsters, You begin as flesh, but end in concrete.

My mother and father hid in the London Underground as skinny German bombs teetered toward their heads and now in tunnel shadow I descend underground into the guts of the gladiators' amphitheatre, the Spectacula, this spectacular place where they died, where grass has taken many sections, as if the ledges are graveyards for those cuckolded by death. Isn't it really wild that we are all basically skeletons walking about with wallets and PINs? Skeletons stare into phones and hope their plan covers calling the dead on an 800-number chat-line or a woman cycling near Dresden.

Pompeii's ancient oval theatre seems intimate, but twenty thousand spectators used to jam inside to watch beast and human dance to the death on the sand. Rome forbade gladiatorial games for ten long years after a murderous riot in the taverns and food stands that once surrounded the Spectacula, a brawl where rival fans moved in stages from jeers and taunts to blows and stones to killing with swords. The locals won the day, but the emperor in Rome took away the games after the murderous brawl. The emperor's dictum: you could be killed on the sand inside the stadium, but you were not allowed to be killed on the sand outside the stadium.

•

Now the next town's blood has vanished. I'm impressed how much the earth takes in like sawdust on a butcher's floor and still stays on axis and orbit. Behind a wooden bench I see a crinkled piece of paper and pick it up, unfold a neatly typed list.

> *Der Polizist = Policeman*
> *Die Weinachtsfeier = Christmas party*
> *Die Zuendkapsel = Detonator caps*
> *Der Sprengstoff = Explosives*

What the hell can this strange list mean? A Baader-Meinhof bombing plot? A Christmas party in June? Today everything seems German, a bratwurst juggernaut — Germans taking over the hotel, taking over Europe and the EU, Germans taking over the art world and the breweries, Germans taking over my head. Is this piece of paper a conspiracy, or simply a scrap left of an innocent language lesson?

And really, what isn't a conspiracy or a lesson? Italian anarchists conspire, men and women conspire against each other, the cabbies and waiters conspire, Madonna conspires to keep her career alive, our genes and mutations conspire inside while in Canada my obsessive neighbour with her measuring tape and trowel digs up a one-inch strip of my driveway while I am out of the country.

And what gentle genetic conspiracies tick away inside our own bodies as we laugh and drink wine and buy tickets online and hop train to train to Sienna and Zagreb. My older brother needs a marrow transplant, and I am tested, but I am not a match. What minor rebellions are brewing inside us, what factions warring inside our bodies and coming to a decision about

us like disapproving parents as we break Starbucks windows
and motor nights of Molotov cocktails outside the embassy.

•

I see my couple from Berlin strolling the vast ruins and see
wild dogs of Pompeii looking dusty and thirsty. We'd kill for
a cold beer, some hop or wheat, a pint of Old Bastard from the
underskinker, but no trace is left of the ancient taverns that once
stood right here. The dry earth around the forum is vacant as
Valium and the jagged volcano with its crown of flames looms
over our burnt tender heads.

"Typical of Italy, no services, no washrooms anywhere," the
man grumbles to me.

"So damn hot," the woman says, "and nothing cool to drink."

To drink we must hike back to the modern side of town.
Don't mention the war! I take a stab at a John F. Kennedy imi-
tation: *Ich bin ein Berliner*, but I don't think they understand
my attempt in their language. *We can be heroes*, I half say half
sing, à la David Bowie.

Looking puzzled, the couple moves away from me. *Gootbye*,
they say firmly.

We'll meet again, I call to the Germans. *Ciao!*

Gootbye. I still think of the woman from East Germany. Arab
warriors sailed to Italy and in tiny ships they found their stormy
way to the west of Ireland to take away whole villages of trembling slaves; where are those villagers now? Their DNA moving
through Algeria and Libya. In my Irish B & B she whispered
that she had butterflies in her stomach, and I was nervous too.
Did I like the idea that she grew up on the far side of the Iron
Curtain and inhaled the Russian language and now with me in
Ireland's stony mist? There are possibilities and there are walls.

Was her farm near Dresden flooded in those last rains? Her land flooded and Pompeii burnt by lava. I wish I'd stayed in touch.

Do you ever have those affecting moments where you crave a service or magic mirror to tell you exactly what someone is doing at this exact second, whether she is sleeping or working a shift in the X-ray lab or walking around the tiny farm with her brother and their doomed rabbits? *Gootbye.*

Mondo cane, so many feral dogs in Pompeii. A dog trots up, pauses to pee in the sand outside the Teatro, and I am reminded of Professor Helga peeing at the plane's exit door, her gushing message from the peons stuffed into steerage. *Gootbye!* Helga called out with her German accent and trim satisfied smile like when you return a rental car with no dents.

The astounding thing was the shock and paralysis on the plane: not a single person made a move to stop the professor walking up the tunnel, to detain her. I know because I saw her soon after, head held high as she waited for her luggage at the carousel. She did have the element of surprise on her side. Had it been a male — a penis drawn out to douse the floor — would there follow a different reaction? A mad chase into the airport and the police asked to supply a few tasers as party favours?

Carousel: what a wonderful word for such a mundane location!

The Italian men continue their ribald exchange, stumbling around the Pompeii sidewalk as I try to pass.

"The widow prefers me."

"You? You are a toothless disgusting old traitor with eyes watering."

"And you are a mucus-stub covered with ringworm and gout!"

"Why don't you go take a shit on some stinging nettles!"

I must tell Natasha. No, I'm not talking to her. I will tell Eve when I get back to Rome.

In the modest Pompeii hotel the unhappy German sighs loudly and pays for his room, pays for his wine and meals and thick marmalade and peel.

"I could buy a flat in Berlin for this!"

"And we've had better Italian food back home in Flughafenstrasse."

"Now we have to get back on board that stinking train. Can't they clean the trains here?"

Soon the two come back, a wildcat strike, no trains today, each train *soppresso, soppresso!*

"What a place!"

The two Berliners are constantly *offended* by Italy (though they like Turks even less than Italians, and now the Irish and Spanish are showing up in Germany looking for work, everyone with their hand out to Angela). The Berliners want to *correct* Italy, to give Italy a makeover, an assignment, they want Italy to be Germany.

Didn't the Germans and Franks sack Rome several times? Perhaps this disdain, this desire to correct someone, is what caused such invasions. In schoolyards and on continents conflicts are birthed by irritants tinier than fruit flies.

And that reactionary German is Pope for a while, an old man eating knackwurst and wearing the white silk cuffs, fur-trimmed *mozzetta* and his red shoes, the shoes' red colour representing the blood of Jesus and the persecuted martyrs, though one might add to this symbology the blood of those the church persecuted and tortured and abused. Pope Rat retires, he's gone, *gootbye!* A white helicopter lifts his raccoon-eyed bulk on high and, as I squint, all our sins and souls are laid bare as cobbles in sunlight (so much more light in Italy than Berlin).

I wonder if I'll ever fly to Berlin or Dresden to see the lovely East German woman with hair tinted red like the actress. My life is excellent, but at times I dream of just slipping away from anything with weight and bills, steal back to misty Dingle and cycling with the woman from East Germany. A ghost can emanate more power and light than the real, a ghost does not cry into her hummus or run to the lawyer. The years slip like bent gears, like bent beggars; does she remember me the way I remember her? Memory seems random, the lobes of my brain seem to rule me, as if I am the sighing servant. Should it not be the other way around, shouldn't I rule my own brain? Yet it doesn't happen.

I must study brains more when I have time. And Mediterranean languages, their rollicking music unfolding on the tongue. And opera, maybe Wagner. And rock operas, they are always so worthwhile. I don't think I'm highbrow or lowbrow — so am I middlebrow? I prefer to think I am sideways-brow or upside-down-cake-brow.

My brain and eye hurt from the sun and sparkling sea and malicious Fiats doing their turbocharged take on chariot races. I love Italy mightily, such a ribald riotous kingdom, but after weeks swimming in noise I also need solace, need a private Arabia, my own private Tibet. Here the ghosts and wonders of the Roman Empire are crowded out by adolescent drug dealers n burping scooters.

But I wonder: when I exit Italy's ancient odours, will my house in Canada seem far too quiet, a spooky silence, will I miss the voices shouting in the streets (*Zotico! Cafone rozzo!*) and will I miss the horns beeping and the dinosaur roar of the Naples garbage truck and trash bins and waterfalls of crashing glass that wake the block at three a.m.?

The man from Berlin insists that no sane person in Germany would dare make all this noise, would dare honk their horn with such ardour as the Italians.

"It is just not done in Germany; in fact, you can be charged by the police for such transgressions. No one uses their horn, it is not civil, and if you give the finger in Germany, the other driver can report you and you will be escorted by the police and forced to apologize to the offended party."

In Italy's pleasing catastrophe they will not report you for being unruly, in Italy 'roid rage is quite normal and one does not have to apologize to anyone.

Outside the hotel, under the latest model of the warlike sun, shade starts to seem life or death, a mortal consideration. I am desperately in love with soothing shade, the clear delineation of a separate more pleasing world inside the existing world, like seeing someone else, an offer of reprieve. My skull is a brick oven and like a heap of bricks my big stupid head keeps radiating heat long after the sun is tucked away. To confirm the shade's cool embrace I creep against medieval walls and veer hither and thither to keep my head under the shade of cypress and umbrella pine, not sure where I walk or when to leave or where I will go next, but admiring wild lemon trees, so bitter but beautiful. I'm attracted to the glittering Bay of Naples, the way the buildings and citizens hug the shore and hug each other in a kind of doubt and hope and love and chaos.

A *terrone* walks among butterflies, strolls rows of orchard trees growing under the shade and shelter of boughs and black nylon hung like wartime camouflage netting to hide a gun emplacement, to hide my dead uncle's position. The worker walks a subdued interior world and with a long-handled scythe he reaches high and expertly lops down a lemon for his lunch or to squeeze zest and sunlight into a cool drink. He seems so relaxed in the dim hallways of this treed subworld, this arena of ripeness, lemons and oranges glowing everywhere. Could my Irish mother make marmalade from his Italian fruit?

Lemon groves left to us in sunny southern Italy by long-dead Arab overlords from another time, hours ago, minutes ago — vanished like parents, like Goth armies, like wars, here and gone, but they left their permanent mark, left startling fruit floating high in branches as evidence, our train a steampunk monster moving its windows uncertainly past endless walls and groves of brains glowing with the heady hues of a language that once ruled us.

Hallway Snowstorm

When old words die out on the tongue,
new melodies break forth from the heart;
and where the old tracks are lost, new
country is revealed with its wonders.

Rabindranath Tagore

My wife sends a friendly note from Canada: everyone is doing well and the Italian heat wave is in the news back home. In the streets of Pompeii I notice the locals' shirts are dark with sweat; so they also feel it, they are not inured to the heat? I am running like margarine. In this oven that is southern Italy, I find myself wondering, does Canada still exist? Why does the heat here not spread and melt the whole world?

Canada's gift for snowy fields and frozen rivers seems utterly impossible, yet only weeks ago I lived through a brute storm where snow fell and fell and blinding winds bent corners and heaped huge drifts against my old house and at night some furious kingdom of darkness descended on us.

My wish is to hunker down, bunker up, but our old-timer team has a hockey game that night, a game miles away in a country arena. Do we dare drive a night like this? Will any other players make it? The insane machinery you'd need to manufacture this wind and snow. The few vehicles visible are spaced out in hesitant half-speed convoys, roads terrible and blurry and the ditch beckons.

Coach phones with the word: the game is on and he will be in my driveway at the usual time. We may be the only old-timer team with a coach.

In the storm we drive back roads and loopy hills and hollows where sawmills once buzzed beside rivers and now the mills are fallen down and the train tracks ripped up and the covered bridge burnt by teens with tires and gasoline. Coach is a good driver and we make it to the old sheet-metal arena that smells of chicken fries and our goalie rubbing on Tiger Balm and, a bonus, we win the game and, another bonus, Darcy invites us afterward to his riverside garage full of canoes and skidoos, to his iron stove and beer fridge and lobster and duck sausage and goose and moose and deer sausage sizzling.

Darcy played pro for Montreal and Ottawa and in Seattle and PEI, he played in Croatia and has some wild stories and salacious gossip about other NHL players and coaches and their wives, including the famous Habs star who was a cross-dresser, he saw him in full makeup and dress at a Montreal strip club. Darcy fought many nights, fought Donald Brashear, Wes Walz, Everett Sanipass, Rudy Poeschek, Milan Dragicevic, and Jim McKenzie, and he beat the snot out of a future Maple Leafs star known far and wide as an irritating rat.

In one town Darcy spent hours sewing an iron rod into his

hockey glove to get revenge on a guy who suckered him from behind. The unseen blow knocked out Darcy and gave him a concussion. But Darcy couldn't go through with his revenge; all those hours spent sewing and then he tore out the iron rod.

Darcy was a fighter, an enforcer, so he can say what he wants and we listen. We eat and drink after the game and he says quietly, "Think about it — people who don't play will never know how great this feels."

He played pro, but we joke that we are bringing him down to our level of play. His friend Chad, a skilled player who played against Sid the Kid, says, "Hard to soar like an eagle if you're playing with turkeys."

Darcy had to stop playing after too many concussions and now goes ice fishing and skidooing and is buying post-crash real estate in sunny Florida, says the market is picking up now. Scallops and bacon go in the stove and he has ribs and boiled peanuts and bottle meat from Newfoundland, rabbit and moose, and maybe we'll shoot off some guns.

Coach says he can take bottle meat if it's cooked, but Darcy eats it raw. We stay up late devouring his victuals in his garage right on the frozen river as the storm rages.

Darcy deals well with winter, but after every game his big toe is frozen a ghostly white. A few years back a neighbour-hood kid tried to steal Darcy's truck from the driveway and Darcy flew outside in the snow in boxers and bare feet and collared the kid, but his nervous wife made him stand outside with the juvie until the police arrived. He had a doormat, but that freezing night made his feet even worse. At our games he tries a folk remedy, putting pepper in his skates to warm them.

Coach sympathizes, says this stormy winter is making him spleeny, he's almost seventy-five, he's getting too old to keep going out late on these cold nights. Like me, he thinks this might be his last year. In the winter some of the players go south to Cuba or Florida. I ask Coach if he ever thinks of going somewhere warm, but he scoffs, has zero interest in some resort. I can't picture Coach without his ballcap and coat, I can't see him in a Speedo on a beach buying beer from a Rasta.

Coach has been a repo man, a meat inspector, a race car driver, trombone player, a goalie and a backcatcher; now his knees are tricky. He smokes like a chimney and I worry when he coughs as he lights up. His car smells like smoke, even in the trunk where I throw my gear and team water bottles. Coach drives me home, insists on driving me right to my back door in the drifts.

"How's that for service?" He treats me far better than I deserve.

I go inside and all night the candid blizzard argues with my house, tries to find me, loose wooden windows leaking air and thumping in their frames (heating this barn by the river will bankrupt me), but I pile on blankets in my cold bedroom and that night dream I'm in a Venice full of puttering Evinrudes and the hot sun glitters on canals and a warm grocery cashier likes me and instead of yelling at me she leaves the till and leans to put her plump lips to mine. A lovely dream of Italy.

In the morning the snow and wind stop. I go to the mud room door and pull it to me, but wind and snow have formed a second door, an exact imprint, every detail pressed in the snow, the rectangular panels, the screen, the handle, an exact white copy of my door filling the frame.

It seems a shame to alter such a creation, but I leap through this new door, destroy this delicate doppelganger. Outside the sky is a forgiving blue, my yard calm and sunny, the wind's fury gone, our world back, our scoured world restored to order.

I shovel paths to my doors. Out front the sidewalk snow-ploughs have pushed through and cut high perfect walls in the drifts, beautiful white hallways that travel miles across the city like some complicated art installation seized with light, like trenches from the Great War, but the war is over and it is bright and clean, no rats, no mud, no snipers in this stunning new world.

Cars pass by, but the snow is heaped so high I can't see them and all sounds are muffled. White walls, higher than I've ever seen, but ceilings of blue sky, like walking passageways in an albino Pompeii, roofless and bright, infinite and surreal, and I can follow these weird perfect hallways all the way across town saying good morning, how you doing?

The new walls glow in the sun and I want to enjoy them before the big dogs arrive to mark their territory, before the bootblack mud and sand and grit arrive like five o'clock shadow to make me forget this beauty. I want to hang a thrift store painting where the perfect white hallway passes my house; in the walls I expect to see light switches and doors and offices with photocopy machines humming inside huge snowbanks, offices printing out more white, and snow and light everywhere so bright it's a form of distilled noise.

Trieste, Trogir, Havana, the Baja. These places boast palm tree beaches and admirable climates and painterly hues, they know limos and palaces and delicacies and glitzy pop stars with thread-count concerns, but they'll never witness this creation of a clean new world, this stormy cold war and sunblind euphoria that follows.

Adam and Eve
Saved from Drowning

When we are not sure is
when we are most ourselves.

—Graham Greene

I remember leaving Canada for Italy's hallucination nation, a late flight over the silver Atlantic and the strange interior night until a new morning's sunrise moves us past dusty Spanish plateaus and ginger points of light, past Barcelona until our plane hangs over cobalt water The pilot announces that we are west of Rome and the phrase rings in my head and I am excited to see such a sharp mountain rising in the water, a peak alone in the sea, can it be Corsica or Napoleon's Elba, then, *look, look*, a much larger island wreathed with talc beaches and azure bays.

My neck bent like a giddy child for my first glimpses of a fabled country, finally my eyes on Italy, my neck bent in the plane to peer down upon boats and pure wakes and glittering seas leading toward speedy voices under a volcano. Do I look foolish in my excitement? I travel alone, no one to share this with, no one coming on like novocaine.

Outside the airport terminal serviettes blow over breezy runways. A careless handler spilled a box of paper serviettes beside a plane, and these folded squares skim the carbon tarmac, pale paper herds zigzagging sullen plains. The grumpy handler will not give chase, matters are officially out of his hands. They *career*, but their travel is so quiet.

I can't pull my eyes away — something spooky about paper serviettes levitating, moving back and forth in dreamscape silence — what is it they seek?

And how have I not noticed this silence before? Miles and miles of glass the colour of glucose allowing no hint of the shrieking decibels of a dozen jet engines. Tell me: are international airports not amazing structures with beautiful citizenry and upright pilots and stewardesses in Siamese silk costumes and so many magic portals! The speaker in the ceiling apologizes to Gate 34. We move along, a doorway to Dublin beside a gate to Singapore right by an entrance leading to Zagreb's Britanski Square, where someday I will say a novena over glowing pilsner. Such different worlds, strange cavern entrances just paces apart. And those serviettes, meant for our lips, and then came the careless handler.

I am happy to share a cab into the city, a couple from Quebec introducing themselves to me in the taxi line. She is a stewardess, has flown to Rome hundreds of times, will guide me, a good omen.

"Where are you from?"

Our taxi driver ferries his three passengers from Ostia Antica into cloudy Rome, the west side of the river, a Byzantine trip in lanes of tangerine stucco and high stone walls blocking any view of the city, driving past cracked walls and hedges and iron gates and swarthy security men in dark uniforms slouching at mildewed guardhouses like roadside tombs, a city of tombs and walls, and in the walls we turn right and left, left and right, until I have little sense of where the driver has placed me in my new alien landscape.

"Clouds in Rome? I've never seen it like this."

The Quebec stewardess is affronted by the cloud cover; she reminds me of Natasha, her worship of the sun, our tenuous love.

"*Quanto costa?*"

We stand in the street and the driver writes the number fifty on the dusty window.

"Fifty!" The stewardess says no.

"Not fifty each. Fifty total."

Ah. I am pleased to put in twenty euro to cover my end and take care of the tip, happy not to deal with this alone. I was lucky; the stew rescued me from an unregistered taxi driver who collared me at the airport doors; seventy euro he was going to charge, but the hack driver ran at the sight of an approaching uniform. So twenty euro is great, twenty euro is nothing in Rome, a city plated in gold. Gilt frames, hammered gold, coins and tribute, sunlight and gold chalices filling family chapels, museums, galleries, churches, palaces; Borgia loot and the overflowing Borghese villa and the Vatican's endless halls and scarlet chambers.

How many rooms of art and how many arrangements and thefts, how much treasure stolen from kingdoms and nations, stolen from other families, Pope to Pope, nephew to nephew. *You first parents of the human race, who ruined yourself for an apple*. Why so much loot in Italy, so many shiny apples.

They are dedicated to Jesus, but do they believe that Jesus would like this display of wealth, would Jesus make his nephew Pope and loot the world and pile the treasures in gilt chambers? Yet that is why the crowds and I have flown here, not for the fine words of Jesus, but to view the piles of loot.

My mother and father so devoted to this church in Ireland and Canada. I wish I had their faith, I envy them. I became an altar boy and took the host and my parents helped build the local cathedral. The archbishop washed my feet at the communion rail. But really, what connection do I have to this series of questionable Popes in such a distant chaotic country? Perhaps as much connection as Jamaican Rastas to Hailie Selassie in Abyssinia or dingbat acolytes with faith in flying saucers. The archbishop washed my feet and later Natasha held my feet. We are all dingbat acolytes.

Ah, hotels: the towels so brisk and young. Can you find Balkan music on the red Bakelite radio? Wowee-zowee, it's a garage band show and that wacky piano solo from "Pushin' Too Hard." It makes me happy. Once my dead teachers had high hopes for me. Maybe I can be happy just being dull.

Near the Spanish Steps I visit my aged aunt and uncle to sip tea from bone china. I must ask where they were during the war. That rich oxblood colour as the boiling water hits the tea, releasing it; it was hiding and now bright as a flag, the sight makes me nostalgic and happy.

"And how are your parents? Well, I hope?"

"Yes, very well thank you."

Why wreck things, why tell the truth?

"You look so much like my favourite brother; it makes me happy to see you."

My aunt and uncle have lived in these rooms forever; the place should be knocked down when they depart, so it remains forever theirs. Their legs are gone, no more tennis and cream. They want to hear of everywhere that I've walked, envious of my rambles in the city. I love being mobile, love walking for miles, and this is what I can look forward to: having no legs.

My aunt and uncle are so kind, they've been with each other so long (I hear the English football chant, *you'll never walk alone*). Why can I not do that, be kind, stay? It seems so simple.

My cousin Eve is here again, my aunt and uncle not sure why. Eve seems free to take time off from her school and it's not that far to the frontier, to Italy. Eve told me that her students live in Switzerland, but their families live across the frontier in France, a short train ride. The parents make good money in Switzerland, but it is cheaper to live on the French side, so they go back and forth. Eve leans in the doorway, does anyone want to walk to the famous Protestant graveyard?

"Now you two watch out for pickpockets," warns my aunt at the arched door. "Things are so complicated now. Did you read the paper where the gypsies kidnapped that poor little blond girl? I don't feel safe anymore, foreigners everywhere and more over the borders every week. There are no jobs to be had here, but they come by the boatload. It can't go on. People have talked about what will happen here soon. They have started to talk about that everywhere, even in the *supermercato*."

My aunt had an operation for cataracts and now can see clearly; she laughs, says her own face in the mirror was a shock, this stranger in the glass, this move from fog to terrible clarity. Eve pulls me, my aunt like Janus in the doorway, in love with us, madly waving goodbye.

At the café I slice my dessert in half; it is too large. "I will save some for later." I don't trust orange shampoo, but I buy a bottle because the price in the shop is so good and Rome is so costly.

"You're so abstemious." I can tell Eve enjoys this word, enjoys laughing at my habits.

Sometimes a glutton and sometimes I know when to stop. Sometimes I am smart and sometimes a fool. We are never just one.

"*Ciao, bella.*"

"This is so good."

"I'm never eating a tomato in Canada again."

Like a fashionable spider, my cousin Eve walks among the tea shops and twee shops, skinny black pants and skin-tight black boots among other solemn spiders parading cobbled boulevards. Do these creatures devour the male or do they love the male? I can never remember when I need to.

Life is a tragedy. Life is a lark. Which mood is truer, finer? A firefly wandered right toward me and the dish ran away with the spoon. After the rain my cousin rides her rental bike through all the puddles, laughing gleefully as water sprays her back, and I find this endearing. I like her body language, though she rides away from me.

My swings, my low hours, low days, convinced that I've wrecked my smoke-and-mirrors life, a horrible sense of regret, a mistake. What have I done?

Other times I think, So what? Few lives stay the same for long, few lives work out smoothly. Why regret what I can't change? I can try to learn, but I cannot alter what has transpired.

A cat-burglar prowls the hotel roof at night, a slim hand in the window, some cash, some jewels, a camera. The thief must be a local who knows his silent way around the top of the neighbourhood; these jaded buildings stand cheek by jowl and most are connected or separated by a small leap. German and Mexican students party on the rooftop terraces and thieves trot the sloping roofs.

Marco, the American intern who works the desk, knows about the thefts. Some residents have heard and some have not, the hotel is not warning the guests. We hear conflicting reports. Eve claims someone on the balcony, a hand through an open window. Tamika says no, the intruder was right inside the room. Ray-Ray heard money and a camera, Tamika says no, family jewels and blown glass from Venice. Tamika says, and I agree, why bring jewels on a trip?

We can see the Vatican walls clearly, like a vast drab fortress beside us, but the rooftop thief does not fear the Pope. God is dead, ideology is dead, and the microwave is dead in my room, Barabbas the thief released instead of Jesus and now a lithe thief strolling above to pluck jewels and cameras and phones from our hotel.

In my top-floor room I am like a hawk perched atop a square tower. Will the thief drop onto my terrace next? I keep a length of wood handy. Knives sleep in the drawer, but could I actually stab someone? I assume the perp is a young male, but what if the thief is an old woman, merry as a grig? Do you still hit such an ancient visitor with a length of wood? What does Emily

Post's advice column suggest? Does Emily Post know a hawk from a handsaw?

"Things are not stable here," says my aunt, returning to a favourite topic. "The Italian economy is the worst since the war. Governments come and go and what have they done? A lot of blather and we're still in the same boat. Our pension has been reduced, they tax everything twice now, demonstrations, strikes, so much unrest, so much chaos, and yet these people come in leaky boats from everywhere, Albania, Romania, Libya, Tunisia, Egypt, Iraq. Why on earth do they come? Do they expect a Shangri-La? We can't take so many. The city is all…" She pauses, choosing her words. "All foreigners now."

"Aren't we foreigners?"

"You can't know what it's like. It is unbelievable. Some are starving themselves, to protest, that they should be classified as political refugees, for asylum, but the government doesn't want them. They all want free health care. Many immigrants are in the hospital now and they will probably die soon. It is very sad."

Is there even a molecule of the poet Keats left in the sacred graveyard ground? All the famous bodies resting in rows under the cypresses, but it's the bloodied cat walking the poet's grave — I can't forget this mangled cat in Rome's Protestant Cemetery, the cat's face sneezing blood and doesn't look like a cat anymore, its nose completely gone, like the faces of so many chipped Greek and Roman busts. Can it survive with such injuries?

At the graveyard is a twenty-three-year-old American who was injured by an explosion in Iraq; we met at an Irish pub in Rome where we'd stopped for shade and cool libations. The American has a Purple Heart and a 30 per cent loss of hearing after an IED blast under his vehicle; he says one day they dismantled eighteen roadside bombs — in one day! He has a crush on Eve (I suppose we all do), tells Eve he is depressed and pissed off because he always wanted to be an officer, to be chosen, but his military career is toast now. I wonder if he unconsciously surveys the graveyard trees to assess where a sniper might hide, where to set up an ambush or field of fire. Does the disturbed soil remind him of an IED planted in the laneway?

"The army discharged me because of my loss of hearing. Which loss came from the fucking army."

"Where was the IED?" I ask. I'm interested in how it was hidden. Was he driving, was it buried under the road surface or beside the road at a soft corner? He seems to not hear me. What, is he deaf? Oh yeah, I forgot, he kind of is.

"They say officers have to be perfect and now after the IED I'm less than perfect. As if they are all perfect."

"That's terrible," says Eve.

"The whole show is a fucking crock," he says.

"Well, why did you go in the first place? Thank God Chrétien kept us out of that mess."

I didn't tell the young soldier to go shoot up some village across the world and I don't like it when they claim that bombing some Podunk hamlet is for my freedom and I should be grateful and tearful for such heroes in our midst.

"Who is Chrétien?"

On the ground by Keats's grave are fallen oranges and on them ants and butterflies acquire their vitamins. I grow weary of heroes and parades.

"You know what," the young American says to Eve, "I don't want to be in any graveyard with mutilated cats."

He got a lump sum of cash from the army, he's going to

golf, going to the beach in Croatia, going to Prague for pilsner under the spires. I can't blame him, I hope he finds some
peace in Prague or Bali. After so many corpses in Iraq this is
not what he seeks, another bone orchard; after the IED and
sniper bullets at the sandy wall he doesn't share our interest in
dead Romantic poets.

Did he study war before he went, has he read of Viet Nam
(*we had to destroy the village in order to save it*), does he know
the war to end all wars? Did he know anything about Iraq or
did he sign up in a Pentecostal fervour to zap some rug-riders?
Each new war delivers some collective amnesia and surprise,
the wrong people go to fight every time. The soldier has been
injured at war, so I expect some wisdom, but he seems a bitter
witness with little to tell that is profound. Perhaps the wisdom
will come later. Or the dreams.

My father never talked of the war, and one day after the cancer it was too late to ask. The warriors return without tongues,
they can't spell out what they saw. Eve has more sympathy than
I do, she worries about the high number of suicides among
veterans, one an hour, she says, an assembly line of suicides,
imagine them all gathered in a gym, the clockwork suicides.

In a grocer's aisle I met the Iraqi woman who fled the same war,
fled the American invasion. She was studying a package and I
had to reach past her. *Scusi*, I said, and she smiled brightly and
asked me if lard was listed as an ingredient, lard might mean
pork. I assured her it looked all right.

Her dark bangs and dark flashing eyes and a soft gold chain
at her neck. Is she local? A Mediterranean face, this might be
the face of Christ's mother or she could be a Spanish Jewess or
smiling princess from Bombay. I could not tell, had to ask her.

"Baghdad."

Now I want to ask about Iraq and the war. I am allowed to walk her to what is now home and she chats easily. Baghdad is past tense. Her parents made her leave her home after her brother was kidnapped and held for ransom. Her mother almost went insane with worry. They paid the ransom, but had to sell their house and possessions at a bad price and had little left to live on. War isn't good for the real estate market. Her brother was found alive in the wilderness, hands bound with plastic cuffs.

"We were lucky. I know of others killed even though the ransom was paid."

Kidnapping becomes a lucrative niche business after the American invasion, a growth industry, anyone can make some easy cash and an expensive car or suit is a target. Suddenly it is too easy to be shot in the skull.

She tells me they phoned the family and in the background she heard voices speaking English. She believes that American soldiers orchestrated the kidnapping, but I wonder if it might be mercenaries and not regular army. I can't explain this idea, though her English is very good. Her brother's silver BMW singled him out; she says he got in the driver's seat and they ran up and put a gun to his head. Her brother became silent after his kidnapping, the man wandering in the desert was an exact duplicate, the same hands and cheekbones, the same fingerprints and driver's licence, but no longer the same person.

She smiles and is pleasant as she tells me her family stories. Before the invasion she drove a gold Mustang, a gleaming American car, but it was crushed by an American tank in Freedom Square and street people had to smash the front windshield and pull her with rough strife though the broken glass as the back of her car was flattened by the moving tank, a violent rebirth with glass in her eyes.

There had been an explosion in the square just as she drove up, and barrels of gasoline were in flames. She told me the barrels of gasoline were left by the Iraqi army as an emergency measure to stop the Americans, but the gas had not been used. Now they were on fire, the square a pall of greasy smoke, and she stopped her car, unable to see, afraid to move in the murk. The wide Abrams tank did not want to slow down. Someone told her an American was shouting that the tank had no brakes, but it is likely the crew inside feared an ambush, another explosion in a daisy chain trap. Her car was simply a dwarf in the path of a massive tank. Trading her life for theirs, they kept the tank rolling in the smoke. They voted on it, they were bringing democracy to Iraq.

Her father came to search for the street people and reward them for saving his baby daughter; she was alive and he was generous, though she insists to me that they expected nothing, they just wanted to help her. She moves my fingers to touch where chunks of scalp and hair are still missing at the back of her head, where she has braided in a hank of hair to cover the scar. Her sister is a doctor, and this sister worked on her at their family home to pluck glass from her eyes and to bandage the abrasions in her scalp. In strong light she must wear large sunglasses.

The Americans offered high salaries to both sisters to work for them, one as a doctor and one as a translator, the Americans liked the sisters, both polite, attractive; fashionable heels, nail polish gleaming on their fingertips, their English superb, but neighbours warned them of reprisals for collaborators, they might be beaten or killed as traitors for helping the American invaders.

Her parents worried their youngest daughter would be kidnapped or killed and drove her to the border to Jordan, made her leave her home, her country. Her mother has not been the same since the Americans came. Her house in Baghdad was a small palace of antiquities and volumes of books and cool marble underfoot, and now in Italy she searches for menial work. Once she drove several family cars and now she doesn't even own a bicycle and worries her money will run out soon.

From her I learn so much of the war and I learn so little from the soldier. Did the two of them cross paths in Iraq, even briefly at a checkpoint? Was he one of the young Americans who asked her to stay and translate, to tell the other drivers what the soldiers wanted? Was he the soldier who asked to see her passport and then tore it up so she couldn't leave the country? After the roadside bomb exploded under him, a mammoth transport flew our soldier to Germany for surgery, and her wounds treated by her sister at home. Now she can't bear loud noises, now she must wear dark glasses in bright light, now she has very specific nightmares. Our soldier is stalled, angry, drinking. She doesn't drink. She has no options. They don't know each other, they are a honeymoon couple in Rome, both heads altered by invasion.

"Here's Shelley's grave," says Eve. Shelley's stone is almost anonymous compared to Keats's star treatment.

"How can he be here? I thought they burnt Shelley's body on the beach."

"Well his marker is here, there must be something buried. I heard that they kept his heart in Italy. Or wait, did they send the heart to England?"

Someone walks past. "Dude, where's Jim Morrison's grave?"

"Wrong city, asshole," says the ex-soldier.

Now he is opening up, now he is communicating.

Eve bends over the headstones. "Corso the beatnik poet buried with Keats and Shelley? So you can just *buy* a spot here? Put it on Visa? How did Corso do this? Can I get in here? I'm impressed."

"Well, I guess as a poet he wanted to be buried beside Shelley."

"The beatnik's last wish. Good name for a band. He hung out with Ginsberg and Kerouac. Didn't Corso kill someone in New York? Look, this grave is Antonio Gramsci; he was a member of Parliament and the Fascists threw him in prison."

"Who? Gramsci? How do you even know of him?" I ask.

"My older brother was really into Trotsky and had Gramsci's book *Prison Notebooks*. Gramsci was a hunchback, terrible health, got on Mussolini's wrong side and he died in prison."

"Mussolini was such an ass." Saved once by Hitler's paratroopers, but then caught by partisans and strung up by the heels at a gas station like a dead hog.

Inside graveyard walls we move past the maimed cat and violets and shade trees, we move past the poets' graves and the strange Pyramid of Caius Cestius and its traffic circle, move past the war in Iraq, we are alive and healthy and jumping on an ugly B-line train that reminds me of Philly, train windows all tagged and bedraggled, but when we climb out above ground the Roman streets are gorgeous again, we climb back into air and afternoon light at a station in Prati, local cafés and grocers and palm trees and peach-coloured buildings radiating in lovely lines.

Sometimes my eyes are wasted; like St. Lucia I should poke them out. All this time walking and only now I realize there are no high-rises in Rome's centre, no brutalist blocks, no faceless slabs. Was I blind? The scale of roofline and window is human and my eye finally notices, my eye loves it. Classically proportioned views run east and west and this new sunlight on ancient stone arches zaps some Luddite pleasure centre in my brain.

"How is the wine?" I ask Eve.

"Very drinkable." She is open, I have yet to hear Eve declare any wine undrinkable. I like that and I like to jump city to city and lose track of exactly where I am on the map of a continent. But I am running low on funds in my jumps: in the daily business of eating and drinking, my money rides off madly in all directions.

Via Virgilio, a pretty café lit at night, an old-fashioned café of golden trays and sea-horse-shaped bottles of oil and golden rounds of cheese and salvers of noodles and bread strewn on the tablecloth and seafood delicacies in her mouth and I like the feeling of forgetting who I am and where I am and the flavours are so sharp; how do they do it? We sit on a narrow lane and my cousin looks as if she has a happy secret, which many prefer to an unhappy secret.

But Eve says over her dark wine, "I don't find secrets that fun." The word resonates for her and not in a good way. She asks the waiter for a spicy dish redolent with chili peppers, *arrabbiata*, angry pasta.

I don't tell her that I love a life of secrets, love her secret face in candles. Everyone has their charged secrets, even her, despite her convincing disavowal. It's the one thing I've learned that is true, all of us nursing worries and secret powers.

Eve says, "I just remembered to tell you, I googled Gregory Corso, the beat poet we saw buried beside Shelley. What a life. I had no idea he was in jail with Lucky Luciano, the godfather, a prison in New York State, right on the border with Canada. And they had a ski hill and Corso learned to ski!"

"A ski hill in prison?"

"Well, a ski hill might be a good idea for every prison," says Eve. "We should ski the Italian Alps someday. Livigno is not far, just north of Milan, it shouldn't cost us too much."

"I'd like that," I say. "Or we could go to prison and ski for free. How did our Uncle Aldo make his money?"

Eve says, "I think he made his money in money."

"Ah, the old-fashioned way," I say.

But what I really mean is the *new* way. Derivatives and default swaps and trading floors and million-dollar bonuses: such astral salaries and then a cool mil on top, such gravy. I worry that making money out of someone else's money has become the last big industry and I am not part of the magic assembly line, I am far outside of the factory gates, walking the weeds and abandoned slabs.

Eve breaks crusty bread, hands me a platter of fragrant salty oil. "What was our aunt saying — odd to think that there are refugees out on the water as we speak, coming toward us as we eat and drink whatever we wish in this beautiful spot. It's the poor children I worry about, on those leaky boats. Do you miss your children?"

"I do. They've been really good kids."

"They seem good. Versus some of the little monsters out there. They're in Air Cadets? Do they still play Hungry Hungry Hippos? Have I made you sad?" She touches my arm.

"No, it's okay."

She holds a photo of my children and their dog. "They are so beautiful, all of them," she said. "Rome *is* so beautiful. Is Rome better at day or night?"

Who can answer, who can think straight after these evening hours pass and we are the last in the cozy café, sated, sitting side by side, my hand slightly pressuring her warm leg, where it might or might not be noticed (*nearer my God to thee*). Did Corso's godfather connection help him get a poet's place in the Italian cemetery? I wonder if he ever skied again after prison. Did Lucky Luciano strap on skis? The waiter has put on his coat and stands by us, the waiter waiting.

At night the blood-red wine presses circles on the starched tablecloth, cobbled blond streets bend under descant melodies and invisible three a.m. emails and the black sparkling river arranges its lights, its candles, its bed of stars. At night our urban universe rearranges itself, seems to be the opposite of dead.

"Are you decent?" My cousin raps at my door, sweeps in bright morning sunshine. Naples is on an exquisite bay, but Rome seems more open to light. Eve is playful, energetic.

"Come on sleepyhead, get moving, let's go out and do something."

"I can't move. I have multiple neurosis."

She laughs. "Do you need help getting dressed?"

"There's no rush. We have all day."

We're in Rome!"

"Rome's not going anywhere. It's eternal."

I add honey to my boiling tea. Within my tiny fridge float such fragrant aromas: smoked salmon, salsa, hummus, Italian pepperoni, berries and apples, all mingling pleasantly. I breathe in the spicy aroma and feel happy about what seems my creation; surely I can bottle and sell this fragrance, Brad Pitt pitching my designer scent on wide screens and in glossy fashion mags.

"You should try goat's milk," Eve says. "Cow's milk has hormones."

"Maybe I need hormone replacement." I laugh, but really I don't trust goats and monkeys. My cousin waits for me while I shower. She carries two Eccles cakes from a patisserie and I feel such tenderness toward her, a flood of associations with this flaky pastry.

The odd thing is I can't recall the exact associations, when I last had an Eccles cake. Who was I with? What port of call, what beautiful kingdom where flags droop like horses and passports open to wow smiling guards and the bright maps fold so perfectly, what ensnaring sunlit coast where I walked as a model citizen? I can't remember specific details, but the pastries affect me. Your old lives wash away in a languorous surf and I am curious what is happening to my mind, my memory. Still, I am so happy to have Eccles cakes again, so rich and sticky.

Eve says, "I looked up Keats dying in Rome, at the end he was spitting up cups of blood, and remember at his grave we saw that poor cat breathing out blood from its ruined face." I must confess to a tiny chill when Eve mentions the bloody cat, though I am usually a skeptic about such matters.

Keats was almost dead when he arrived in Rome, delayed by a long quarantine in Naples. The poet came to Italy for warmer weather, but Rome was freezing, damp. The doctor in Rome bled Keats and starved him. From Moorgate and Gravesend to this agony on the Spanish Steps. Avoid the Spanish Steps, I say, a horrible part of Rome. Keats was born in the Swan and Hoop inn and his father fell from a horse and broke open his skull and left no money. Keats made love his currency, his religion.

Love, I think, is admirable; what else is there? My aunt

in London took me to the poet's house in Hampstead and, a malcontent, I didn't appreciate her efforts, her love, I wanted to see the Banshees and the Jam, not Keats; I didn't know I'd stand at his grave and think of my aunt and love her when it's too late. The poet's room in Rome is now a tourist trap, but I'm not sure how original the room is: after Keats died of his illness, the Italians tore up the flooring and windowsills and burnt his furniture.

I remember the fallen oranges and swarming ants near his stone at the pretty Protestant Cemetery, the Cimitero degli Inglesi. In the nunnery yard below my room oranges or apricots lie on the ground, but there is broken glass set into the top of the wall. We are separated, we are partitioned. I can look down into the garden of orphans and no one picks up the apricots.

Eve sits cross-legged on my bed with my tiny new digital camera, figuring out the buttons. She says she dreamt she went on a date with Salman Rushdie; he was a perfect gentleman, but when they arrived at a palatial estate house another woman started yelling at him, so Eve had to go find her car, but where was it parked? He tried to help her, but the woman kept yelling.

Sleepy and relaxed in the heat, I lie flat on my back, a pillow under my head, a white towel wrapping my midriff. She takes random photos of my hotel room, the flowered terrace and our tea and cakes, takes photos of me in my towel.

My cousin leans over and opens my towel. She holds up what is beneath with two fingers and peers at it, as if intrigued by a curious new toy.

"*Senti com'è morbido al tatto!* Feel how soft it is to the touch!" Her Italian accent is so much better than mine. She lifts it and lets it drop several times to see if it falls over the same way each time. Her expression is studious. And the old Adam grows larger with her attentions.

Do people act differently in hotels in Europe? There must be a study, a doctoral thesis underway. Did I try to engineer this situation with the shower and towel? Natasha used to joke that I should have an engineering degree.

"Are you decent," Eve asked at the door. Now she asks, "Does it point one way?"

"Well, I dress left."

"What on earth do you mean?"

"Well, it hangs to the left. My left."

"It's really curved."

She seems to forget that I'm even there as she moves it this way and that. I sense that this is the first time she's been relaxed enough with someone in daylight to really look at one and move it about and feel free to ask questions about this odd object. I am strangely happy to be part of this study, even if I am literally only a part. I can tell that playing with it is making her amorous.

"Weren't we going to go out?" I ask her. "And do something?"

"Later," she says, eyes focused, serious, a dedicated student. "We have all day."

Yes, we have the day, we have the great George Jones singing to put your sweet lips a little closer to the phone, George Jones sings and a grinning George W. Bush visits Rome at the same time as I do, the President visits odd corners of his troubled empire at the precise end of his sad reign. The President is a religious man, seems a decent sort. Does he think of all those he's touched in the head, all those walking around and cursing him and all those dead and all those with nightmares? Does he toss and turn and need little blue pills to bring on rest? Or like me, does he sleep like an oafish bear? George W. insists he is a new Winston Churchill, he says history will look back and judge him a visionary warrior, a prince. And it's true, history will judge him.

"Weren't we going to go out?"

Two cars packed with eighty kilograms of ammonia nitrate explode outside a crowded market in Iraq and ignorant armies clash by night and the dead in their postures in the rubble by the river and the living wearing night-vision goggles — that vision thing.

"And do something?"

Choppers circle the rubicund Vatican and rotary blades whump and drone like weird gods hovering above my rooftop terrace (and Roman gods line the silhouette of each building), the sky solid with metal and rotors (*here come the warm jets*), choppers supplying that hot LZ soundtrack, and irritated travellers are delayed as Rome's da Vinci airport shuts down for this puzzling man's security. Ah, the President, our shining example when cynics argue that you can't change the world.

My world is changing in its small way. In the Court of Queen's Bench, Family Division. Financial Statement Form 72J. I hereby make oath and say the details of my financial situation are herein accurately set out, to the best of my knowledge, information and belief.

And verily, Eve saw the fruit of the tree was pleasing to the eye and tasteful to eat and she took it between her lips. The Chaldeans listened to reggae and conquered and ruled Babylon in biblical times, well before 7-Elevens and ammonia nitrate and drone missiles. Chaldea, the southernmost Tigris and Euphrates Valley, may have included Babylonia and the original Garden of

Eden, where the young Iraqi woman had to flee the American soldiers and a giant Abrams tank tupped her golden Mustang.

Tiny Canadian tanks burnt here in Italy in 1943, burnt in the grain fields, the Canadians had popguns and such thin armour compared to the German armour and 88s, take a hit and boys trapped inside the burning hull, the crew brewed up and no one climbed out. Now touts and tourists with bare legs and iPhones and vineyard passes. Medium tanks hid themselves in the orchards under the hills. The soldier who was in Iraq said that sometimes it's better to be clueless. Thou shall kill, thou shall not kill, thou shall not lie with her, thou shall not put a pillow under her ass. Eve and I steal past ladders in the orchard and I look up and stars are fucking pulsing!

Fireflies and jets blink overhead in the stars and a firefly moves deep in the black riverbank verge, the firefly swerves happily toward us and flutters right over my brain. I enjoy that the firefly flashes then blinks out, disappears, so I have to guess where it will blink to life next, a pleasing game. We hold hands, I like Eve's small hands. The firefly almost wanders into a wall, and we worry, but the charmed firefly rises at the last second and clears the barrier.

Bats too move in the dark air, driving at us and skirting the giant swaying tree. Eve and I both like bats; I believe bats wake up feeling peppy and want to show off their flying skills in the dusk. What a marvellous night to be outside in the dark, simply staring up, so content to sit. My modest empire of weeds and flowers, bats and beetles and fine beer. What more could anyone want?

Bats fly and students riot in the street and I love the look of her face asleep so close to me on the pillow. I see a tiny spider on the ceiling making a mini-fresco; I will not tell her of the spider. My anxious cousin dreams a hedgehog chases her, starts beside me in my starched bed. Her sleepy voice now like a little girl, describing the hedgehog dream: *it was awful*. She sounds English, favours words like *sozzled, dustbin, loo, horrid, naff*; lying in bed with lager and wine is, in her eyes, a naughty afternoon and I'm a naughty chap. I like staring into her lovely green eyes, I touch her and she vibrates.

She asks me if I'm a fox or a hedgehog. Before I can reply, she says, I think you're a hedgehog.

We are learning about art in Rome, learning that too much art is like too much salt, too much doctrine. More Canadians died fighting in the streets of Ortona than died on the beaches of D-Day, but who knows anything of Ortona and the Italian campaign? All the dead Canadians and no one cares, D-Day is more widescreen, Hollywood. Is Ortona on the east coast of Italy, the west coast of Italy? And what of the fighting and rubble of Monte Cassino, the Liri Valley, and the gory Gothic Line? Dropping bombs did not help matters, the heaped rubble from the bombs made the fight more difficult. I will try to learn from this; I resent the constant memory of Natasha but will try to give up my ill will, my desire for revenge, to make Natasha suffer. Bombs do not help.

My bachelor uncle died near here, Italy, Christmas 1943; he survived the debacle of the "raid" on Dieppe in the summer of 1942. He was one of thirteen kids on a homestead; he was not trying to save the world, the army was a way to get off the farm. At Dieppe the Canadian guests were expected, mobs of green soldiers trapped by seawalls and cliffs and cut apart by German mortars and heavy machine guns intimate with each inch of the holiday beach, Churchill tanks stuck on the stones, men's tears and blood on the steep stone beach and at the conclusion of slaughter the dead men's corpses directed to a mass grave. I would have gone mad on the beach at Dieppe, but my uncle kept his head and stayed alive.

My uncle is also Eve's uncle, he is one reason we are both in Italy for a visit. In Italy in 1943 he was using a solid stone wall for cover and the wall exploded and my uncle vanished. Our uncle left behind several cedar canoes, sleek vessels like vintage pieces of art, and Eve ended up with one, her cedar canoe hung upside down in her carport, thwarts and polished ribs gleaming inside like the best maple syrup.

The food in Rome, our love letters to the market stalls, to bright heaps of fruit and peppers, to pasta sliced on wires and wondrous wines and gleaming grapes. Honey for my tea! Olives and oil, figs and dates, hazelnut cookies, loaves and fishes. *Brava!* This giant orange is going to change my life. *Molto bello!*

Eve says, "The thing with the pillow is *hot*." But she also says I'm insensitive, aloof, Prufrockian. She said that.

"Are you on the pill or anything?"

"Or anything. Don't you think it's a bit late to ask that?" Still, she smiles.

Halfway across the bridge in Rome there is a sharp cracking sound, not the bridge under us, but an explosion just past the other end, blocking the way to the piazza. The first sound is blunt, but it is also the loudest noise I've ever heard, soft and hard at the same time. A yellow-orange flash leaps high into blue Roman sky while pulverized dust rushes sideways, the air cleaved, a frenzied blur, a tertiary sandstorm beneath the sunny orange mushroom and a small shockwave making my eyeballs tingle. The deafening noise ricochets away off ancient city walls, holding and gone in bald daylight.

In the dust we are nearly run down by the corner of a red truck; an elderly woman slowly crossing the street is brushed aside by an escaping Vespa. The older woman seems to not notice the panic of fleeing cars and scooters. I also have to recover a bit, reboot. She lies flat on the road as if nervously kissing the ground and a tiny Fiat 127 tries to avoid her.

We lift the tiny woman, a weightless moth, and she looks to us, puzzled by our hands; a taxi driver cups her ribs, eases the woman into his cab. Fleeing cars flash by so close to my legs, an inch that way, an inch this way and the cars can shatter our light bones, they can kill us in the smoking light. Will my hearing ever come back?

Some humans run toward the explosion, some run away. I have no plans, as right now I am made of jelly. Some humans run, but my cousin and I stay still, my head aching from the concussive noise, almost a sinus pain, my ears not working right, my monitor needs way more volume.

In the shade of a pine tree a woman sits, her forehead cut and blood falling into one eye in slow heartbeat cadence. An ambulance with blue flashers loads up an embassy employee; the poor guy started opening the morning mail and now he has no hand. Our dear old uncle killed in Ortona: was the wall where he took shelter booby-trapped or did he hear a German 88 shell whining closer as he hugged his heart to the earth and thought of his horses in the foggy hayfield, his Chestnut canoe crossing right through flooded islands, his canoe bumping trees and behind the canoe the big head of his dog swimming. In a

high willow two bald eagles study my uncle and his dog until
they vanish.

We cross the river just to get away, to not be there, and then
my cousin and I sit down as soon as we can, attempt to relax
by jittery fountains, to forget in the liquid light of the piazza,
water falling on stone statues and water breaking in heated air.
The knifing at the party, the bomb in the street; am I some sort
of jinxed magnet? But we are not hurt; so does that mean good
luck? I remember my euphoria in the pulsing night orchard,
around us our minor whirlwind of bats, and I remember her
clean form like steam in the tiled shower, a pleasing image.

   "That was really fun yesterday," I whisper as if we are in a
chapel.

   "Yes," she says in a flat voice, "and that's all that's important."

   Behind Eve's dark glasses — do I detect a new critical tone?
I wonder if you can ever pin such things down to a precise moment, the first shingle blown off the roof, the band no longer
playing "I'm Just Wild About Harry," a small boat about to tip
and when do you leap from the gunwale.

On a train near the Rebibbia Metro station, the driver finds
a "device" made of metal tubes and powder. Perhaps it is an
al Qaeda device, or perhaps a device connected to the rioting
Roman students and anarchists. Or perhaps it belongs to one
of the Italian Prime Minister's famous underage girlfriends,
could it be Ruby the Moroccan belly dancer who steals hearts
at the PM's ribald *bunga bunga* parties in Milan? Ruby the
dancer's brief moment.

   The train will not leave the station, though the device is
not a true bomb, there is no detonator, and the Vatican says

The Martyrdom of St. Lawrence is not a true Caravaggio and now the Pope is on Twitter, but you cannot confess to a priest on an iPhone, despite earlier statements leading some of us to believe that you could confess on an iPhone.

But what if I need to confess?

No one speaks of Caravaggio's *The Martyrdom of Staple Gun Guy*, no one says who sent the severed pig's head in a parcel to Rome's Great Synagogue.

"This heat. It's always so damn hot."

Her voice sounds more stressed than I'd realized and I decide I better pay attention. Her walk is so confident, but at times she lacks confidence.

"All these amazing antiquities, but then look at that apartment building. Zero aesthetic sense, not a thought about design, and honestly, these bombs are freaking me out a little." She pauses. "Can we maybe get out of the city a while? What do you think?"

Yes, we can, surely we can go where we wish. We are free. Bombs now in the road and the knife party not leaving her mind, the world a flower, the world a floating dagger, a chalk-face Noh play-acted in both our heads. Her tension breeds tension in me, perhaps both of us a little freaked out and the melting city pavement (what glorious ruins paved over a few feet beneath?) packed with more and more people and tiny cars powered by teeth and hatred and the temperature higher with each summer day that opens an eye and unrolls its arms.

I want to please her, really it's all I want. So yes, we can get out, we can exit the holy city's crowded streets. All I need is a T-shirt or two. So the coast, the sea, the skuas and scoters and shady vistas somewhere cooler, a tranquil bay, a beach, a full red moon glowing on the strait and glass-green waves collapsing on pebble beaches like a constant industry. To a harbour's scattering of picturesque skiffs and ropes and rattling pebbles and mute swans and a moon drowned and the sea pulling its milky weight around the globe.

My cousin and I rent kayaks for a week and pack our picnic and sunscreen in watertight compartments, a tiny seaside village clinging to the face of an uncooperative cliff, houses above us stuck like colourful mussels, people's lives; how do they hang in place?

The coastal world holds audacious islands, pyrite-yellow strands lacing glowing red cliffs standing over us in the sea and Iceland gulls and jagged peaks of dark lichen and cold seawater running down the paddles onto my arm and my hips soaked in the easy waves and this cooling breeze so welcome in this murderous greenhouse! It's lovely on the water, the shallows such beautiful shades of emerald, azure, jade, and cobalt.

Eve and I kayak a new coast threading islands and greenshanks and whiskered terns and we see so far and glide so smoothly and cover such distances without engine noise or oily exhaust. Our long, conjoined paddles dip in the sea and lift dripping in the sun. Kayaking is like snow skiing in that it alters me quickly, makes me happy that the natural world can be so exhilarating, my lungs full of fresh air and my eye full of beauty. Sand, cliff, sand, cliff, the sun setting as Eve and I spin in easy circles and drift and drink water, kayaks tied together near gatherings of pygmy cormorants and noisy mobs of pale-throated birds; that night we sleep like children undersea.

•

In our chamber we sleep so warmly and a larger night ship waits off the coast in strong seas; a smaller boat moves away and struggles in the darkness, the open boat bobs and yaws, tilts in the rocks and pours them out before the passengers are at shore, they are thrown from the boat as it capsizes in white surf on the dark land like lace at a neck.

On a beach we share black cherry juice and pale bread and buffalo mozzarella and then we kayak past cliffs and a sun-lit village and beach and over there: should we stare or look away? We glide past men roped to each other in the surf, men searching the water for bodies and three bodies already laid in a row on the sand of the beach; three bodies in sodden coats drowned near this narrow accumulation of sand under the cliffs.

Men with mustaches, with suitcases and wet sand glued to their black coats; this crescent beach was not their destination, but now they are stopped on the sand, their mouths stopped, now they are at their destination. Their skiff sank in riptides and long lines of spray, their hands let go and their mouths let in the sea and sky.

Far offshore a red Zodiac inflatable lifts on rhythmic waves, scuba divers surfacing around a boat. Why all the divers gathered like gleaming black seals? Diving for pearls, diving for our café's seafood? We paddle closer and then Eve steers away sharply; her eyes are better than mine. I don't know if I can understand this scene on the water, divers and floating bodies tethered to a boat, a rope tied to each body so they don't drift away from the red inflatable.

A drowned man lies on his back beside the Zodiac in a short-sleeved shirt, his face under the water, his face almost under the bobbing boat. I don't want the hull to hit his face. The man's face is under the waves, but two clenched hands reach out of the waves toward the sky. His head under water, but his big arms lifted up in the air; now does that make any sense in terms of evolution or human design? A rope is tied to the man's shirt and runs through the open fingers of his left hand, as if he is grasping the rope, doing his bit to help the divers.

Herring gulls float on the rolling surface as a diver holds up a small girl from the water and a uniformed man balancing inside the boat takes the girl in his hands. She is perhaps ten, has a long black braid, and seawater runs from her braid into the boat, her jacket and hair dripping water, water running off her face. A gull stares.

The girl's eyes are closed as if she is calmly sleeping, her large closed eyelids, her small fingers, the sea a beautiful azure, and she is so quiet in the man's tender arms. This drowned girl makes me think of the Pietatella chapel hidden in that Napoli alley, the delicate details in stone of Sanmartino's Christ lying under a thin shroud, how can it be, one piece of marble suggesting both body and light veil.

Eyelids and fingers, a mother gave birth to a daughter, this tiny wet creature slipping from between her legs like a tadpole and pulled from silky water and now a man stands in a boat, a girl lifted in his arms, a lamb as offering to the wide summer sky.

This uniformed man's motor-launch and its strange cargo, this turquoise sea and golden photo light of tourist brochures — can death visit here, this pleasing sea rolling under the summer sun, the water muscled, like muscles and curves on a living body. A diver visits the sea and ties a person to the rise and fall of a motorboat.

Will the mother grieve or did the mother also drown here, thus spared this sight of her daughter? She and her family were so close to the shore, so close to Hotel Europa. Daughter, mother, father. Tell me, did you learn to swim in your village in the far desert? No. Their flat desert was sea bottom once, but that doesn't help these travellers with this sea bottom. Where are they from? Who knows. Sand blowing in the desert and sand roiling under the sea, the surf comes strolling to them, sea ringing to the stars and comets. They brought nothing with them, they are moving, untethered astronauts. Hurry, get to land, get sand under your boots. But where in the riptides is the bottom? We begin in a warm sea and we end in the cold.

The girl with the braid so peaceful now, but villagers heard screaming in the dark under the cliffs; the villagers couldn't see where the migrants rolled in water and rocks and now in daylight these people collected on ropes, now in daylight the girl's long dark braid dripping seawater and bodies and babies roll in the waves like glossy dolphins. Are they from Iraq? Tunisia? The family came so close and I wonder will they be buried in Italian soil, remembering words carved on the gravestone in the Protestant Cemetery: *Here lies One Whose Name was writ in Water*.

Eve can't watch the divers do their work, Eve glides away in a bright kayak and I follow her, hearing an old blues tune, Reverend Gary Davis's raspy voice stuck in my head, death don't have no mercy, death don't take a vacation in this land. In this land of vacation, in this perfection, our bows whisper water's music and Eve whispers childhood prayers under the walled cliffs and I try to remember the childhood words, and our dead uncle and his dog follow us on the water in the ribbed Chestnut canoe.

•

A village appears an hour later and I want a drink, a really big cold bottle if possible. Under a long pier the black water seems alive with jellyfish, our seas heating up and jellyfish made happy by the warming. They have lovely oscillating blooms, jellyfish the colours of stained glass, like big Tiffany lampshades, glowing by the dock and pulsing under our kayaks. Swimmers can't relax near them and local fishermen slash at the jellyfish, trying to kill them, but more and more arrive, thriving on violence, unease, warmth.

A Canadian pilot died along this shore in the war; so warm now, but it was Christmas when the pilot parachuted into the freezing sea. They found him quickly, plucked him dripping from the waves, but he was already frozen blue, another cold body in the sea, his girlfriend on Charlotte Avenue waking with a chill and when he didn't come back the other pilots calmly divided up his kit, his socks and tea and tobacco. All the tea tins and forgotten names who fall like harriers from sky to sea.

The sun is low and a jellyfish stings Eve's small breast and she holds herself where my hand has held her. I hold her on a beach, a kind of venom in the stingers. I'm hungry and thirsty and we must climb to find a room, a meal, see if we can buy some ointment and Tylenol or painkillers.

From high on a cliffside path we look down and can still see the three men's crow-like coats in the foaming flood, *twa corbies*, three travellers drowned in the night and still lying on the beach, strange sunbathers. What are the names of these young mustached men? These Adams in a new world moving to imaginary jobs and city apartments and city lives in Lyon, in London, to Eccles cakes and curry takeaways in the new world, wanting what I take for granted: decent shoes, a roof, and fruit and food for your children, for the girl with the dripping braid.

I move for work, my parents moved for work, my grandparents moved for work, and some for war. My great-grandfather was an Irish cavalry man and dowser, finding water with a forked branch, and my grandfather a cooper, crafting beautiful oak barrels in steam and smoke, and my father an artist and a coal clerk in Oxford; they are gone and their trades all vanished. Horse and wagon selling milk and blocks of ice in the brand new suburb, pickers of rag and bone, gaunt wanderers sharpening my mother's scissors and knives — all those worlds of work vanished along with the tinkers, all the exiles expelled from such modest yards and gardens.

The world does not stay the same, the world rearranges and turns inside out, old lives washed up and whooshed away like my father's bent jetty or a skiff dashed into pieces with you in it, water pouring over lapstrake planks and rocks revealed in their iron-green troughs, in their lair where the jellyfish wait to lay their red welts. We gamble on our arrangements of patches and sticks, we settle down for a suburban moment and forget we are nomads, forget that our particle-board ranch houses are constructed over hidden kindred underworlds, forget that we are racing engines, a race of émigrés, *una faccia una razza*, the Italians say, one face, one race, shoved about the world on strange currents like horses in a swift mountain river.

Our illegal aliens have escaped the future, left the flat desert, found water like a dowser, like me, found a beach in Italy, found the curve of Eve's breast. Her pretty green eyes in my room, her curves everywhere in my eye, her name on my lips, my narrow interests, our delicious after-tremors. They drown in the surf and her period arrives, generous with blood the colour of my best geraniums.

"I can put a towel down under us." The towel is dark blue.

"There is too much blood. In a day or two we can," she says, "but not today."

There is one kind favour I would ask of you.

"Usually I don't like this," she says. "Why do guys like it so much?"

She arranges herself on the bed in a pleasant businesslike manner as if agreeing to learn a new card game at the cabin. She sits and I stand before her, but who is supplicant?

She stops, says, "I've always hated this, but I actually like the taste of yours."

I stand over her, but she controls me, moves me with her mouth and hands, my body a big doll tilting forward and back, a balloon animal moved this way and that, feeling closer, closer, a low gravitational force moving up from the floor through my ankles and knees, through my thighs, a concussive conclusion nearing, and sweet is the death that taketh end by love. I rock three or four times in involuntary motion until my legs sag under me and she has to hold me up. The feeling is far more powerful when standing up than if lying in bed with her, but I don't want to convey that information. Both of us are surprised, we are related, we are bound.

Bound to each other with dripping ropes, villagers move like line dancers in the surf; ropes tighten and go lax as the villagers walk the surf together, a row of living men and women and children searching the water in case there are more aliens hiding in the sea.

•

Sunburnt and spent we return from days rented on the water. Wet ropes lie coated with sand.

"Do you have any lotion?"

"Your poor skin. I think I have some."

Eve sleeps on the bus, her face so peaceful in sleep, her nerves relaxed; refugees hit a wall of cliffs and surf while we move so easily through Italy. I love her peaceful face as our bus corkscrews through tunnels and mountains, the driver's horn as musical as a trumpet at the blind turns.

We've been in the city and country and sometimes she says, *That's it*, and she leaves me. She leaves me and comes back, leaves and comes back. Times I can't relax with Eve, wondering what's next, she keeps me on edge in my own rooms. Perhaps that's good, perhaps that's what I need.

Tunnels and faith: that moment when you enter a tunnel, when you move from bright light to darkness, you can't see a thing, but you keep going with faith that the pathway is safe, that there is not a wall there, but an opening and a lane, and the same hope when you burst from a tunnel into blinding light, wondering what is beyond. That the grill of a bus isn't filling your lane, that the earthquake didn't drop that small section of the road, that your children will be happy, that their lives will be good.

Like skiing in a blizzard, the light declines and you can't make out the dips and moguls and start wiping out, but you have to ease yourself down the mountain, find a route a foot at a time, or the light returns and you didn't know how much you loved the light, needed it. And when you ride a scooter, enter a party, a club, buy a cellphone from a crack addict, ease your doll-like head out the open train window — that moment of faith as night and wind flow and you offer up your face to the forces.

At a wooden table in the courtyard two Italian children laugh and slurp soup from yellow bowls. An adult made the soup, the children would die without the adult, but the children laugh and the adult does not exist. How long since I saw my own children? I don't carry a phone, but I email them and they sound happy in their summer pursuits.

An American woman stands by her car, yelling to another woman.

"I cain't find him," the woman complains in a loud nasal voice. "I call and call and he won't answer. I'll try calling him again." How many of us are hiding from that voice, that place, that jagged coast. They can't find the vanished bodies, the submerged swimmers.

Before my cousin left the last time, she read to me, read lines from a strange guide to speaking Italian, a guide she found in a hotel lobby.

"Who wrote this? *Ha spesso le palpebre gonfie?* Do you often have swollen eyelids? Who the hell travels to Italy to comment on swollen eyelids? *Con l'età siamo diventati un po' sordi anche noi.* With age we too have become a little deaf. *Ti ama alla follia.* She loves you to the point of insanity." She stops to consider. "Or would that be *folly* rather than *insanity*? *Follia*?"

"I like that last line. Say it again."

"*Ti ama alla follia.*"

"I like that."

•

My cousin and her lotion in a room so small we end up on
the bed. Three bodies lie so close on the beach. They do not
proceed to the luggage carousel to retrieve their bags. The
red Zodiac offshore dangling ropes in the water, keeping the
bodies close as family. Her pyjamas washed to indifference,
translucence.

She says, "I had a dream in which you were very mean to me."

"Eating too late cause dreams like that. How is your beautiful little pussy?"

"It's been lonely," she says.

We move on the map. Are my polite old dead relatives watching us, uncles and aunts and sweet grannies? I hope not. Does
she really have MS? She told me she did, as if it was a minor
matter that might affect her driving at times, but she seems fine.

She was down by the village graveyard and I followed her,
fog rolling over us into lovely dark green parkland and evening's
dendroid silhouettes, a sweet season with green hath clad the
sylvan hill, the sunny peak and the valley depth so close together
and my hand on her. I know we shouldn't be together, but she
is better than meth, than mirth.

She was mad that I made fun of Sylvia Plath, but then at the
bar she says happily, "Vodka goes right to my vagina. I'm going
straight to video. Or to hell." She went to a piano and played
"The Crystal Ship" and the room applauded. Time passes, a
city of gold awaits us, an eternal city, an eternal question: are
my eyes on the prize? Hell if I know.

She goes out walking. Does she really mean to meet me later
in the village, or did she know when we spoke that she would
not be there? When does she have to be back in Switzerland? I

don't know anyone with MS; what are the symptoms? I worry that something might happen if she drives alone on the coastal highway, all the tunnels.

But this is not the first time she has disappeared, tried to save me or save herself; she comes and goes. My cousin was mad at me a week or two back, complained that she was almost my age but I was treating her like a fourteen-year-old, treating her like a call girl. Why did she say fourteen? She walked away, but a day or two later, she showed up saying, Let's go upstairs, ordering me to follow her and I did so.

No parley or preamble, no chance to reconcile, no polite chit-chat or cup of tea. She walked to my room and I followed her. I've never met anyone like this. Back in bed I called her my fourteen-year-old call girl and she laughed. It's almost puzzling how much we enjoy our time in my bed; we do nothing weird, nothing kinky, but we seem so compatible, nesting dolls, perhaps the best ever, her face in my face and her bright eyes so close, her eyes looking startled as it builds, her body closer and closer, and that one time her teeth biting the pillow so those in the hall won't hear.

Taxis, movement toward or away from stimulation, from her crosswords. She is gone this minute, but on my sheets I am left a bloody imprint the shape of a butterfly; I treasure the faded menstrual imprint, my shroud of Turin.

Like my sheet, like a clamshell, we add layers and insurance policies, we accrete. I am a measly planet struck by passing worlds and haunted chords and fragments of silver moons, a long process of erosion and addition and meat draws and comp lists. My pocked outer casing, dusty craters, but a smooth child buried inside, strange weather inside us and furnished rooms and a rat inside us reading Proust (such memorable pastry!) and perhaps a rat nesting inside your inner rat.

In town it's strange to see such a massive red Buick in Italy, a big convertible shipped from North America by a Milanese car collector before the economic storms and cutbacks and collapses. Eve wants to drive it by the sea. I daydream there might be cocaine hidden in the doors, all for me, perhaps a taste for the Cobalt Woman whose hair caught fire. The motorcade speeds up, but you're no Jack Kennedy.

That bomb by the river in Rome, at the embassy: we never found out who was trying to kill themselves or attempting to kill us, was it domestic or foreign or from flying saucers, the message is never clear.

Before she left, my cousin said, "I think I'm getting addicted to you."

Is that so bad?

Yes, this addiction worries her.

I notice that she hugs me tighter when she is about to leave me. I need a change, she said. She cut her hair into bangs that made her look like Pippi Longstocking. Using my scissors in the bathroom and singing softly, something about the desert where she can't remember her name.

Then the handwritten letter and envelope sliding under the door when she knows I am not in my small room, when I'm out at the internet café, where no one writes me.

I've had to make some hard decisions, her letter claims. *But, it's been wonderful, true mad deep abiding stockinged scattered love.*

She's come and gone before, but this time she seems serious about no communication, no attempt at contact. I admit I laughed when I saw the letter on the floor, saw my name. *Not again!* I thought. But I'm not laughing now. Now she is under my skin. They say you must separate sex from love, that they are not the same; I'm slightly confused on that matter.

The thought of never seeing you again is intolerable, but might be best. You do make me happy, but I can't seem to feel calm.

Beyond the pale curtains there is traffic and the earth wobbles so quietly on its bent axis that you barely notice. By the river some gypsy kids sniff glue from a Kleenex, they don't know how to mend tin pots and pans. My worries mean nothing.

Eve said I was detached, difficult, maddeningly stubborn.

I thought I was easygoing.

No, you're difficult.

Me difficult? Well, this is certainly news to me.

Natasha said, You're so lovable, but then she left me.

Always these exits and always this question: should I follow to make peace or go the other direction? Should I follow Eve's footsteps along the seaside road, or let her go alone with her fear of spiders? Each way seems the wrong way. I want to move, ride a buzzing red scooter, see the shimmering Amalfi coast and cliffs, one foot in the sea and one on shore. I worry something might happen to her; how would she tell me? Once Eve almost fainted using the phone in my room. Am I attracted to affliction? Or is affliction attracted to me? The East German woman said I was calm. Eve's note said, *The time I spent with you was some of the happiest of my life, I hope you'll always be happy.*

I like a kayak's separation from shore, moving away from established things. This movement reminds me of fast downhill skiing; I feel more accepting of the exhausting world, movement helps when things don't go my way. I ski over a ridge and get some air and the view goes forever. At this altitude flowers may take years to blossom. I must stop on this high table of land and look and catch my breath and rest my legs. There are legions of dark pines and far below are lit glass triangles by the tranquil river and I am alone in a swerving sky, the soft powder a dream.

When skiing I work tiny patches of a giant mountain; I map it out and add all the parts together: ski to the right to avoid the hidden rocks, then veer to the left and hug the treeline for untouched powder, drop down that bowl and up that lip to fly off the round white cliff and don't land flat, keep my balance and keep my gleeful speed and keep my ass off the ground.

My kayak is so low in the water that I feel the sea's pressure on my rump. Water drips into my lap from the raised paddle so I tuck a towel over my legs like a skirt; this works perfectly. With no keel or rudder the kayak zigzags (*by indirection directions find out*) side to side with each paddle dug in the water, no choice, paddle on the left side and go right, paddle right and go left, as if waddling across to that opposite beach. A keel may help, steering my life crookedly, hither and thither. Sometimes I am direct, sometimes not.

On my own in a seaside village, she is gone, but I refuse to be sad, I rent a glamorous wooden speedboat, art deco lines, no charts, no maps, no problem, I'll follow the coast to the next available village and tie up for a tasty meal and a drink and assemble my rakish reptile thoughts in a clean well-lighted place with a sympathetic waiter or waitress, but I fail to notice that the coastline I follow is an island and islands can be round and all the glowing cliffs look alike because I'm passing the same cliffs over and over and where the hell is the stupid village and café, going around and around in a circle until the speedboat sputters out of fuel, and my little wooden boat helpless into the rocks and the rocks grind into my ears with a sound like a frailing banjo. I'm sure my dead uncle is laughing at me. They do not laugh at the rental kiosk.

"Was the hull damaged when we gave it to you?"

"It may have been. I did not think to inspect the hull. It may have been weak, undermined by mussels or worms."

"No, I assure you, no worms, the boat was not damaged. You were careless with what was not yours."

"I was not careless."

"Perhaps so. But tell me, who will pay me if not you? Will the rocks pay us? No, a rock will not pay."

I think he is losing steam, but it's like arguing with a movie star; there is no point. Round and round we go, round we go day after day, my life, the same beautiful coves, boats getting nowhere.

Silver cliffs stand in the sea's frenzied cities and you rode upon a steamer. Azure, aqua, cobalt: how to describe such deeply pleasing paisley colours of the warm sea? Delicious greens and prism blues mixed in curves and lines over a shimmering sand bottom and sunlit mica rocks. But how does anything grow on such jagged rock?

Boats tilt, water leaps in over the gunwales, the transom, over something, and the passengers choke on water. From the cliffs above, helpless villagers ran to open their salt-bleached sheds, blindly threw cork life jackets down to the drowning aliens, enemies and sudden allies. I am a simple animal: I feel bad when things are bad, feel better when things are good. I love you like towns under wet smoke, rooms that never dry out.

Step outside and the front door swings shut behind, locking you out; I hold my mug of tea, but my brass door-key is inside, there it is, I can see the key clearly through a glass pane. I was careless, I wait and wonder how I will get back in, if anyone is around to help.

It's funny. Most mornings I lie in my room listening and wait for others to scurry away to their worlds and demands, waiting for the footsteps on the stairs to stop so I can enjoy an unrushed shower. And in the afternoon I wait for the lunch hour ebb-tide to flow from the café so I may pick a solitary seat in peace. I spend so much of my time waiting for others to disappear.

The Troubled English Bride

*The distance I felt came not from
country or people; it came from within me.*

*I am as distant from myself as
a hawk from the moon.*

—James Welch

Clouds pile high over the Vatican like horses biting each other, clouds rising over Rome's glowing peach walls and tiles and television antennas. One white gorgeous mushroom cumulus lifts higher and higher — I love looking at it, staring into the ruins of this God-like face.

The blue Italian night turns darker and darker and a stranger's ebony piano plays near my flowered terrace. Rome or Naples or Pompeii or Positano: a piano trills or a dog barks somewhere near me, perhaps the apartment across the way. A sense opens inside my brain or ear and needs to know where the sound is formed, to know more of this mysterious envoy from another home.

At home in Canada our household is divided, literally and figuratively.

"Turns out I don't have room for the oak bookcases," my wife says on the phone, "but I'd like to keep the big quilt."

"Okay," I agree.

"And the car."

"Okay."

"You can have your roll-top desk."

"Okay."

I, the bad husband, find myself agreeing to anything. In Rome and Sorrento, that divided home seems so far away.

In an Italian town south of the excavations, high above the sea, I spy God in a lawn chair. He calls to me in a hoarse voice. "English," he says. He calls me English, he wants money.

A church dome looming above his alley catches my eye, a rougher Arabian or Moorish structure clumsily hidden behind a façade of Roman pillars and triangular portico, a cleaner classical façade imposed on the place of worship like a movie set's false front. Was anyone murdered in that transition? This church is jammed into a tiny space, one more tooth cramming a walled lane.

The old man calls to me, "English."

I stare up at the church's warring components, though the Mediterranean sun does its best to knock me down. Even the locals are wilting, soaking shirts and dresses.

When I first arrived everyone complained of clouds and rain, not typical weather for Italy.

Always clear blue sky, said the stewardess from Quebec.

Now I'd love some cloud or rain. And this is not the height

of the heat. August must be unbearable. Natasha would thrive here; she is heliotropic, worships the sun, loved Spanish Morocco and Northern Africa. I wonder if her hair is still long? Someday I'll stop bringing her up, her spectre, that triangle I didn't want to be part of.

At the ancient church the ancient Italian man calls to me from his chair.

"English, give me five euro and I'll go up there and pray for you." His hoarse voice in the lane. "Believe in me, English, believe in me."

I don't believe in him. Go up where? The rough eastern dome disguised behind the newer triangle? Do I understand this god? But do I understand anyone anymore?

A seagull dangles over uncertain cliffs: such faith in air. Dazzling seas of mythology and fable, sirens naked and billowing sails and deep blue grottoes and men into pigs. Do I want temptation, do I want Circe? Do I understand myself at all?

Too much time on my own, staring at Greek Orthodox anguish, statues and faces in arching giant vaults with gilt tile and tortured Christs. On my own I walk past glowing Italian fountains and on my own I worry about my stray dogs and my orphans of the mountain and I jump on a bus to Positano by myself to shudder at cliffs and hairpin turns and stunning views of the Amalfi coast stretching south.

The old man shows coins cupped in his hand, evidence of his offer's merit.

"I'll pray."

Who would delegate such a thing as prayer? Should I pay hammered coins as a kind of insurance policy? But what if delegating prayer is a sin? Then I'm worse off.

"Believe in me, English."

This is religion, this is our hoarse God, a grizzled man in a lawn chair. Or a real God is watching and this is a test.

No. If I must pray I must do my own praying, not pay someone else. I walk away in this stone lane past the English brides, not sure where I'm headed.

His rough voice follows me down the echoing stone. "English! Believe in me!"

Nietzsche was misled; God sits in a lawn chair in a set stone lane over a writhing ancient sea. I'll show you the place high above a harbour.

I want to believe, but I do not believe. It's all such claptrap.

But then another day I really do believe, it makes perfect sense.

Am I two different people? Twenty different people? Believe in God, believe in sunny Natasha; it changes hour to hour. The blackberries were sour and the yogurt too sweet, but together they are perfect. I believe in her, but I have to pull the plug on her, *no más, no más*.

My wife can no longer believe in me. The talkative women on the terrace in Rome no longer believe. Perhaps it is our collective lack of confidence that eats at the ozone. Seneca said to make each day a separate life. I like that idea, but really that notion changes little for me, I live the same life over and over without learning.

Hooves echo loudly, the troubled bride approaches, a wagon and horse clopping noisily in this narrow lane; I duck into a doorway to make room and the blonde wrapped in white passes, her face right by my face, *clop clop*, I see skin, bare shoulders, our lane so narrow her white wedding dress touches me. The narrow lane of her long shaven legs, her sad face turned to me.

Run away with me! I want all women to marry me, to love me, to get to know me. I just do.

A wedding in Capri or Sorrento, this was her inspired thought last winter in grey England. Italy! How exciting, how very romantic! But something is wrong. In this African heat the wedding party sweats uphill in matching cobalt metal dresses and funereal Prince Edward top hats, sweating as they climb cobblestones and cliffside paths up from the rolling sea's waves and the hydrofoil's surly staff and the faded fishermen's church right on the narrow beach under the cliffs. The bridal party's backless cobalt dresses have an unfortunate way of making their shoulders look chubby and these chubby British women shine like sweating horses as they pass. When she planned the romantic Italian wedding, sweating like horses was not part of the vision.

The troubled bride passes me twice, twice I have to hug the wall as she rides past, I could touch her, her dress touches me. Perhaps her father beside her, going with her to the church the first time I saw her. Not yet a wife, then a wife when next I see her. Not looking happy. Either time.

Two different laneways, yet the new wife passed me both times — I have doomed her marriage. My eyes are to blame, I saw her and I am jaded and cynical and I have disappointed my wife and my friends and my sisters.

I represent separation, the imminent failure and dissolution of marriage, though I also represent love and fervour and blind optimism and blind pessimism and a very good nose for bargains (look in my fridge at the very reasonable berry yogurt and tins of German wheat beer).

•

My eyes see the troubled bride and I wish to approach her here on the coast under the palm trees and I'd like to have us hie to my cool third-floor room like a cave carved out of icy marble and there my eyes wish to see the bride slowly strip bare for me and only me, oh to witness each slow shoulder become naked and my fingers touch each slight elastic garter bisecting her loins as she waits for me to move over her and I will levitate, just my face brushing her blushing silk triangles, silk caught on her body and my hand fanned on her high hipbones and my hand breathing heat from that tiny isthmus between her legs, the cusp of entrance, and a white fan turning a breeze on our liminal forms and a soothing shower if we want streams of water running along our blessed bodies.

But I do not breathe of her and my eyes see no silk or triangles. We're not in my room or shower.

No, that's me past the palm trees and hundreds of scooters, alone at a shady table with a bottle of Peroni and staring out at scooters parked in domino rows and on my right dark cobbles of the amazing road zigzagging steeply down to the fishermen's church where she was lawfully wed.

And in this Italian summer I can see her English future, her English winter, the lost sparrows, I see that in a cold English winter someone will approach her cluttered desk at the agency where she's worked for some months now.

On her desk perches a small blue-sky photo, the frame of gold trees, bright metallic dresses on the plump bridesmaids, the wedding in sun-swathed Italy that seems another life than England's gun-grey mists.

Hullo, going out with us after work?

Not today.

Do. We're all going. A bit of fun.

She studies his face, his eyes, wonders what he's like, what he means. English rain at the Venetian blinds.

They do go out after work, a pint, a cocktail, more drinks, a curry, then an after-hours club that someone at work knows.

Weeks later the blond English bride will confide in her best friend, I feel alive again.

And it is my fault, I have this in my head, all my fault, for she passed me in the cobbled lane with her horse and snowy gown and her uncertain face. I now pronounce you alive again, that mix of guilt and thrill, and then the moving van waiting at her door.

Which sofa is yours?

Can I have that painting?

Sure, take it.

Her desk at work. Come just for one, someone says.

I suppose I could, just one.

What's the harm?

Ah sure, this work can wait until tomorrow.

Sure, I don't need that long sofa or long marriage or long green riverbank.

I did this to my wife and then Natasha did the same to me. Are you familiar with the familiar tale?

Life altered in a few seconds, an entire world gone in Natasha's few words, like the American man who flew all the way here to leap off the cliff or the beautiful scooter couple from Rome smashing into the bus on the hairpin turn above the sea.

We made plans to meet in Rome, I'd meet Natasha in Venice, in winter we'd ski the mysteries of mountains. Natasha knew a family hotel, amazing risotto with her every lunch, and fondue in a chalet. But now there is someone else. What I'd hoped for, for so long, gone so quickly. Fast as a car crash, a scooter.

And so easy for him to be beside her. So hard for me to get near Natasha, two years, her crippling guilt about other parties, her caution, but he has the whole world I wanted and makes it seem effortless, simply by being there in the same city and asking once.

Natasha said she loved me, said, *Buon giorno* my darling, you are all mine on all levels. Was I to not believe her very specific words? Now I feel I was a distraction, a curiosity, some vague zoological interest until the real thing was evident. But the real thing for me, unfortunately.

Torture took the place of sleep, I who usually sleep so well: was it her place or his? Had to be her place, the door, her cloudland bedroom, where I'd been, our private code. Did she invite him over knowing what was next? His girlfriend left him and then he professed love for Natasha. She rebuffed him; next time they didn't talk and she was sad, thought she'd lost two best friends, him and her.

Then the birthday party; they did talk, they both got drunk. That tiny zipper on her jeans like an on-off switch. Her living room sofa first or did they go right to the bedroom duvet?

Two creatures create a new time, just one move, one hour, one drink, just one finger brushing another finger, her creation, her ceiling of Sistine, one overwhelming question coming to life there at the threshold. I know her: she is too polite to turn away from what is offered to her. And I am absent, I am thousands of miles away, I am like Othello fearing the horns of a cuckold, horns bursting from his head, pointing, my head hurts *here*.

They know all and I know nothing. It is humiliating and erotic. Was it good for her, for both? He is younger than me, eager. I felt a stud with other women in the past, lifting them in the air, but so insecure with her. A sign that we were not meant to be? A world of omens: to believe or not? The Gods punish me. They enjoy it. The myths punish us as we enact them, doomed to repeat the same lame moves, the same ludicrous stories.

A volcano floats over Italy's silver sea, a volcano hovers at Pompeii's shoulder like a permanently drunk uncle. Pompeii swelters under the volcano, days in the odorous ash and ochre stone and roofless ruins, baked excavations the colour of excrement, past the Villa of Mysteries and ancient brothels. Miles of giant paving stones — like I'm stepping on the polished backs of so many tortoises. Sweaty trains sway back and forth like fates, and the coxcombs try to gauge if I'm worth robbing.

Train tracks run on both sides of excavations; clearly we ride dust clouds over the outskirts of a dead city, clearly not all this ruined city is excavated. There is more: dead families and homes and hidden lovers live on under our wheels and rails. Stone and more stone; all these walls of stone remind me of the Aran Islands in Ireland.

In Pompeii a fast phone call from a ghost: the exact spot where I met her and my phone rings. Can't be her. It is her, but her cell dies, her phone always unreliable, unreliable as her. I call back but she can't hear me over the miles of fields and snowy mountains. I can hear her eager voice: *Hello! Hello!* But she can't hear me. The wind blows ash and dust, tourists covering their cameras. Then the click as she gives up and the machines break contact.

Will I ever be able to listen to Vic Chesnutt's murky songs without thinking of her?

I leave the excavations, pass the exit like a border. I walk away from Checkpoint Charlie and am set upon by merchants outside the temple, grabbing my sleeve, hungry for my money. Always a hand out.

Cold drinks over here, very good.

Sir, this way!

No, *grazie*.

Good meals and good prices, all you can eat, right this way, sir.

They think I am alive because I cast a shadow, carry a passport, a wallet with euros. When it rains, which is not often this summer, Asian men magically appear with umbrellas for sale. They are polite, soft-sell. In the heat Africans selling knock-off sunglasses and heaps of purses. And in the rain Asians with umbrellas.

Have these foreigners reached a secret accord, a division of spoils? A local Yalta. In Italy the outsiders have divided the weather: Africans own the sun, Asians own the rain, and Croatian chambermaids own the tile floors and buckets of water. The tiles of my hotel room resemble the sea. The Italians own themselves, their speed, their buzz, their voices, own everything right around them. The Americans own Iraq. In the rain Asians ask me to buy an umbrella: the marketplace deems me weary of the examined life, but alive.

I buy sunglasses in the rain.

"Believe me, English!" calls the old man in the cobbled lane.

Don't believe me, I now want to tell the bride. Your odds have nothing to do with mine. Get married, you'll be fine, you'll beat the odds, beat the banks. Have confidence, have faith, I want to tell her.

I am an atheist and separated, yet I believe in the mysteries of God and marriage. Troubled, I believe in peace. Hated, I believe in love. Unhappy, I believe so devoutly in happiness.

Party Barge

Never confuse motion with action.

—Benjamin Franklin

Late one night Eve follows the banks of the Tiber to find her way home from a tiny restaurant, a hole in the wall with amazing seafood, was it the Black Tulip, but on her way out the door Father Silas pointed her in the wrong direction. His poor directions steered her miles out of her way, and the Roman riverbank at night is an altered world from daylight. Boisterous crowds funnel in lanes and steps from Trastevere, crowds block her way, and on the Tiber party barges float under Vatican spires and windows, and drunken animals wander everywhere: these creatures of nature party, chill, urinate, wave to the Pope.

The barges so empty and silent when she walked past in daylight, she felt sorry for the owners, they must lose money, poor sad failed bars, I should go aboard, she thinks, have a cold drink, make them happy, but now at night she sees party barges packed to the gunwales, at night the economy is booming, euros to be had from hooligans, Italian emo bands out on the water and floodlit barges raucous with drinkers as industry, too many inebriated males crowding the walk and dark stone edges of the river, on the creeping edge of sex or violence.

It's like passing through a nerve-wracking Serengeti, tip-toeing a grass lair of hyenas or wolves; don't rouse them. Is it feeding time or can she creep through without being noticed or pinched on the ass or attacked by a drunk or flecked by projectile party vomit that is part and parcel of The Big Hormonal Trip to Europe?

In Ireland you see signs pleading, *No English Stag Parties*. In Berlin, *Noisy Tourists Go Home, No American Hipsters*. The local citizens resent young drunks falling off cheap Ryanair flights not sure what country they are walking in. Shelley called Italy a paradise of exiles, but neighbourhood families now strolling their placid river are outnumbered by exiles, by drunken foraging armies on bargain pub crawls. The locals would like to stow them away on the barges along with the plague victims of old.

I have to go pack! yells one son of the football fields and cornfields, a college quarterback with a blond woman clutching each arm, at each ear, they won't let him go pack, forget it, they all laugh, ha ha, no packing for you tonight, two party women farded and larded with makeup, elbows held close to their toned bodies.

Seven hills of Rome above us and our quarterback views four breasts shifting in bright tube tops as if directional devices, first this way, now this way, cobbled lanes twisting through all of Europe to the next nightclub or piazza or party barge, and he knows he will kiss all four breasts before dawn, they'll play Romulus suckled by she-wolves. Our QB laughs and buys rounds, he still has to pack his suitcase, he has to kiss the girls, he has to down more shooters and neon martinis, he has to scream PARTY!!!

He has to text his good buddy, more shooters, dude, where are you!!! How 'bout them Hawkeyes!

Wait, he has to hurl in the Tiber, dude, where am I, oh no, puke on a silk Italian shirt, that's *harsh*, man, where's my phone, I lost my new phone and lost the new dudette girls.

Morning comes and our Iowa boy didn't kiss four breasts, morning comes and his buddy finds his phone and calls his room and yells PARTY!! and the QB says Dude shut up!! He still has to pack his suitcase, fuck the suitcase, fuck the hotel, you know what, I'm not even paying these greasy Eye-tal creeps.

With zero shut-eye he taxis his throbbing hangover head and burnt throat to the airport, what do you mean there are two airports! How the hell should I know which one, and the taxi driver rips him off and oh Christ he left his passport at the hotel desk, he still has to pack and curse every Italian and every blond skank and he still has to punch every wall in Italy, then he has to grasp his broken fist, his throwing hand the Big Ten coach will be furious, *ouch ouch ouch*, he has to grasp his groaning head, has to buy shares in Tylenol, and why the fuck won't you let me on the fucking flight, I'm not drunk, and what do you mean no more flights today, that's it, no more trips anymore ever, screw George Bush and Homeland Security and screw all of Europe, Europe sucks in hard daylight.

But at night on the Tiber river other quarterbacks are alive and at large like animals among gorgeous party barges and all our glowing faces and from his lit window our Pope waves back and winks, our world full of razors and orphaned brain cells, but wonderfully wild and generous in nature.

Exempt from the Fang (Aircraft Carrier)

Our sincerest laughter
With some pain is fraught;
Our sweetest songs are those
that tell of saddest thought.

— Percy Bysshe Shelley

Pope Rat watches Euro Cup, the blind man wanders our hotel halls, and I wander Rome's swarming city. I soak my head and T-shirt in cold water to escape the Roman heat, I inhale cold bottles in a dark bistro, then I creep into another empty church — simple, not a rock-star church, but I must look. The streets burn in wild daylight, but inside is shadow, inside my eyes rise to a blue dome where a young Italian artist painted night stars inside the cupola before spilling from his high scaffold, the falling man ending his art and life in one downward stroke.

Ever so slightly sunburnt and intoxicated, I am in the precisely right state to take in the swooning gift of these stars glowing in a tiny compass of sky, this is exactly what a place of worship should do, lines of light guiding my eyes from the well bottom up to these high stars in a circle.

My cells vibrate happily, my mind and eyes ready to receive this perfect sacrament. Light like blocks of white stone fills the church windows, and in my head Gene Clark's tremolo voice singing, *ain't it good to be alive*. This temporal bliss won't last, but in the moment its echo is beautiful.

Our world revolves about me for a few hours until like Galileo I know — what heresy — it doesn't circle me, I remember I am millions of miles from the centre. But I'll survive, I have options. What of the woman from Iraq with her injured eyes? She was once so happy, on her way to school she steered a blinding gold Mustang through the heart of Baghdad and courted bright ambitions, but after the invasion she has nothing, finds herself so far from the centre.

American soldiers liked the woman from Iraq, and Americans ran over her gold Mustang with a tank while she was trapped at the steering wheel and then I meet her in her new life in Rome, in her exile. Birds and countries flying through the air like scalding shrapnel, all these wax nations, all these melting borders and missiles into homes. Our hotel rooms have teensy televisions bolted to the ceiling and mine pulls in a German MTV channel, *rock und roll*, the VJ's narration an unsettling mix of Teutonic Girl and Valley Girl. Our alliances and kingdoms change so quickly, fidgety as a blackbird's eye.

Loaded down by buckets of dirt and rocks, men trudge out of the earth, carrying rocks by hand through the hotel atrium, lugging buckets to a tiny truck the size of a scooter. In a silent prayer I call upon the backhoes of the nation to help them.

I want to chat up the soft-eyed Spanish woman who inhales cigarettes in the atrium. Under her white sundress blood speaks in her skin and she reminds me of Natasha, a similar face and hair, as if I know this person, a sister-messenger, though Natasha is too health-conscious to smoke, Natasha is more green tea than Pall Malls.

Angelo owns the rambling hotel, Angelo delivers to our atrium party a giant vat of purple-black wine that resembles Welch's grape juice, a giant ham, *prosciutto di Parma*, and a giant knife; Eve and I glance at the knife warily. Angelo moves slowly to a long table, his grey hair slicked back, a beaked nose like a hawk; he is generous to us, he is regal.

"Tonight we have a super-big party!" exclaims a smiling Angelo.

Eve can't take the wine's sweet taste, but Ray-Ray and the others like the hooch well enough. We also carve up a spicy sausage the size of a small pig and an amazing cake filled with light custard. Food is so good in Italy; it's like being stoned.

Father Silas makes a toast, "Thanks to the hotel owner for a *festa* with real Italian girls." And it's true, Angelo did arrive with smiling Italian girls with big hair like Amy Winehouse or the Shirelles.

"The bigger the hair the closer to God," says Eve.

"*Grazie, grazie,*" we all intone. *Grazie.* Am I saying it right?

Basta, Angelo says modestly. Enough.

Father Silas whispers to me, "If Angelo says *Ciao* to us, then we can say it to him." Otherwise Father Silas worries we might be too informal.

•

The Spanish woman says Angelo's men are digging a cellar for a basement café and gym. Angelo is ambitious, owns many buildings, and I find myself wondering how much real estate he has in Rome. Or how much does he owe, is he overextended. The crew has no jackhammer or BobCat. Excavators and dump trucks are too wide for the narrow lane. So the work is done by hand and back and legs, like labour scratched out thousands of years ago. Will the men's picks and crowbars stab into artifacts, find bones in a well? Will our hotel collapse?

Every time they dig in Rome they find something, the Spanish woman says, reading my mind. It is impossible to do anything. If they try to expand the subway, they can dig a new line — a tunnel is narrow, that is okay — but a new station means excavating a much broader space and then they find a temple to Saturn, to Venus, they find a villa, they find rude frescoes, and work is halted. A stray cat crawls into lost catacombs and they must bring in specialists in archeology and incest. So apologies to the world, but Rome will have no new subway lines.

Bottles of champagne arrive, like the hand-cut prosciutto, courtesy of generous Angelo, and the champagne thrills Tamika, she scrambles for her camera to snap photos of the large dark bottles. I find this endearing, and wonder if Tamika wants the photos to show her parents or grandparents that she moves in champagne circles. Or perhaps they worry she isn't having fun in Rome and here is evidence to send them, truthful or not.

I feel guilty lounging around with Eve and Tamika and the Spanish woman while the men work in this heat, passing by us with buckets of rocks and earth. They must think me a rich tourist, that I am lazy, that I am lucky. Am I lucky, I wonder. They dig under the hotel and I hope the undermined foundation will be all right.

Angelo's cured ham is scrumptious and the soft-eyed Spanish woman sips spring water inside her cigarette fog, says, "I am here from Madrid to help a friend at the hotel, a woman. I am not staying at this hotel, I am staying by Termini. Do you know my friend? Do you know Madrid?"

"Madrid is a beautiful city; I was there many years ago." I struggle for memories: such striking architecture and art deco and oil paintings in the Prado and parks and *tabernas*, but what I recall mostly is summer heat ballooning in an airless upstairs room by the Puerto del Sol, the temperature driving me from the old hotel and driving me from the city to a cooler sea and a smaller harbour town. Perhaps the Spanish woman loves the heat, like Natasha. The Madrid hotel was shelled during the Spanish Civil War. And I remember San Sebastián and the threat of bombs in Basque country. Does Natasha still keep her hair long, light striking her like a saint?

Eve wears a fichu cape and a cute Oriental coolie hat to fend off the sun. An Italian man in the courtyard stares at her white T-shirt, a low scoop top. He speaks to her breasts in heavily accented English.

"Ooooooh, look at you! That is a very nice shirt. My wife has been in the hospital for eight weeks, that's her over there." He points to a weary-looking woman glued to a phone, but his eyes stay riveted on my cousin's chest.

"She was really sick. Yes, her kidneys I think, I'm not sure, but oh she was in so much pain. It was hard to take, but she'll be all right." His eyes never lift from Eve's T-shirt. "You look so goooood!"

My cousin backs up, trying to get away.

"Oooooh yessss, I very much like your beautiful shirt."

I chat with the Spanish woman several times in the atrium but find I cannot ask her out because I am sure she is waiting for me to ask her out and I hate the moves and the knowledge and the lack of knowledge.

"Are you interested in zombies?" the Spanish woman asks me. Her name is Elena. How do you say dinner and drinks in Spanish (the dream of a common language)? How do you say that you are so very tired of zombies? I wish I had my old phrase book from years ago in Spain. *Mucho gusto.*

Whenever I walk onto my room's terrace I hear two women talking on their terrace.

"We went to Australia," one woman says. "We went camping, it was fun. They offered me all kinds of seafood and I said no. We didn't have money to buy. Well, we had some."

"Don't you wish you'd done some of those things?"

"You look back. There are memories."

"Those are positive memories! Mary, you still have memories to come."

"You think so?"

"Absolutely! Life isn't over. It's a new chapter. And another chapter. A set of problems is just a new chapter."

I make noise with a chair on my side of the terrace so they know I am there, but it has no effect, the two women keep talking, so I abandon my comfy terrace to zigzag over bridges crossing the Tiber.

I step inside out of habit and curiosity; every church has a relic, fragments of the true cross, bones, thorns, nails. What chance that they are real? There is Christ's alligator suitcase retrieved from the Holy Land, there is Christ's hair dryer, and his first report card, signed by Mary.

On the terrace Mary the nervous woman says, "In the old days I'd talk to men. Now I hold back."

Her more confident friend says, "You've forgotten who you are."

"I lost that. You understand?"

"Absolutely! What if he knew you were looking for someone new. I'd be interested in his reaction. I'd be very interested."

"Maybe we'll meet some Italian men!"

Ray-Ray says to me, "I hear you're running for Pope. Very cool. If there's an interview, just remember he's human, he puts his pants on one leg at a time."

Ray-Ray, so tall and smiling, has a girlfriend and a baby waiting back in Canada, but in Italy he's on a quest for an Italian woman, even asking the Spanish woman for advice.

"Where can I meet them! What do Italian women like, what should I say?"

"It will not happen," she says, "they live in another world. My apologies, but you must be Italian to seduce." Ray-Ray has a few words of Chinese, but little Italian.

"One leg at a time," she says, "yes, I understand such a motivational concept, but does a Pope even own pants?"

"He probably wears sweatpants at home," says Ray-Ray, "you know, to chillax, eat chips and watch Euro Cup on the boob tube. But the man's from Düsseldorf or somewhere. So what team does the Pope pull for? He's hunkered deep in this crazy-ass palace in Italy, but, really, the man's from Germany, right? And he's got these Swiss Guard dudes, who do they pull for?"

"Is there a Swiss team in the Euro Cup?"

"The Swiss Cuckoos?"

"The Swiss Army Knives?"

"Ye gods," mutters Father Silas, shaking his head while enjoying cake and custard.

South Africa is killing Italy in the Euro Cup; Angelo and the girls with beehive hair grimace as one. The goalie moves the wrong way with his ski gloves outstretched. Italy has a gifted team, but they seem jinxed, they lose every match. For the locals this is heartbreaking and suspicious: are the matches fixed?

Angelo holds one hand up high: "How the team should play," he says. Then a hand low: "How they are playing instead."

As a child in Nigeria Ray-Ray went to old-style British schools, obeyed a headmaster, wore school uniforms in the Nigerian heat. I try to imagine him in a blazer. Later he may try to kill himself in the Don Valley, but how can our group know that?

Ray-Ray says to the Spanish woman, "Did you know the Etruscan language was never deciphered?"

"That's really a shame," she says.

Ray-Ray keeps saying that he was a celebrity in China, the girls on campus loved him, flocked to him, thinking he must be an NBA star because he was so tall. But he is not so well loved in

Italy. In the hotel Ray-Ray doggedly pursues the chambermaids room to room, his big wolf teeth in a grin.

"How you doing today, ladies?"

The chambermaids' boss, a severe Aryan-looking woman, shoos the towering Ray-Ray away from her staff. "Go! Go! Let them do their work!" And we smile at the ribald drawing-room spectacle.

But what of my gaze, and my crush on Irena, our Croatian chambermaid? Am I so different than Ray-Ray? Every day I speak to Irena on the stairs or when she knocks on the door to ask if I need my room cleaned.

Irena gently scolds me in the hall: "You should not walk about in bare feet! You might step on broken glass! You are a free spirit. It is America."

"It is not America."

I delay wearing socks as long as possible, not to upset Irena the chambermaid, but because in bare feet the day remains somehow mine, I feel the chains when I have to don socks and shoes and move out into the world to take care of something dubious or pay money to someone when I'd rather not pay. When I get in the door I can't wait to peel off shoes and socks, especially in this hot climate. And what chance of stepping on glass when Irena guards our sparkling halls? Being scolded by Irena is enjoyable. She first showed me the long route to my rooftop room. Why do I feel my pursuit of her is not base, but is high-minded, a noble romantic quest? "It is Canada."

Marco the intern laughs about the hotel's Croatian chambermaids. Three women were washing a floor and Marco had to get in the room for inventory, so he took off his shoes to tiptoe past. They were incensed; the clean wet floor should be made dirty rather than Marco take off his shoes. A man should just walk through.

"When I had to move out of my room and stay with the chambermaids I made my own bed every morning, but they would unmake it and make it their way. They are still very Old World."

On my way out of my room one fine morning I see Irena making up the beds next door, in what I think of as the sex room, as this room is used by so many mysterious couples. Irena pauses by the bed, looks over.

"Do you need your room made up?"

"No, thank you. My room is fine."

She asks me every day and I have the same reply. I have everything I need. *Grazie.*

You are lucky, she may say. That is the usual extent of our talk. But today she stops her work, today she wants to chat.

"You are wearing shoes today," she notes with approval. "You are from Canada," she says, "what is it you do in Canada? What is life like there?"

She knows some Croatians who like Canada. She says, "Canada has more interest in culture. Here in Italy it is all business."

"It is?" I'm surprised.

"Here it is who you know. Want anything done? You need a friend, a connection. And if you have no friends? Nothing can be done for you."

"I think of North America as all business. With Italy I think of art and culture."

"No, no. Clearly it is the other way around."

Now I'm puzzled. Irena tells me of her home in Croatia, the hills of white stone above the sea, she says in Croatia there are mountains, but not too high, they are just *perfect*. Her town once a Roman colony and now she is drawn to Rome, her town once a key port in the salt trade, but now a marina and pale beaches covered with roasting Germans, Germans everywhere, the EU accomplishing what Hitler could not.

Irena says, "I'd like to move to London and go to school there, but it's hard."

Irena has been working in Rome two years to save her pennies. London a magnet for her, but London is so expensive and school in England is so dear, thousands and thousands of pounds sterling. She worries, she worries about the crash of the euro and the terrible economy and the backlash in Rome and Athens and Madrid and she sees TV news of arson and riots and jobless males battling police and attacking foreigners (do we have that in common, Irena, we are both foreign?). She is an immigrant, as were my parents, but her hill town is close to Italy, she did not need to step into a sinking boat, she rode into Italy by fast train.

Irena says she worries that what is happening elsewhere is sure to spread here and become far worse. Greece is a disaster, Spain, Tunisia, Libya, Syria in rubble, Iraq in convulsions.

"It's not over yet," she says. "On the contrary, it is just the beginning."

She has worries and hopes, Irena seems impossibly nice. She asks where else I'm going and I mention Naples and Pompeii.

"Ah, Capri," she says dreamily. "And you must go to Elba. Though Napoli has the best food. It is the best city."

I wonder if Irena lives and works in Italy legally, but can't bring myself to ask. Irena has three languages and I have none. I heard her speaking Croatian and the language sounded like jagged Russian colliding with musical Italian. How long must Irena clean tile floors in Rome, work in a hotel and save a few euro to put herself through school? She has no iPhone or tablet, no college-student pub crawls, no fast Bimmer or fake-and-bake tan, no Mom and Dad paying the credit card for a trip to the capitals of Europe.

Irena served and fed Marco when the hotel was overbooked and he was kicked out of his room and put up in the apartment shared by several Croatian chambermaids. A male guest in their home was not allowed to lift a finger, they cooked full meals and fed him plums from a mother's garden in Croatia, plums a storm-cloud purple, taut yet dripping sweetly with juice, and sliced wrinkled apples that tasted like summer wine, as if the apples were ready to ferment. The young chambermaids treated him like a lord.

Irena's stern blond boss bursts out of the coffin-sized elevator, an unwelcome genie with dyed hair. She stares, suspicious of a shirker, suspicious of what I am after. Irena's face alters, eyes scared, and she scampers back to cleaning the sex room.

Sometimes I feel like an exact saint of restraint, sometimes I worry I possess the virtues of a dog running loose. At times I've been called a dog, but my mien leans more to milquetoast, surely I am more custard than canine. Galloping miles of halls and stairs to the Roman street (I don't use the elevator), I hope that Irena's Aryan boss won't make trouble because she spoke to me. But I am happy Irena wanted to chat with me about her future life in the UK.

A sickle moon hangs over the curved brick portal arch, moon and brick permanent fixtures both. And statues everywhere in Rome, long lines of anemic statues peopling rooftops, huge armies of silhouettes and future suicides crowding ledges, arms spread as if losing their balance or to leap from the ledge and get air in their beards, fly off and shudder like shaky kites around the white columns and spires and tourist piazzas.

I stare at chalk-white eyeless statues and older Italians in the subway car stare baldly at Tamika's dark round face and wire-rim glasses and dainty dreads. They are not shy, they stare wide-eyed, as if Tamika is some amazing piece of furniture perched beside me on a subway seat.

Tamika is super-shy and doesn't fit into the group of young drunks and Tamika is very aware of the open stares as we ride buses or the Metro. In Philly she fits in fine; in Rome her dark skin draws unwelcome attention, eyes on her.

Tamika asks me, "Do people stare at you here?"

"Not really." I am becoming invisible and to be invisible has its uses.

Tamika tells me that she ate something that disagreed with her and without warning she became sick on a moving public bus.

"I felt horrible, but I couldn't get off in time. The driver stopped the bus and he called the police."

"The driver called the police?"

"They took me off the bus and I sat for ages in the police station. No one seemed to be paying any attention, so after three or four hours I slowly stood up and walked out the door with some other people and came back and hid at the hotel. I get nervous when I see any police or a uniform."

Shy Tamika the outlaw. Italy has an uneasy relationship with colour, with Africa, Africa once part of its old Roman Empire and still so close, a slow boat-ride away from Sicily or the Italian island of Lampedusa far to the south where refugees swim to shore at this moment or they fail to swim to shore.

•

Some citizens in northern Italy prefer the north, would like to be part of Switzerland or Austria or Friuli; Venice wants to be an independent serene republic. Italian cousins in the south are seen as uncouth, un-north, they are *terroni*, of the earth, swarthy peasants, lazy, corrupt, brutish, violent, invaded and tainted by Arabs and Moors and Algerians, by heated kingdoms of darker blood, by invasion after invasion.

Men ask Tamika, "Are you *africano* or *americano*?" They want to be sure.

Father Silas surprises us, saying, "Some Italian men have a fetish for black prostitutes."

"A fetish? North Africa? West Africa?"

"I really can't say, it is not my fetish."

"It's not that I've been cold to him."

The two woman talk on the next terrace and I imagine my wife saying similar words to her best friend over a glass of shiraz, adjusting decades of memories. To hear this is depressing.

"You ask yourself what happened to all those years."

The years of connections and cities and good times don't alter or disappear. But now those years are different, tainted, to my wife, though not to me. The women talking on the next terrace are a vocal reminder of what I've done wrong and how I will be misunderstood and maligned over a glass of shiraz, perhaps at this very moment.

"This new therapist, he lets me come to my senses, he doesn't *tell* me."

"I like the advice this doctor gives you."

"Is it out of fear I'm doing this or out of love?"

"You do what you have to do."

"I don't want my kids to be vulnerable. Damaged people gravitate to someone alike — to damaged people. I can empower my two children by standing on my own two feet. Or they'll step into the exact same scenario. It's a valuable lesson."

"You know in your heart you did everything you could."

Don't the women know that I'm on my side of the trellis and vines, that I hear every word and sigh? Again I make noises on my terrace to alert them, but they are like oblivious shoppers who block the whole aisle with their carts, no one else exists.

"What if he came back? He's not open, he's not going to be expressive or lively or please me. He can't find it in himself to be happy."

"Can't go down that road. Tell the kids when they're older."

"If I'm giving 150 per cent and he's giving 80, it ain't gonna work. Is that flame too high?"

"I don't think so."

"That fire worries me. Should we get some water?"

"It's citronella. It smells nice. Ah, this is the life. Shopping in Rome."

"Can we put it out?"

"Okay, okay. Feel better?"

"I do."

Jesus, I think, let the stupid fire burn. I've lost my euphoric mood under the perfect cupola of chapel stars.

So once more into Rome I wander footsore, that one church on the edge, marble underfoot, tombs underfoot, reading graffiti, stepping over graves, over a lost city. Eve and I gaze at *The Conversion of Saint Paul*, but the canvas is so dark for an epiphany, it seems more the reverse of an epiphany, I see no light or illumination.

Saints line every rooftop and I pass the spot where the dead rat has been resting every day on cobblestones and when I wander back the two women still talk on the next terrace. Like me, like the woman from Iraq, these two women so dedicated to their dead country.

"I told him, 'Wish you were here,'" she says. "Why did I say that?"

"Because that's how you feel. Mary, you're allowed your emotions."

"If he was here he'd know every temple where Caesar was stabbed. I think women a generation or two back were stronger."

"Hey, we're two powerful women — we put out the fire."

"Safety first, ha!"

"This is fun. More vino?!"

"We are having fun."

"Be grateful for small things. The here and now is important."

"You're wise."

"Life isn't over. It's a new chapter. Life is a book. And each chapter…"

"See, in a marriage…well…he betrayed me. But I'm more angry about the car than that woman."

"Tell him you're looking for someone. Did you do that before?"

"Fool around? No."

"To grow."

"No."

"I did, I went to someone else. I felt those feelings. It scares me that I don't care. Is it because I've dealt with it? It's wonderful to feel that close to someone. If I stumbled across her in a social setting, what does she look like, I don't care. It's almost creepy. It is creepy, a creepy creepy feeling. Every day I wake up and expect it to change."

"The Mole called me back."

"Who? Not him."

"Turned me down, but he called me back."

"You're better off without him."

The woman's last words make me wonder: in the long run, am I better off without Natasha? I resist, but I need to believe this, need to take it in like an arthroscope to the knee.

Something in me can't accept the finality, some part of me still wishes for contact, to hear of Natasha's mother and father, the farm, her sisters. "My dad's youngest brother died, only sixty-two; my poor dad, such a shock for him. My crazy sister is okay, but her boyfriend bonked her on the head with his laptop and she's depressed a bit."

And I want to tell Natasha all my Italian news, I feel a wave at times, a physical command: lift the phone, click *Reply* on her last email. But I have decided: no more.

It's difficult, as we were so comfortable with each other; how to find that lost empire again in the stone mountains? It seems impossible. The anatomy of desire and the anatomy of loss — I have them mixed up in my sunburnt head. Brushing my right ear is the fever song of mosquitoes, then a mosquito frittering inside my ear, wanting my brain. I smack my own head hard, then cry out, "OW!" And Eve laughs at me: is such slapstick exactly what this mosquito aims for as evening entertainment? Like me, the mosquito has a soft spot for the Three Stooges. Rome's hills and marble temples built above a marsh, and winter mosquitoes felled an emperor. In Trogir I leapt off a water taxi to see a Norman fortress in palm trees and walked Malarjia Park. In Rome we will devour delicious blood oranges and pray to Madonna della Febbre, the protectress of victims of malaria.

At night in the hotel stairwell I bump into a thin blind man. The blind man is shirtless and wields a long white cane, a slim stick, a pilgrim of sorts. His pale wonky eyes aim into deep space.

"I'm above you on the steps," I say.

"Are you with that group?" His voice is assertive, angry about noise in our hotel. Would I be so confident if I might plunge down an open stairway?

He says, "I have a wife and a two-year-old trying to sleep. Can you tell them to stop chit-chatting?"

He may mean a noisy group up on the roof. I don't know them, but I lie to the blind man, saying I will pass on his message. Is it more of a sin to lie to a blind person? Or is the sin pretty much the same?

Eve and I are crossing manic streets like expat experts, we're leveraging complex transactions in fruit market bedlam. When was it I met the exiled woman from Iraq in a *supermercato*? Later she told me I did something that convinced her she could trust me, she told me that she can read people, was trained in it.

Was it posture, I wondered, how I clasped my hands?

She wouldn't tell me what it was, but it was enough for her to believe in me.

I had no idea what I would learn about her family, her fiancé. At the time she was simply someone interesting I met by chance, one of Iraq's numerous exiles, Iraq coming to pieces and so many forced to become gypsies, wandering like brimstone butterflies, the first to appear after winter.

She worked in a hospital in Jordan after fleeing Iraq, liked her job and the people and the dialect was similar, but Jordan was overwhelmed by refugees from Iraq. Every month she had to make her way to a police station and pay a monthly fee to stay legally in Jordan. The fee rose every month until it was too high for her to pay and she had to leave her job and had to leave Jordan and look for work in Italy.

She does not drink, is devout, well-schooled in the Koran, but she does not wear traditional garb, does not wear robes or a veil. She can look very Western in stylish jeans, makeup, nail polish, even a Mickey Mouse T-shirt if she is in a happy mood.

The woman from Iraq told me her father had kidney problems, she worried about him. She said to me with a serious face, "Drink only water when you wake up, and cleanse your kidneys." No one else speaks to me quite like this. I enjoyed such times. She was always very clean, concerned with health and hygiene. At one café she wouldn't sit on the seat cushions because they seemed dirty and she was used to better.

I bought her tea from Ceylon, Akbar big leaf, and one afternoon over tea I guessed her age.

"How did you know?"

I said I liked the henna tint in her hair and she asked, "How you know that word?"

"I know some things."

Much of what I said seemed to surprise her. I told her about Natasha and she did not approve. "So she left after causing trouble with your marriage?"

"It's not that simple."

"No?"

She showed me the ring her brother gave her years ago. "He loves me. He is very handsome. And in Iraq it is real gold, twenty-one karat, not like here, ten or eleven. In the Middle

East men don't wear gold. Only women. Men don't have earrings like here. If men wear jewelry, or a lot of gold, we think, eh, no."

She looks at my hand. "There are no rings on your fingers? All those years, did your wife not give you a ring in all those years?"

The women's voices continue on the next terrace.

"I fall for people. You understand? I fell into that trap."

"Are you mad at me? What I said about the Mole?"

"He was nice. He's okay. He had the Asian wife. He did seem interested in me."

"He's a microbe, a creepy little creep. He had an affair with the cleaner, can you imagine — creepy, on the desk."

"No."

"Yes. He's a pervert. She got pregnant."

"Maybe that's why he was so hot and heavy to get a vasectomy."

"He's a perv. He has to send her cheques and his other wife has to get up at five a.m. to catch a bus and work at a factory."

"She probably has no background."

"Treat your spouse like that. It's unbelievable. A perv."

I listen to the women and think, Now I have joined the club of those sending cheques, joined the club of those termed a perv.

The woman from Iraq says, "Everyone I meet here, divorced, separated, divorced, separated. I think our system is better." She may have a point. My drunken question to popular opinion: why does the phrase "night falls on Rome" sound cool, but "morning falls on Rome" sounds clunky and wrong?

She doesn't drink, but young males stagger our hotel halls shouting, "MAKE SOME NOISE!" Rome has no history,

Rome is a drinking binge with no parents to harass them. They lug huge jugs of rotgut wine, yelling, "Yo Yo Yo Yo!"

Young and loose and full of juice, drunk with what seems possible. Their shop has not yet been bombed to molecules.

In the Roman night someone is insisting over and over that she is not a hollaback girl. My high room is well removed from the inebriated and industrious fray, but poor Tamika's hallway is the epicentre of several open-door party rooms.

Eve walks by bent to her tiny clamshell phone, her face serious, saying, "She told me three of the drugs she was on."

Tamika says, "I can't get any sleep with their drunken racket."

Father Silas says, "I'll see what I can do," and walks over to a noisy open door.

"You ain't my daddy," yells a drunken female voice inside, "and you sure ain't . . ." And then the voice trails off, seemingly stumped, and we all wonder: what else is he ain't?

Tamika does not like the drunkards, Tamika a lone wolf roaming Rome while the others seem blind to the ancient city, see Europe as a hotel, an outlet shop, a humongous nightclub. They are the same age as Tamika, but she dismisses them with a world-weary wave.

"It's so awesome here in Rome, but all they do is complain about everything, they bitch about the food, bitch about their room, bitch about walking through amazing cathedrals. They complain if they have to walk uphill! They bitch about having to look at Bernini's marble and paintings by Caravaggio."

Tamika mimics their voices: "It's not *fair*! You can't tell me what to do. This is *boring*. I'm *hungry*." Tamika pauses for breath. "Rome is not boring, they're boring."

From my backpack I dig out a tiny sealed bag from my days in a loud band: the baggie is not drugs, but a packet of disposable foam earplugs for Tamika. Eve asks for some as well, worth a try to help her sleep and she is wary of depending on sleeping pills.

Tamika takes the earplugs with a skeptical look on her face, and eases the door closed on the drunken mayhem. She longs for sleep.

My cousin Eve has an uneasy relationship with sleep, uneasy with Morpheus and Hypnos, the father-and-son team running our sleep and dreams. I never know if she is awake or asleep, she has a night language, uses her hands to make a point or ask a question, wakes up laughing. It's odd to watch. Eve dreamt the two of us were trying to find our way out of a city-sized department store and I fell down an open elevator shaft.

"People were running down stairwells to find you. Is that a 9/11 dream?"

Is the blind man's sleep a steep grey cinema? Has he ever seen stars at night? Can you imagine colours and faces and fields in your dreams if you are born blind and have yet to see colour or a face? Can you dream light if you don't know light? When the blind man is in a better mood I must ask him.

To shutter my own eyes at night seems not always to deliver quietude; my sleep chaotic, unnerving, festive. I close my eyes to a strange movie-house in my head, fragments and half-lit clips, an unseen projector constantly grinding. A huge cast and the footage never stops. I have no idea where these night films come from, but I like them.

"Someone called him, 'Did you hear of the bomb downtown?' I begged him not to go."

The woman from Iraq told me about her fiancé, though

she did not tell me this part right away, it took her some time to get to the chapter of her fiancé.

"His business was in the bombed building, he wanted to see if his shop was hit. 'Can't you wait?' I had a bad feeling, I pleaded with him."

"Sorry, sweet one," he said, "I must go see the damage"; perhaps his shop would be spared, God willing. His shop was his livelihood, his hope, their future, her fiancé was worried and he drove into town to see the damage.

The second bomb exploded later, timed to kill those who came to walk the rubble of the first bomb. The second bomb exploded and her fiancé vanished and she was a widow without yet marrying. As Trotsky said, "You may not be interested in war, but war is interested in you."

"He was good to me," she stated calmly, "he was modern, he told my parents when asking for my hand that he didn't mind if I wanted to go to school or have a career." The bombs had detonated only months before, very recent history, but she stared off, speaking flatly. It happened to someone else a long time ago in a world that no longer exists.

Thursday at dawn our art group rises grumpily to inspect the Sistine Chapel. Father Silas has a connection, he knows an ancient Irish monsignor who arranges a select viewing, but we must arrive very early, before the mad throngs block St. Peter's Basilica.

Eve and Tamika crave more sleep and the party animals cradle monstrous hangovers from their dubious cooking wine. For a few cents more, decent plonk can be had, but they scoop up huge jugs of cheap cooking wine, amazed by bargain prices, but this is stuff the Romans don't drink. At dawn they feel the hurt big-time, at dawn they can barely move, can barely text or kill aliens.

In my arms I once carried my dead dog from the street where it had been hit by a driver who did not stop: my dog's beautiful brown eyes lost their light to a machine, the brown eyes had no depth, no engagement, no awareness. Some in the group have that dead-canine look as we shuffle down the block to Michelangelo and the vaulted ceilings of the Sistine Chapel.

My head! Man, why does this asshole make us go out so fucking early? Who wants to see some stupid Listerine chapel? Dude's seriously harshing my mellow. And we're missing the coolest Shark Week like ever. Got any Advil? Man, I can't deal with fizzy water, going to hurl.

Father Silas hates alcohol and some suspect he has made us rise early to punish those with piercing hangovers. He reacts strangely when I happily tell Tamika that Eve and I found an "Italian-American-style Irish pub" called Fairytale of New York, a great little underground bar.

"American and Irish and Italian?" asks Tamika, interested. "What was that like?"

Before I can answer Tamika, Father Silas gets right in my grill.

"A place for American college students to get DRONK!" he shouts, his big reddening face in my eyes.

I want to say the pleasant arched cellar is not for drunken college students, but he won't give me a chance. Everyone I meet in the cellar is Italian, lives in the neighbourhood, and the young musicians are local. But Father Silas hates any mention of pubs and pub crawls and Rome is crawling with pub crawls, posters and ads everywhere; Father Silas is furious when he spots Ray-Ray in a souvenir T-shirt from a pub crawl that reads APPRENTICE ALCOHOLIC.

Ray-Ray complains to Eve. "Man, why does he get so mad like that? I'm not a child. I can travel and check into a hotel, he'd be surprised. I can do all sorts of things." The younger people in the art group hate it when Father Silas lectures them on how to behave in Italy.

Father Silas may not win a popularity contest, but he finagles us past the massive lineups in front of St. Peter's, skipping mobs and security checks; his Irish connection in the palace of Popes pays off. As early birds we have time to check out the Sistine Chapel before the throttling crowds. How many times have I joked about some half-assed project, "Hey don't worry, it's not the Sistine Chapel." Now it's the real article, now it *is* the Sistine Chapel!

Father Silas expertly guides our eyes through each brush-stroke and painted image on the ceiling, nude bodies and fresco skies of pale pink, robin-egg-blue, pale canary-yellow, Noah drunk and disgraced and martyrs and mild saints flung about hallucinatory heavens floating in this chamber. I love it. Grotesque figures and dizzy prophets lean out from high corners and sinners pulled to hell in this ecstatic artifice.

"Noah a drunk! News to me."

"Don't let Father Silas know," jokes Eve.

The guards yell at us, "No fo to!"

A young German backpacking couple elbows me, pushing past me to cram closer to Father Silas and hang on his every word; they are not in our group, but they are eager for Father Silas's narrative of the Sack of Rome in 1527; some of our group couldn't care if the Sack of Rome is in five minutes.

Eve nudges me, signals with her eyes at a bench where some of our disgruntled comrades perch: one art lover cradles his

pained head in open hands, one holds his giant Dr. Dre headphones tight, one poor soul manages to tap out a text. In the
Sistine Chapel they are all looking *down*! I will say this once
and then let it go: the fucking Sistine Chapel and they can't see,
can't lift their eyes to Michelangelo's *The Last Judgment*, blind
to the arches and lunettes hovering above their dehydrated
heads, blind to miracle and treasure floating over their trauma
brains. Youth is wasted on the wasted.

Above us God divides light from darkness and we linger
in the centre of the chapel, Father Silas ecstatic, the longest
visit he's ever had here. But as the room fills with travellers,
guards spring up to move the crowd along the marble, to herd
us to the exit.

"Keep moving. No fo-to." Does the blind man know Michelangelo's chapel? "Keep moving! No fo-to. Keep moving! No
fo-to."

A woman from Delaware asks me, "Where is Noah?" And
I have the answer! I show her the ark and his drunkenness and
she charms me as we chat, looking me in the eye — how to describe that permission to engage her eye, the face, that magnetic
connection? But her tour group is gone from the tidal room
and she worries she has lost them.

"Bye!" she says hurriedly, eyes still on my eyes. "Very nice
talking to you," she says.

I want to say more: woman from Delaware, you seem important. But what to say quickly that doesn't seem lame? I fail
to utter key words and she vanishes from sight. Sometimes I feel
my own mind staring at me and judging like a separate person.
Delaware: I'm picturing a river, a green valley.

•

In the Vatican café Ray-Ray buys three sandwiches and three drinks and thirty euro vanish in seconds; Ray-Ray puts it on plastic, does this over and over, Ray-Ray is always hungry.

A button on his tote bag says, *I Was Raised by a Pack of Wild Corn Dogs.* "Does the Vatican sell corn dogs? I'd kill for a corn dog."

I don't know if the Vatican has corn dogs. I will return from my travels to be murdered in the bath. It is the fortieth anniversary of the White Album; the *Osservatore Romano* says that the Vatican forgives John Lennon his "boast" that the Beatles were bigger than Jesus.

"Weird to drink beer in the Vatican."

My parents loved the church and hated the Beatles. I am going to get me religion, maybe I'll start a church, the church of cold toast. Natasha likes cold toast and cold butter, as I do. No one else likes cold toast. It's a sign, she sank her nails into me, haunts me still. Like Pompeii after the volcano, the shore altered.

Through marble halls and chambers we find our way and stumble outside to battle sunlight in our slit eyes, we are in the vast pillared piazza in front of St. Peter's Basilica, the floating dome, the silver spaceship, the mothership and its rows of myriad Doric pillars moving out like great arms enclosing a flat open space larger than a football field.

This is not the way we entered; this morning we slipped in the north side, and now we move under the church of churches, the rock of Peter. Byron admired this view, this architectural marvel, Melville stood here, Goethe, Dickens, Dostoevsky, Jethro Tull.

"Are there any zombies in Rome? Yeah, zombies in the Vatican! That'd be a very cool movie."

Ray-Ray yells, "HEY" and runs across the space to question an Italian man who is missing one leg and has an amazing comb-over, his hairdo a monument to tenacity.

"Hey man, is it true about phantom limbs, that you get an itch in the limb that's not there anymore?"

Non capisco. He doesn't understand English.

In the endless white light, in the corner of vision, a bear cub gallops through the forest of pillars. The bear must be panicked, but it looks very cute: dark fur, a pale brown muzzle, outsize ears and that rolling stiff-legged lope past our hungover group, past St. Peter's, and barrelling toward the sidewalk men selling leather purses and sunglasses.

"How did a bear get here in the city?" asks Eve.

Is there a gypsy circus camped in Trastevere or the Piazelle del Gianicolo? The poor animal swiftly crosses a road, speeds down a narrow medieval passage, and I can't see it anymore. People scatter before the bear cub, but some follow behind attempting shaky photos and videos. A tiny blue police car joins the chase and when the men selling sunglasses see the police car, they gather up their squares of cloth and footstools and vanish, a form of magic.

"Oh shit, where's my iPhone?" calls out one of our group, half of a star-crossed couple who have fallen for each other on the trip but are betrothed to others back home. They spend much time in Rome pacing and staring at each other and sighing like tragic silent film stars.

"Did someone steal it? I put it down for like five seconds max. My mother's going to freak!"

In Italy eyes are on us, waiting for the moment when we put down our laptop or briefly ignore our camera on the table. The thieves love us.

Eve says she was mugged for her phone in Chile: she laughs telling us, says the man asked for her phone, looked at it, an old clamshell with a duct tape hinge, and handed it back to her, her phone not worth stealing.

"What's it like to not have a phone?" They ask me this question with genuine curiosity, as if finding a lone survivor of some polar expedition. Discarded phone cards litter the ground at our feet. They are so afraid of not being connected. I once left room for my guardian angel, they leave room for their device, uncomfortable if alone with themselves for a minute; everyone consulting a tiny magic lantern of a screen in that slow zombie walk.

Our hungover group walks away from the mothership's giant field of pillars. Taking our place, a new batch of amiable tourists line up to display their girth and sunglasses; we are all part of a giant art installation, the pure products of America abroad, trodding leather and considering miracles in marble and wondering about hotels and drinks and dinner menus with no inkling that a cute bear cub rambled past us moments ago.

Ray-Ray stops me: "What kind of pants is this?"

He's studying a woman swishing past in gold harem-pants; her walk has a pronounced twitch, fabric moving around her like shimmering drapes.

"Looks like MC Hammer."

"Who?"

"You can't touch this."

"Touch what?" He looks suspicious; what am I talking about?

With the harem-pants woman we try our limited Italian. *Dove un* internet café?

There follow many speedy sentences and in seconds I'm lost.

Wait, *non capisco. Holdo, signora, parla lentamente per favore, lentamente*, please speak slowly, I am a foreign simpleton in your speedy empires of talk. Our group did not invent stupidity, but we are the latest visible practitioners.

Eve leans conspiratorially toward Tamika and says, "Those Italian men on the street! Their eyes, they look right into your soul."

Tamika mutters, "It's not your soul they are after."

Amore, amore. Look at the eyes here, eyes like slow sunsets and foxfire and friar's lantern, eyes like the feral cats in the temple ruins, diamond-eyed cats after rats.

My eyes roam the world too, looking for stars held in a cupola, looking for the right person, a person who likely does not exist, like my childhood guardian angel, an ideal that may lead only to disappointment. I'm not unlike the two women on the next terrace in that respect.

The promise of Rome and the promise of the Spanish blonde in the leafy hotel atrium, her adherence to smoke and water bottles; I work up my nerve for the question. And I never do this.

"Would you, um, care to go out for dinner?"

"No," she says too quickly. "I'm having dinner with my friend when she gets off work." So Elena was expecting the question and ready to say no. What is it like to believe in an anthem, I mean really belt it out?

I need a wee drink. The others keep working away on vats of sweet wine. In the laneway a few feet away a sweaty man with no shirt hits a motorcycle with a piece of wood, setting off a loud alarm. The man tosses the piece of wood and casually lights a smoke to wait for the resulting beneficial social interaction.

His hope: someone will approach and fight.

Our hope: he will go away.

All our tiny wretched hopes like cartoon thought balloons over each block of Rome, multiply these across the city street-map, across the wide world, all these hopeless little balloons of our hopes, like markers on a board game, like hotels on Expedia.

We are not always pleasant, but we all have our tiny hopes.

The blind man wanders the stairways in search of culprits and the women's voices continue on the next terrace.

"I asked that nun for the time. In Italian."

"We fit in."

"We're doing so well, we went right to the edge of our map!"

"No one would know we are tourists."

Sun beats on our skin, leathers our lives of quiet desiccation, sun on lovely hours of fountain spray as Hotwire and Orbitz fight over my soul, and then the strange lost look of my street before dawn.

Get some sleep behind scrolled blinds and rise late and the sun always there until it must enter the horizon like a burning airship and a million emails jetting out to everyone in the world say *A Special Offer Just for YOU!* and at dusk swallows circle and blur in a mosquito frenzy and in her famous T-shirt my cousin walks out in the garden of green parrots just before rains sweep in from some distant sea.

The Italian man has eyes. As do I. I resent him as cousins might.

"It's so cozy here," says Eve. "I love the sound of the rain."

Night and the light on Eve's face may change your mind about the world. I have to gaze, to compensate for the blind man who can't see her. Behind the city a wall of rain like green glass, like some remnant of hurricane season. Once she climbed above me in the fig tree and I was allowed a vision of her muscled legs and beyond, I see Paris, I see France, I dream of her at the beach, half nude at the shore, her freckled skin so lovely, to live inside it, to kiss her in the eelgrass, light under the harbour swell like light inside a fountain, to see her at the sea where she is almost naked with strangers, but I never go with the group to the beach, it is too scorching or I am not inspired.

Perhaps I'm a winter person, a touch of winter in me always. I should drop everything and be a ski bum in the blue glaciers before they melt and vanish, I could work on the hill, work as a liftie putting skiers on the Angel chairlift.

Eve knows the mountains and resorts, says, "No, don't quit your day job. Being a lift-operator is a killer on the back and people are always falling over and poking you with their ski poles. Definitely join a band. Chicks love musicians."

The lifties use shovels to level the snow where skiers load onto the chairlift, like shovelling coal, and Eve says at shift's end they set their asses down in the scoop shovels and race each other in shovels to the bar at the bottom of the mountain.

God is irritable, God recently gave up cigarettes, At our subway stop I let Eve and Tamika step out first, and the doors close hard on my arms as I step out. Why do the subway doors attack me when I was so chivalrous? Perhaps the gears and sensors know something of my true nature, gods alive in our machines and devices. I must have offended the elders of the internet, a major disappointment to YouTube. I need to learn to love technology, must dab data on me like cologne from a dollar store.

•

In the neighbourhood café, Francesco knows our faces and gives us free morning coffee. Angelo, the aged hotelier, joins us for a late breakfast. Eve picks up an espresso and an Italian newspaper.

"Tell me, Marco," Angelo says to the American intern. "Is it true that Americans eat donuts for breakfast? That is *wrong.*" But for his breakfast Angelo fills a sweet croissant with layers of whipped cream and chocolate.

Angelo says he used to know the Vatican crowd, but no more. I assume those men he knew are dead now (*and there rose a pharaoh that did not know Angelo*). He doesn't look that old, but Marco says that Angelo is over eighty; he never stops working on his hotel, moving walls, refurbishing rooms, digging a cellar.

Eve and Tamika run off to a pro-choice rally assembling in front of Pope Rat's place at St. Peter's; Angelo finishes his whipped cream and Nutella and leaves; Marco lowers his voice to tell me of an old friend of Angelo at the hotel.

"The man paid me cash for *three* different rooms. Seventy years old if he's a day. He books the rooms for four hours and I swear five different women showed up."

I wonder if the noisome couple in the next room paid by the hour, the minute, or down to the second. Or hotel staff who know the room to be free? Or was it Angelo's old friend with his harem? Does his harem wear shimmering harem pants?

Every hotel, every guest house, every B & B has offered me an "arrangement" to pay cash. No receipt, but the room costs much less. I find it hard to say no, as it saves me so much — hundreds easily; perhaps thousands, given enough weeks or months.

Factor in millions of tourists wheeling luggage down Europe's cobblestones and dropping cash only, and one sees why law-makers and accountants have such trouble chasing their cut of the haul. As a spoiled North American I am so used to plastic, but cash is king here and my best deals are off the books.

Marco's work at the hotel has to do with the books; Marco's task is to nudge the hotel into the computer age. The French woman still consults a huge old-fashioned ledger with our names and reservations written by hand. Marco is setting up a computer. Businesses in Italy often need two sets of books; after Marco is done, will the hotel need two sets of computers?

God enriches, but cash is king, so we all must stash envelopes of cash, cash on my person or hidden in my room, more cash than I am comfortable carrying or hiding.

Eve's purse was stolen from her hotel room a year ago; she found a small footprint in a flowerpot on her balcony and her bag tossed to the next balcony. Luckily the young thief missed euros she had hidden in the WC. The art historian's phone lifted as he walks a crowded street, a religion teacher's wallet eased from his front pocket on the bus, a beatnik backpacker swarmed by children, turning and turning, a dizzy whirligig to keep their nimble fingers from his pack pockets, and a pink rental car stolen from a woman from Banff as she opened its door for the first time — she possessed the car for seconds and then the car was gone.

Marco and Eve travelled to the police station to interpret for the hotel's American family who lost a ring handed down from a great-grandmother, lost blown glass from Venice. A sweltering night, an open window or balcony door. The police type up a report, but what can they do, a waste of ink.

Who expects someone from the roof? In all corners of Europe such a complex economy dotes on our purloined phones and cameras and we oblige, we carry cash, wallets and laptops, and we deliver them to the thieves. How they long for us like lost lovers in their damp winter and each year we come back like the blossoms of spring.

Angelo had to sack an employee who lit rubbish on fire in a stairwell; the employee hated the guests, the noisy party animals, and he wanted to get off work early. So a fire against the exit door is the answer. Could he be the hotel thief? Or is it the blind man, bounding like a cat across the roof?

Father Silas tells our group a farmer's-daughter joke. And Natasha sent me email from her parents' farm in northern BC. Why did I not think of this all these years: Natasha is a farmer's daughter. I broke off contact with the farmer's daughter, for my own well-being, but every day I have a physical urge tell her what I see and do in Italy, a habit.

In Canada Natasha said we must stay in contact, an unbearable empty place if we stop talking, a huge hole in both our lives. She said those words, admirable thoughts. But in her life, in her distant city, she has someone there to turn to, to say she had a bad day, to say, He's really upset, I just don't know what to tell him. She can say to someone, Let's go out for a drink, can say later, Hey, love you so much.

Irena the chambermaid greets me, *Come va*? She does not ask, *Come stai*. Is she being formal with me as a hotel guest? Irena is always so friendly with me. Is she just as friendly with the others? I want her to like me. She wears cargo pants with numerous pockets to hold cleaning gear, waistband low on her belly from weighted pockets and pulled tight on her round rear. Irena's shirt rides up as she cleans the room and I notice a puckered scar on her belly like a hieroglyph, a story scripted in a scar. In her supple hands a large sheet rises and settles as if on a breeze: her levitating art.

Come stai? I ask.

Sto male. She is sick. But she is working anyway. Maybe she caught whatever Ray-Ray had when he arrived from China. Some afternoons I see the chambermaids walk away from work in their street clothes, altered in their clothes, happy to be free on the sunny avenue, happy to be free of us.

I hope you feel better, I say. She nods.

Irena leaves the sex room, Eve leaves Italy like a merry sleepwalker, Excuse me, says Our Lady of Madrid, I must go. Soon all leave the city, the mountain frontiers, leave Europe's stone quarters and catacombs, say goodbye to the orchards and marble excavations.

It seems so long ago that Natasha phoned after silence to say there was someone else. I knew something was wrong but did not know what. I was married to the sound of her voice, talking to me when she was almost asleep, part of something beautiful and spooky and rare and rich, but part of nothing now, and another woman in a doorway or an airport says, I'd hate to lose touch with you, you know I love you in so many ways; says, It's been wonderful. My half-buried past, my layered Pompeii, my quiet buried city.

That day my faith was tested. Phil Ochs in exile from Ohio, kicked out of Dylan's car, no more songs and the rope on the pipe beckoning. The snake-handler's look of disbelief as he died in his own church, as he recalibrated his idea of being exempt from the fang.

I KNOW I AM NOT SPECIAL: I must repeat this until it sinks into my head like a spike into a rotten log. Exiled from dopamine, from the snowshoes of yesteryear, I tape a piece of white paper to a mirror: *For sleep, riches, and health to be truly enjoyed, they must be interrupted.*

On a map I showed her Canada, showed the woman from Iraq where I grew up. She is well educated, but has rarely seen a map of Canada. And America on the map right below Canada.

"They have so much space; why did they want to invade our country when they have so much land?" She peers at the map of America with utter puzzlement.

The billion-dollar question: why did Bush and cohorts invade the wrong country? Oil an easy answer, or they got their Auto Association maps mixed up. Or, rumours suggest, the invasion was revenge for an earlier plot by Hussein to kill Dubya's father, George Bush Senior, and if the oilfields fall into friendly hands, that's gravy.

"Bush is in town; you could ask him."

"Bush is here? Where? I'll go see him. Did you see him smiling on the aircraft carrier, he was so happy while we suffer. Bush is always talking of terror. My brother is not a terrorist. I am not a terrorist, I want to hurt no one. He has killed more than anyone in the world. Will someone hunt down Bush and hang him on a rope?"

The woman from Iraq is very charitable, she is not anti-American, has relatives in Chicago and wonders about moving to live there.

"I hate no one," she says, "but I hate that man. When they threw a shoe at Bush, I was glad."

I do wonder about Bush, what he really thinks. "Did you ever see your Mustang again?"

"Oh no, nothing was left."

Blow upon blow, her pleasant world dismantled by this stranger, this man Bush, her fast American car transformed into a tin can, her brother kidnapped and dumped in the desert in plastic cuffs, her mother's breakdown and her fiancé dead in the rubble, her happy life stolen as if by a hotel thief. And on TV in Iraq the family reads the banner on the aircraft carrier: *Mission Accomplished*. After meeting her, I swear I'll never complain again.

Her mother misses her bright laughter in the house, now the house is quiet but for the noisy generator running outside the house; the power off and on since the invasion, so they must run a generator in the yard.

"I was always laughing then," she says. "Now I only laugh with you." And somehow we do laugh a lot. Our odd connection.

She says her mother needs to go to the hospital, but the power grid is so damaged that doctors are afraid to start any complicated surgery for fear the lights will go dark while a patient is cut open. She grew up in a prosperous, stable country, her father a professor, but now he can't leave his home and risk the roadblocks where a human in a mask may execute you if you say the wrong word or drive the wrong part of the city.

She misses driving her car in Baghdad.

"Was your Mustang fast?"

"Oh yes. I'm not a crazy driver, but on the highway one must go fast."

Marco convinces Angelo to lend me a two-door Fiat so I can take her for a spin and let her drive a car once more. I am nervous in Rome's traffic. Sniffing Rome's oily exhaust, she claims the petrol in Iraq is so pure that her car's exhaust was sweet as perfume. Before the war every road was brightly lit and the roads smooth and broad, not so narrow as here.

She asks me, "In Chicago, are there many blacks? I've heard there is work in Chicago, but it has many blacks." She worries about blacks. "They scare me," she confides.

"Winters can be cold in the Windy City," I say, "and you're used to the heat."

"Yes," she says, "I don't know how you go outside in that cold. You whites are tough!"

I get an inordinate kick out of being called a white. I put my arm by her arm and her skin is lighter than the skin on my tanned arm.

"Summer must be very hot in the desert. You must need air conditioning."

"Desert? Iraq is not desert. There is a river, how can that be desert? There are plants, a hundred varieties of dates and olives, such flavours." She is offended. "Iraq was a great civilization. Why do you say desert?"

Sorry, but on TV with the rolling tanks and dust it looks like desert. When her car was too hot in the Baghdad sun she kept a special aerosol spray in her purse to cool the hot metal so she could touch the car door without burning her hand.

Sipping leafy tea, we chat and laugh and by accident I discover my power over her: if I reach out in conversation, touch her shoulder or neck, the woman from Iraq swoons, falls into some half-awake state, not used to touch from a male who is not a cousin or betrothed.

I ask, "Has this happened with anyone else?"

"No one else has touched me but you and my fiancé. How you do that?"

"I don't know; it's never happened before."

"Please don't right now, I want to go out, I don't want to be sleepy."

I touch her and her knees buckle, but she acts as if it is normal to have such power. She casually asks me to be careful. Yes, I will be careful. I have the strangest life.

I strum a quiet Townes Van Zandt song on guitar and she says, "That's nice, soft music." The woman from Iraq jumps at any noise, even the sound of feet running on stairs. She can't listen to loud rock or rap, she can't take bright light, must wear her big sunglasses.

At night she wakes from nightmares, has a frightening nightmare immediately after telling me the story of her fiancé and his bombed shop; her eyes closed in sleep, she relives the scene and I feel guilty for bringing on the nightmare. Any noise in a room above, a shoe dropping or a door slamming and she jumps in panic. I'm no physician, but these seem classic symptoms of trauma. The young American soldier in the graveyard may suffer from the same set of ailments, the war that always follows the war.

Odd that I meet both in Italy, two brains creased slightly by trauma, two brains moving through train stations of beautiful flowering vines and thuggish teens.

I heard the Iraqi woman weep on the phone to her mother, when a connection worked. Often her phone rang briefly and then went dead. I bought her time at a grubby internet café. She told her mother all was well in Rome, she didn't want her mother to worry.

We'll talk soon, she said to her mother, God willing. She often ends sentences with this careful phrase: *God willing*.

"If there is a God," I commented once.

"No if!" she said. "No if. Believe me, there is a God."

Is it the same God George Bush believes in? Perhaps my childhood faith will return and I will believe, will be an instrument. Am I taken care of? Sometimes it seems so.

The woman from Iraq has such faith in God, that God will care for her, but she must sell the gold ring from her handsome brother who loves her, she must enquire into jewelry or coin shops. She can't understand why this has happened, her father trapped in his eerie house, the old land of Persia laid low, his daughter exiled in a strange land, an orphan who is not an orphan, a widow who is not a widow, Babylon destroyed and giant tanks lumbering through the garden, tanks in the garden where we began as Adam and Eve. Then Adam and Eve forced to pack their bags, exiled to a less fashionable suburb.

The woman from Iraq's last email to me: Happy Birthday, I wish you the best wishes, I hope I'm the first one who remember your birthday, have a nice day and might be when I have time will do it again coz I will be busy tomorrow, have fun and wish you the best.

Her name translates as some kind of desert blossom. And like her fiancé, she vanishes as if never there, like an ancient civilization, like dew leaving a blossom as the sun rises. No answer on her phone, no reply to email, no answer to a knock at her door. Weeks walk on and I finally receive email from her, but it's spam, her email account hacked. I see her name, but it is not really her, she has been taken over, a regime change.

At a hockey arena in Canada I heard a man say, "My truck's got the same tranny as a tank in Eye-rack." I never thought I'd

meet someone who'd been crushed by an Abrams tank in Iraq.
I hope the woman from Iraq finds a home, perhaps with her
relatives in Chicago, a quiet home in the world.

Bush stands on an aircraft carrier in his flight jacket and Father
Silas is working in his curtained hotel room when I drop by
to return a book on art in Naples. Out of the blue Father Silas
tells me that his favourite sister is a serious addict.

"She wakes up each morning and it's a fight to not have a
drink, not use something. I've seen it first-hand."

So Father Silas detests levity about staggering drunks or
stoners and he loathes people profiting from giant pub crawls.
My eyes open: so this is why he is always angry at the group's
manic moronic drinking, so angry at Ray-Ray's *APPRENTICE
ALCOHOLIC* pub crawl T-shirt, this is why he got in my face
when I mentioned the cool little Italian-American Irish pub.

"I worry some in the group will be on that same road because of Rome, and I don't want to encourage it. That boy from
Madison, blotto every night, but he makes it for every class
or trip, up wearing dark shades in the morning. He's coping,
which is a bad sign. I don't want something like that to start
on my watch."

What about me, am I also coping on his watch?

If he told the group about his sister they might understand
his anger, not dismiss him as a Puritan out to kill the party, to
ruin Italy. Can one hold up a sign? My sweet baby sister is a
heavy-duty addict; please cut me a little slack.

"More vino?"
    "Yes please."

"I like to do a good thing now. Like today at the elevator, so they think about it and pass it on and it keeps going. It makes my day, it really makes my day."

"A good feeling. I think I'm getting to that."

"Mary, you're almost there."

"Ninety-five per cent?"

"No."

"Ninety-one?"

"No, eighty."

"Only eighty, only eighty."

"Sorry I'm so mean, I'm terrible, but Mary, I couldn't lie to you."

Go ahead and lie, I think on my terrace, *please lie to Mary*. For fuck's sake, tell her she is 90 per cent.

A lightning storm hangs over the dark mountains, an X-ray shudder, a heart attack of bleached light, then the world brought back to dark purple, back to now, a form of time travel, two worlds at once. Near our high terrace an invisible dog speaks in an urban cave and the barking sound echoes into every neighbourhood wall. Which window or room is the dog? The woman from Iraq was not used to dogs; in Iraq they are stray curs or guard dogs, associated with fangs or power, not a favoured pet in your bedroom and never on your bed.

Eve loves animals, bends to address every dog and cat she spies. This invisible dog speaks to something in the night of lightning and the two women on the next terrace speak their lines to the night as if in a play and I hear every word, yet my eyes never know their keen faces. Now I stop, now I close my terrace door on their secret mix of bonhomie and sadness.

•

We all believe we have a corner on sadness. In our Jetson future perhaps sorrow will be valued as a renewable domestic resource. The immense power of sorrow will light our giant glass houses and pay the tab for our therapy and plastic surgery. In our jeremiad Jetson future they will mine our misery the way we frack the earth for shale gas pinned there like a cage wrestler. Our sorrow will fuel beautiful sports cars and sleek machines to Mars, our sorrow will employ our children's nannies and reverse invasions and rescue the euro and dollar and make shuddering markets rise in joy, our reliable sources of domestic sorrow will make brokers rejoice with champagne smiles behind their complex buzzers and floodlit gates and blank limos.

An animal speaks to lightning and a piano echoes tidy counterpoint. My small room sways above you, orbiting in a beautiful Roman sky, and the blind man walks our clean halls with his clicking white stick: *Will you please ask them to be quiet!*

He can't stop the raucous partiers, those who drink themselves blind. I close my eyes and see Eve at the black sand beach in the bay under the volcano, her pale form stretched to the black sand — like looking at a negative. The blind man wanders eternally, I expect him to carry a lantern at noon, Diogenes searching the halls for an honest man, Diogenes searching the deck of an aircraft carrier lurking in the gloom offshore.

I walk down the stairwell with my eyes shut, I admire the blind man, I feel I owe him that much, but on the stairs I fail, I have to open my eyes, I have to look. Train your eye, he seems to suggest, see better, live better.

I will try. We try on mysterious shoes, have mysterious offspring. One child wants to be a priest, one wants to be a pirate.

The snake-handler and I are like Adam and Eve; we felt exempt from the fang, then something changed. We sin and are forgiven, we fly to and fro, we are on earth, then we are in the heavens, then we are not, we are on earth, then we are back in the silent cup of stars, then we are not.

In this world tiny things make me irritable and tiny things make me greatly happy. Like a stone in my shoe, like stars inside a chapel ceiling, or my high window in the night sky, its glass moon shape, and moonlight over arched doorways and ivory rooftops, moonlight making shapes seem profound and unearthly, but only for those who have a moment, this staggering light so secretive and brief and only for you and me.

Pompeii Book of the Dead

Thin walls divide the hotel rooms and one morning I hear a couple's amorous sounds through the wall. The amorous voices are clearly not the older couple renting the room right now. These wall voices are younger and Italian.

Did this couple stride off the elevator naked? I hear absolutely no pause between the sound of their hotel door and the sounds of their sex.

Someday I will be spiritually perfect, will free myself of the physical plane, free of appetite, but right now I can hear the woman's sounds in a bed just beyond my wall. My ear, my aroused listening, the membrane of the wall, the honeycomb rooms we curl within, our beehive brain with us living like a great guest inside, my blood rising with this strange woman so close to me, a woman so open and willing just past a wall so thin I could drive my hand through.

Thou shalt not covet thy neighbour's illicit paramour, but perhaps she'd enjoy another friend when the first friend is done. Why not? We all want more than we have. *Amore!* The second orgasm may be more intense. That is, if she has a first. The man next door is very fast.

Can I whisper to her through the wall? *Signora*, excuse me, I can't help but hear the revealing human sounds you make. And I have no one. So perhaps I'd be welcome?

Of course, you poor soul, come to me, she will whisper back in Italian, and somehow I will understand her language. Of course I will take you in, you poor, poor lonely teddy bear. First let me get rid of this skinny peon, this nonentity in a loud purple dress shirt — there, he is gone and I will float like a spirit to your room. And why would I not?

Here, put your hand here, and here, and here, brushing like a moving breeze, yes, yes, we have all the time in the world, a hundred years to each breast, let us live new lives in this beautiful Mediterranean bed, for bed is the poor man's opera. To callipygian Aphrodite, to Apollo, to Bacchus, to Dionysus! To kiss a golden face, her red lips, and hear her soft song.

Hold your horses, am I going insane? Do I really think some woman will welcome a hand through the fucking plasterboard, a cock through the wall?! I've become a lunatic in Rome's bacchanal opera, I am in a world that worships beauty, the body's form, my eyes blinded by form and flesh, by smackwarm plenty, by *amore, amore.* My cousin's bikini and Titan kisses a dish of butter and my brain is toast, Rome all flashing skin and bosom and eggplant and olive oil and tomatoes and tongues and lips in a contest with the grape-fattening heat. In hallways, rooftops, sidewalks, my God, the amazing skin my eyes take in around this mammose mammering holy city!

This city brings on the swell of memory, overwhelming memories of skin that gain power in retrospect: my girlfriend's ponytail down her back when she came to visit in such hot weather, to walk under the sun by a cold sea where black ducks dove and a seal popped up its old-man skull to gaze at us, curious as we swam sandbars and gravel bars.

The vision of my girlfriend's curved body and me at her side, laying a wet face cloth on her to cool her, laying on hands, this vision haunts me now. I want someone with me in my hotel room, have hit the point where I would pay, need to bite one of those big Italian bums I see passing every day. I have hungers, appetites, I crave food, drink, her letters, her mouth. Yes, I would pay right now. Of course I would pay. Does it not make sense?

All of the world's money directed to gilt chalices and decanters of burgundy wine, money aimed at ghosts and stained glass and eyeless statuary, money to trifles, to hapless burgers and fries, to lottery and accident and hope. Hope and commerce are the way of the world. Why would I not join in, why would I not pay for a companion?

You really want to pay for a woman? God asks me this question and God dispatches the answer quickly. By train I travel to Pompeii and in Pompeii God tests my theory minutes after I arrive. In Pompeii I check in easily and bound out of the small hotel, thirsty and excited by a new town and the famous volcano over the glittering bay and sea views lurking for blue miles before evaporating into light haze, that milky horizon with no horizon.

The ruins of the old city also seem to stretch forever, roadside tombs and mausoleums and villas and walls and sand-coloured excavations. Pompeii is so many worlds, so many levels, a strange village below us, families caught like an underground zoo, mothers and children frozen in their poses, then a breathing world built just above their heads, busy footsteps on the dead's ceiling, roads and tracks and our sweaty slum train's noisy motion just one level above the digs, we live and move above their heads, wheels and engines rolling over graves.

What is it like to live in Pompeii as an ordinary town? Is it strange for the locals to know this shadow city below and to one side, this destroyed duplicate in the basement? I must ask someone. Like Las Vegas, like New Orleans, no visitor cares a whit about the real city. In Pompeii we want the visceral proof of someone else's apocalypse, the tourist attractions of roof-less ruins, ancient cafés and bedrooms and brothels and shops broken open to the sun and the old aroma of sulphur and fear. I wonder if locals resent this favoured twin, this magnet shadow so close to their heart.

And we are the same, that other place shadowing us here, the lost place we left and must return to, return to a questioning face and cheques written at the kitchen table and deep leaves raked past the backyard swing, a return to winter and shovelling a driveway and a new battery and heavy-duty windshield wipers, a return to providing and caring and staying put in one place. Will that cooler world stay put while I am absent?

Pack on my back, I walk the layers, the strange ruins and excavations open at my feet. Why am I so fascinated by Pliny the Elder and his fiery demise in Pompeii? I travelled to Pompeii because of Vesuvius the volcano and the excavated ruins, but also because Pliny sailed here to his death.

On a morning just like this the sky grew dark and the sun stood still; a volcano woke the vineyards and all of this life was buried deep, left to sleep so long, an entombed amphitheatre and villas and cobbled avenues, cowering families caught on their broken plates, mothers clinging hard to babies, suffocating in seconds, lamps extinguished, then discovered by chance after so much time asleep, ladders and lanterns down into holes and villas dug out and exposed once more to the harsh sun and tourists like me, an ancient roof peeled back like a convertible, sun inching forward into the rooms a crimson ribbon at a time, the living come to walk the long avenues of the dead, the living and dead come to visit each other on this shore.

Near my hotel in Pompeii I spy a café called Irish Times. Nothing Irish about the café, but in this heat it offers cold Italian beer. In the interior shadows they pluck a beer from a dark wooden icebox and I walk out into electric white southern light. Tiny tables out front, but someone is at each table.

A woman at one of the sidewalk tables looks at me with bright eyes. She has long curly hair, a pleasant face.

"*Come stai?*"

"*Bene, grazie.*"

I point to an empty chair at her table.

"May I sit?" I ask her, with a mix of sign language and English and Italian.

She motions to sit.

Both of us face the sunny street, our backs to the shop windows. I check newspapers and a map, happy to be in Pompeii in a pleasant café with a cold beer.

I took a fast train to Naples and changed for Pompeii, away from the others, having fun on my own. Hercules lived near here, Spartacus, the Sirens and grottoes, Pliny's naval fleet was across the bay. There are no tourists around, other than me sipping at a cold bottle. And I am not one of those who pretend they are not a tourist — I know what I am. Locals glide by me and children play by the tables, perhaps Pliny's descendants.

In front of my family home the moving van opens its padlocks and doors. I am glad I missed being there for the moving van. My separation arranged and lawyers and bankers consulted minutes before I hurried to the airport. Waiting for a crucial fax from the big city, waiting to sign the papers and then I can flee, roar off to the plane at the last second, and I almost missed my flight. Later I hear about my banker also getting separated, it is a virus you can catch, it has gone viral.

"Three hours," the Italian woman says, looking at me. I think that's what she says.

"Oh really," I mutter, smiling stupidly and turning back to my newspaper.

What does she mean? *Non capisco.* This woman at the table has beautiful eyes. It is a sunny day and curly-haired children line up for cold gelato from the café. Are those her kids? The same curls. A dark-featured man talks on a cellphone at the curb. Is the man with her? Three hours, she said. Did her husband keep her waiting for hours while he talks at the curb? Yes, that is a long time.

I return to my newspaper and my Peroni (*Birra Superiore*).

Across the bay at the naval base at Misenum, Pliny the Elder spied a massive cloud rising high, the cloud taking the shape of a tree. Pliny took swift galleys to Pompeii to help old friends stranded on the shore of the bay, to help them escape. He died here, gave himself to the people.

"Thirty euros," she says.

I look up, look into her face.

A woman beside me at a café table is talking of money. Is this what I think? *Non ho capito*, my Italian is very poor, I lack language, lack the secret code.

Thirty euro, thirty pieces of silver. This as a possibility should not surprise me. Venice once had twelve thousand registered prostitutes. A few blocks away from our table are ruined frescoes of Roman orgies and cunnilingus, and ancient shop entrances boast their good-luck charms of erect penises, and pictures of Priapus, the minor god of gardens and fertility, Priapus proudly weighing his giant cock, balancing it on a scale like avoirdupois, goods of weight, his cock stuck out in front of him like the neck of a goose.

But what if she is not one of them, what if I am misunderstanding her? This scene is so *public* — a sunny street, kids tasting sweet gelato. Is that her man there at the curb on a phone? I am on my own, no one knows where I am and I could be punched in the face over a woman's honour, beaten or stabbed over an insult.

"Thirty euros?"

"*Sì*," she says, so calmly.

"For you?"

Again she says yes, as if all is obvious, life so simple. I can have a person for the price of a few coins. But I don't know what to do.

The woman with curly hair speaks to me again. It sounds like *quindici*, or is it *dieci*? Fifteen, or perhaps ten, or is it nineteen? I'm lost. Why would she say an odd number like nineteen? I wish I knew for sure what was happening. She seems to be bargaining, dropping the price rapidly. Did she take my words *for you* as a ploy, an insult? I don't want to insult anyone, I just arrived, I want to wait at least a few days before insulting anyone.

It seems very inexpensive to own a person for a few hours, *if* that is what she means. How long since I touched anyone's skin? I complained so much about that in Rome. But what if she is discussing the temperature, the stock market, the ages of her children? Why did I not try harder to learn Italian from that CD in the car? Perhaps I'm like the fishermen who refuse to learn to swim so as to drown quickly, as swimming only delays the inevitable.

An elderly nun walks past us, leaning forward as if her huge shoes are snowshoes and she crosses some windy tundra or white taiga. Her shoes are so large she must drag them along rather than lift each foot. I understand her: the shoes do not fit the nun's tiny feet, but they are the best shoes she has ever held and she wants to make them work, and in this the tiny nun is like me.

My room in the small family hotel — can I waltz in with a strange curly-haired woman from the street? The son or daughter or mother would see us traverse the lobby with its polite wicker furniture and blind dog from Asia Minor. Would they know her? The Italians say to not trust a woman with curly hair. Beware: *ogni riccio un capriccio* — every curl a caprice.

Should I take the leap? Why not? This is very possible, this is interesting, an adventure, I'm in an amazing foreign country and a woman has offered herself to me, one of the linen-lifting tribe, one of the seraglio. I know my eyes crinkled in stupid amusement when I first understood her offer. It's exciting, exotic, it's possible.

But then my cautious side touches the brakes and I regret my initial levity. I don't want to give the impression that I'm laughing at her, that she is amusing. What if she has a man waiting to roll me for my tourist cash and bank cards? What of the promise of disease?

1. Yes, an adventure.

2. No, this is trouble.

One or two: which number is true, which number is me? Is there even a singular mind? How many voices and voters make up a brain, how many rivals, how many factions and gangs? How many cells clamber in the riotous Balkan parliament in my head?

I flirt with the Croatian maid, I flirt with the cryptic Spanish woman, I stare at my cousin's form, I stare at every waitress. Then a woman and I share a tiny table in Italy, in Europe, on the planet, and for a handful of euros I can do certain things to her for an agreed time. How perfect it no longer seems.

No, I say, No, *grazie*. I say it several times, trying to be nice, trying too hard to be polite, that I am grateful for something, her attention, not wanting to insult her. *Grazie*. No.

Pliny the Elder sailed to the shore in a fast cutter, rescuing citizens from the hellish volcano, the air getting worse and worse until he couldn't breathe, a saviour overcome at the shore by sulphurous gases. Pliny died a hero. Or so I thought.

Because of this woman in Pompeii I find I do not believe what I believed. I find I cannot just buy someone, despite thinking I was fine with the idea, the *theory*, find that I cannot pass across a sum of money and have my way. I want a travelling companion, want to be comfortable, stay in touch, want a girlfriend, or my cousin drinking sour San Pellegrino Limonata at the Hotel Europa.

How old-fashioned it turns out I am, how straightlaced, that I need some simpatico conversation, some connection (*these Digby scallops are to die for*), touching a knee, a neck, an ear, and talking of singers we like (*you lent me* Veedon Fleece, *remember?*). Not a simple transaction with a stranger; I need a complex transaction.

I sound like a moony schoolgirl: *it should be special*. I'm as bad as the whining teens on exchange in Rome with their puppy-love crushes and swooning. I have had love and affection and kindness and talk and all it did was break my heart. Special, not special, what is the fucking difference?

Disease crossed my mind (*the canker galls the infants of spring*), or I could be robbed, a trap for a traveller laden with euros, cankers and thieves everywhere. Pompeii has a bad rep; my guidebook says quite seriously to see Pompeii, but to not stay there.

This woman seems accepted by the locals in a way I am not; those running the café must know her if she frequents their tables. They don't drive her away from their tables, they don't spit on her the way my cousin was spit on miles to the south.

The café woman walks away, looking hard at her phone, leaning forward toward the square eye of her screen. Is the screen a handy prop or does she really have a pressing appointment? Her eyes are changed, her face no longer friendly. I've seen that look before, that strange sea change. And the town changes with her.

A man with cropped hair sits down to show me his hands, his mangled hands. A refugee from Tunisia, he crossed the desert and then he floated in a jammed boat to the island of Lampedusa, now beset with refugees. In Italy he tried to obliterate his own fingerprints, he burnt his hands, perhaps with acid, afraid the police would ship him back south. The authorities have his fingerprints registered.

Will I give him five euro?

No, my nature is not generous. Perhaps the nun's shoes will fit him. Go ask her.

I stand, no longer wanting my place at the table, I want to walk too, a street walker, I walk the city, walk and turn into an alley as a shortcut to the basilica and central piazza. I think I know my direction, my landmarks, but the alley curves the wrong way, turns away from the centre and keeps going and going and I'm alone and start to get jumpy, paranoid, the alley connects with nothing, I've made a bad move, entered a box canyon. Where am I? I can hear the train's air horn over there. Keep moving and let's get out of this blind alley.

These encounters with this woman and the man with the burnt fingertips have thrown me, my mood altered. I was so happy to arrive here a few moments before, but I am edgy now, walking an endless alley with cash on me, waiting to be jumped by lurking strumpets and stoned thieves. Finally I find a way out of this maze and immediately spy her at a table in front of another café. I nod to her and keep walking toward the ruins just outside of the city.

Now my world seems strange and dangerous. What if the guidebook is right about Pompeii: a world full of foul deeds and sneaking mischief, a mousetrap, *miching mallecho*, a cold beer and a knife needling between the ribs. All around the bay the Nuvoletta-Polverino cartels open suitcases and sell groceries, garlic, hash, relics, leather coats and high-fashion gowns, moving bricks, ecstasy and cocaine in the northern suburbs, stolen antiquities and jewels in the narrow lanes.

Beat-up trains move and stop in bleached grass and iron stations blotted with graffiti, so many trains, so many stops, Vesuvio de Meis, Scavi di Ercolano, Madonna dell'Arco, Torre Annunziata.

Our furnace-hot trains forge past arid ruins, past prickly pear cactus by the track's sandy ditches, as if we move through Mexico, and a uniformed man calling for tickets, tickets. Yet I ride the train for free most days, my pass expired, a Unico Campania Three-Day Travel Ticket. I am rarely asked, trusted — or I am invisible, of a certain age and appearance. The police do not check my ID in the piazza to see if I should be deported, I don't have to burn the prints from my fingertips.

The train circles the placid mountain that broke open and killed so many, the mountain filling the train window as our headphones fill our head with mumblecore and shoe-gazer. Millions live in the volcano's *zona rossa*, the nervous red zone. The volcano blew during World War Two, March 1944, adding to the woes of starvation and typhus. If it blows again we are all dead, the peak held over us no matter where we go, until I feel Vesuvius has been looming over me all my life, leading me to this cratered place where fumaroles fume steam and ancient vineyards rise in long perfect lines to the volcano, a series of triangles and convergences and my eager eye follows, pleased by the sightline.

The fields around the Bay of Naples are fertile, deep soil enriched by repeated eruptions of volcanic ash, crops leaping up in eternal sun. Old women draped in black work the fields, how do they do it, sweaters and long skirts, all in black in this heat! Arbours and grapes and orchards and orchids, beaches and marinas and all this beautiful coastline, this emerald sea stretching away in the sunshine, all these stunning islands, all this potential, the Bay of Naples could be a new California, an Eden. So I wonder, and my apologies to the locals: why do these sprawling suburbs under the volcano seem so fucked up?

Trash piled in cul-de-sacs and vandals and thieves and graffiti, graffiti like ugly tattoos, and no work and larceny and kidnappings and extortion and payoffs and murders and sewing machines singing. In suburbs and exurbs men drink peach wine, sweet *pellechiella*, men cut packages into vials, kilos roll in and the kilos roll out. And all the euros, all the money being made? Where does it go? Like water, like affection, like affliction, it has to go somewhere.

At the station in the centre of town I greet Ray-Ray and Tamika at the train. In Rome I was so weary of the art group at the hotel, happy to slip away to a pub on my own or travel down to Pompeii solo, but now it's so good to see someone I know; let me hug them both. As we chat on an outdoor platform, a high-speed train pulls in to stop very briefly, a train so much more streamlined than the boxy Circumvesuviana carriages we sweat inside most days.

A stray Jack Russell terrier dances around the train, full of pep, the stray dog checks us out but quickly loses interest and wants to move on. Jacks may seem the epitome of living in the moment, but really they live in the moment just ahead, the moment just one second from now. Now the dog wants to cross the tracks from our platform to see who is at the station door, but the streamlined train blocks the dog's path.

The train must be going all the way down to Sicily, where these cars will be uncoupled in a cumbersome dance and ferried across the strait.

The little dog peers this way and that for a way to cross the track. The diesel will leave any second, we know; these high speed trains never linger. We all groan as the dog places his head under the iron wheels of the idling train, where he will be crushed or sliced in half in front of our eyes.

"Don't."

We see his quick terrier eyes and brain working in tandem: *Might a dog sneak through here?* The crowd tenses as if the curious dog awaits a guillotine, the lull between beheadings.

"No," I say out loud, "come back." But the stray dog does not know English. Tamika turns away, she can't watch the dog be killed.

"Here!"

The dog turns, runs back to our platform, the diesel train shrieks and train wheels scythe over the space where the dog's nose was under the engine.

"Come here. Good boy!" He has bright eyes and brown ears soft as gloves. I saved him, I am Pliny the Elder. Eve would like this dog. Do I have a treat in my backpack? It's a Jack; it doesn't want to be petted; it wants to run, it wants to run and work until it dies. I know this dog will die. It has no one.

Tamika and Ray-Ray ask me to hike up the slopes of the volcano with them.

Sure, why not? Any height here brings an amazing view.

As we climb Ray-Ray tells us of suitcases full of gifts he brought back to Canada from China; odd to think of Ray-Ray hanging out in Hong Kong's meatpacking district, it seems to him only minutes ago.

"Shoes incredibly cheap," he says. "Brand new electronics, shuffles, hard drives, man, they cost nothing there! The customs people wouldn't believe me when I declared the total value, it was so low they thought I was lying. Man, it was harsh, those dudes at customs held me for hours."

•

For hours we walk up toward the bulk of Vesuvius, sweating like mules in slanted streets, in dark rock and sun, the drugging sun. This is harder than we thought.

"Isn't there a bus that comes up this way?" asks Tamika. "Like, up to a parking lot?"

"I don't know," says Ray-Ray, "It looked so close, I figured we could hike it. Man, I hear you can see right inside the volcano. I want to look inside."

I'm lost and wobbly and my scalp is toast. On her laptop back in Rome Eve showed me satellite photos from directly above the volcano's cone, the strange opening, a black hole in the planet. We can see paths high up the slope above, but in a stretch of scrub brush and flowering broom we halt; we're not going to make the peak, the Gran Cono.

Pliny died doing this almost two thousand years ago, roof tiles breaking in the heat, in some corner of a foreign field Pliny fell and didn't get up, covered in ash and molten lava. The poet Shelley burnt on the beach, I burn in Pompeii. Too long in the sun, my head hurting, and the scored mountain defeats us.

Below the mountain such rich fields and bright sea and scattered islands running off to the glittering west. The volcano and bay sculpted by tectonic collisions, the African plate forced below the Eurasian plate, and below the mountain African men sell new sunglasses to an ancient nation. Tall men set up tiny tables on a street or a cloth spread on the sidewalk outside the glowing church and gather their goods and run when they see the handsome police uniforms moving toward them.

Southern Italy so warm, a boot aimed at Africa, a long fashionable boot, so close to Tunisia, to Cleopatra's Egypt,

Cleopatra's golden breast. North Africa is so close, part of Caesar's empire and Mussolini's empire, artifacts from Nubian locales scattered everywhere in Italy, yet Ray-Ray and Tamika seem like strangers in the living room.

"Italians treat you like family," Father Silas said at a restaurant in Rome. "Italians are wonderful, so warm."

This is not always so for African street vendors, and locals think Ray-Ray is a purse-seller, an illegal. My old Irish uncle used to say, We are made of the same dough, but we are baked in different ovens. And who among us in any country is consistent or perfect? Some nights we are the drunken bozos bellowing in the street and some nights we are the voice in the window telling the drunken bozos to shut the hell up.

Ray-Ray and Tamika catch the milk-train down to Sorrento, but I travel alone to a smaller excavation I want to explore. A second-class train, baking inside, but a good price. Coming back toward Naples, I find a seat in a compartment with two men and an elderly woman. Two seats left. I sense each passenger's unspoken hope that no one comes into their compartment. Then a young woman with a heavy case; I mean, it is large and in charge. She struggles awkwardly and I jump up and help tilt her giant suitcase to the high rack above our seats, where I hope it won't fall and kill us.

She sits beside me, her face flushed from exertion and heat, and we make our introductions. An American, Abby has been teaching art in Istanbul, but now her contract is over. She is travelling for a month and will meet her parents in Venice; next year she will teach in Asia.

I'd like to see Istanbul, sail to Byzantium.

"Any Italian links?" Abby asks me. "In your family?"

"Not that I know of."

"I have an ancestor," Abby says, "who was a sculptor in Italy."

"So art runs in the family?"

"No, I'm the only one into art."

When she hears "Canada" she asks if I know Quebec's Gaspé Peninsula. She says, "I went there as a child and still remember it. It's so beautiful."

I agree, I love the Gaspé. It reminds me of the far west of Ireland, the Blasket Islands, but I can drive there: no Heathrow Airport!

"I want to go back," she says. She has lovely memories of diving whales and dazzling light and sea air. Wiping her perspiring face, she says she'd pay to have such fresh sea air supplied on this train.

I usually hate about 98 per cent of the world and then once in a while I see someone I really like. She has lovely eyes. That way of talking or looking at me. On a train, here let me help with your luggage, a woman walking into a room, or you walk in and she is there and looks up, or passing in a street, every once in a while it happens — a glance, a hope, a chance, all moments of a possible life described and unfolding and held in that quicksilver second in the eyes.

Abby asks if I can translate a sign she sees. She knows Latin, but not Italian. When did they switch? We speak English in the compartment and an older man stares at us. I practise Italian phrases daily, but when I try to speak to native Italians my tongue is struck dumb. No wonder Italians think we are all morons.

The older man says, "You come to Italy and can't speak Italian?" The man has a dark upswept pompadour and leans forward, head deep between his shoulders, like Elvis with osteoporosis.

So wanderers and travellers must speak every language? Then I could never see Russia or China, Croatia or Greece.

"Be very careful in Napoli," the man says to Abby.

He points to his eyes. At first I thought he meant they'll go for your eyes, but then I realize he is showing her that he has seen it all with his own eyes. The old man is a retired detective, jaded by all that he has seen over years of police work.

Abby does not understand what he says and I try to decipher. Another man joins in, a well-dressed young Italian filmmaker who has more English than the detective.

I ask if they are sad about Italy's loss in football.

No, the filmmaker does not care.

The detective says football is a very bad influence, all business and piles of money. The matches are fixed, it is contaminated.

They surprise me, so far I have met only devoted fans. I talk with the filmmaker about Wim Wenders, Bertolucci, *Besieged*, *The Passenger*. He made a documentary about a Victorian writer, English, in Calabria. I will try to track it down. He says it is hard to sell films, he has to take other jobs in media.

Abby asks me, "Is there some kind of trash problem in Naples?"

"A little bit," I say to her quietly, not wanting to offend our hosts.

"A little bit!" Both Italian men laugh ferociously at my reply. "A little bit!"

It's as if I've fired a starter's pistol for a race, the two men leap into a wild discussion of Italian governments and elections and communists and mobs and trash collection, both men waving hands and yelling. I can only make out snippets of the speedy animated Italian.

"This is not a normal country. Here up is down, down is up. Here matters move like molasses and everyone wants a share off the top and a share off the bottom and a share off the sides and then what is left? Since the war? A new government every nine months, as if having a baby. But what is the result? The new baby never arrives. Nothing changes."

"No, nothing changes ever."

"When the *americani* voted for that fool Bush I laughed. But now we have elected a *buffone*, a clown. Now I can no longer laugh."

"A clown, yes," says the young filmmaker, "but a very rich clown who owns all the television stations and newspapers. A clown who does what he wishes."

"Still a clown. This is a country run by old men, you have to know someone, what matters is who you know, not your talents, and thus the talented leave us. My nephew writes me, he has a job in New York, he had to leave, *la fuga dei cervelli*. How did we get like this? In a normal country the government governs. In a normal country criminals are arrested. Here the police do not police and villains roam free in gangs, here trash is not collected and taxes are not collected. Mister So-and-So drives a Ferrari and has a swimming pool, but he pays no taxes, the priest arrives at mass in a Lamborghini, but he pays no taxes. It's no secret. Everyone wants to take and no one wants to pay."

The detective argues that Mussolini and the old ways had benefits, that at least the Fascists kept order.

The filmmaker politely disagrees. No, he cannot favour fascism or Mussolini.

"Believe me," says the detective, "in the old days they knew what to do. Mussolini would take care of these *banditi*. If you stepped out of line back then, this is what happened to you." The detective makes a motion of slitting his own throat.

Again the young filmmaker tactfully disagrees with the older detective. "There were more *banditi* then than now."

The filmmaker turns to Abby and me. "The centre of Napoli is free of trash, but…" He struggles for words in English. "The outside districts, there it can be worse. But you are fairly safe here. The violence is exaggerated. They'll happily lift your wallet on a crowded bus, but no one mugs you. They want crimes of opportunity, something sitting there, something easy."

The detective scoffs. "Are you insane? You haven't seen what I have seen with my own eyes!" And they are off again, arguing about shootings and car bombs and the Camorra.

I whisper to Abby that the Camorra is a very powerful mob; I think the word *camorra* means quarrel. I am glad that I didn't travel first-class on a sleeker, air-conditioned train, I would not have met any of these people. The elderly woman in the compartment glares disapprovingly at all of us, foreigners or *italiani*. Her stern, lined face asks, *Why* did we have to sit with her on her peaceful journey?

A wandering woman comes to our compartment, *buongiorno*, asks for money. I say no, but to my surprise the detective and the older woman wearily acquiesce and give her coins, the older two more charitable than the younger passengers.

I like them all, like the detective; he speaks his mind. I like the filmmaker; he is closer to my age and political leanings. And I like Abby from Texas who sits close to me all the way to Naples, named by the Greeks Neapolis, their New City. Both of us unsure what is next as the train slows to penetrate the perplexing fulcrum of Naples, the huge harbour and wharf rats, the crowded troubled buildings by a beautiful bay.

Naples was an independent kingdom for centuries. Naples was never as rich, never ruled the world, but also was never flattened the way Rome was. Rome such a centre of riches and sin that it attracted armies bent on setting Rome straight, on breaking its bones: aqueducts cut and lovely fountains dry, monuments and pillars toppled like tenpins, and the vandals took the handles, Rome left a ghost town, sheep grazing the empty tumbling temples and Rome's lovely marble fascias burnt in rude kilns by scavengers.

The kingdom of Naples was taken over by every touring barbarian — Viking, Goth, Frank, Norman, Hun, Slav, Saracen, Arab, Byzantine, Magyar, Nazi, and recent Eurotrash— but the city spires were not brought flat, Naples made arrangements with its strange bedfellows. Which approach do you lean to in your private kingdom? Cut a deal or be sacked?

In the railroad switchyard we move under blue sky and a ceiling of wires and Abby points at big block letters spray-painted on a yellow shed, WELCOME TO AN ANTI-FASCIST CITY, accompanied by a hammer and sickle.

"Why is it written in English? So the tourists can read it?"

I wonder if the Soviet hammer and sickle looks odd to her American eyes.

Abby and I walk the crowded Naples station, peering inside and outside the glass walls at the piazza and taxis; there for moments and we see police chase a man through the glass doors, where others wait for him outside; cat and mouse, they are familiar with each other.

Attenzione Ai Borseggiatori — Beware of Pickpockets!

Cat and mouse, boy meets girl, the train comes in the station with a blue light on behind and we sit for a cold drink near the station, an eye on our bags in the noise of a shambolic urban mob. *Vorrei una birra, per favore. Vorrei* many beer, *per favore*. Look at those faces; that family of four walked and bickered in Pompeii and were smothered by the volcano. The same handsome faces walking past Abby's face.

In Dublin I met a couple from northern Italy, near Pisa. I mentioned Naples and their faces altered, they rushed to look up the English words for theft, danger, worry. Do not go to Napoli, they begged. Yet the owner of a bar in Rome and his best friend show me where I must go in Napoli, the best friend circles spots on my map, writes down names; he lives in Rome now, but says Napoli is his favourite city, says Napoli is the true capital of Italy.

Napoli is volcanic, scary and strangely endearing, flea markets with no tables or booths, hawkers and hustlers holding up smokes or soccer balls or simply laying shirts on the dirt of a vacant lot. The street people are not upwardly mobile, not on their way to better things. They say Christ didn't make it this far and neither did a middle class, the place looks harsh, Napoli has endured plagues and quakes, cholera and cruel overlords, but Napoli also shows off wonderful antiquities and art, sleepy catacombs and blunt campaniles, with gourmand treats around every corner, clams, mussels, swordfish, eel, tripe, hunks of buffalo mozzarella, and hefty pizza. Abby lifts a big wobbly crust, trying to hold the fluid crater in the centre. I think of Rome's pizza as thin and simple, almost dry, Napoli's pizza liquid and, like the city, more complicated.

Another bottle of beer and the usual questions of the past, but Abby surprises me when says she has just ended a long-term lesbian relationship and ended an affair with an older man where she worked. She worries this man has a pattern of staying with a younger woman until the woman is past child-bearing age and then he moves on to someone else.

"I'm celibate right now for a while," she says, "having a moratorium."

Moi aussi, I think, though the moratorium is not my choice.

"But now I prefer older men," she says. "I don't think I can go back to younger guys, they're so goofy." This last idea from Abby was not expected.

Abby still remembers her childhood trip to Gaspé, the massive sunlit prow of Percé Rock, crazed gannets diving for herring and whales lifting and sounding and so much light and fresh salt air like wine. The small motel was perched on a cliff; placid whales directed themselves below her balcony and she heard the whales snorting as they surfaced in the bay. I may have stayed in the same motel. In town I drank glasses of lovely cold Blanche beer after kayaking on the windswept sea, now in my head both Gaspé and Naples in a minor key.

"Where is the sea? Is it by the station?"

"You can't really see it from here, but the harbour's that way. We're close."

"I want to see the bay and the islands. Ischia, maybe Capri. I'll meet you in a day or two in Pompeii. Where are you staying?" she asks.

Abby has already booked a hostel in Naples to save money. I am too old and cranky for hostels and bunks. It is on to Pompeii for me and the small family hotel. I have my hand on her neck, it seems so intimate. Her head is so close that I can see down her top and spy her black bra and small breasts nestled within. She doesn't mind my touch on her shoulders and neck. Yes, I must go there, the Gaspé is so beautiful.

I know it's impossible, but I want to skip the awkward courtship steps and calls and restaurant candles, watching plump scallops shuck their bacon wraps. Can't two people simply look at each other and know and walk by the milky sea, can't one just say, *You and me*. And both would somehow know.

And it can happen, it has happened to me, a matter of days,

perhaps minutes, and it seems we know. But then all the other bad times. Do I have luck or do I not?

"Email me," I say to Abby, worried about cementing things before she walks away into the chaos of Naples, before I catch my train to Pompeii. "I can check at the internet café."

"No need to check, I'll see you in Pompeii soon."

When she says these few words to me I am elated, suddenly I adore our world, my step light and posture improved and only yesterday I was ginger with vague grief and drear glaucoma.

Abby buys a train pass, we say our goodbyes and she walks past taxi drivers waiting like wolves for the lambs, she walks into buzzing Naples to find her hostel, repeating my directions to the veiled Christ's spooky chambers and Capodimonte's Bourbon palace far up the hill.

On a dark subterranean platform (Milan would never tolerate such a Stygian substation) I catch another slow train out of town, the windows on the right side suddenly full of light and unspooling views of aqua sea and up lift the tribal cameras and always a church like a narrow knife in the blue sky, a view of water on my side of the train, but also afternoon sun beating on that side so you pay for the view, body heat increasing markedly inside the crowded train as it travels the curve of the bay down to Pompeii and Sorrento (why is Sorrento so serene and Naples so lawless?), prickly pear cactus and wild lemon trees in the windows and Abby and a Smiths song in my head about fifteen minutes with her.

I wouldn't say no, I resolve that I will stop again in Naples and learn more of the harbour and the Spanish Quarter, the weird high avenues and that steep ancient alley that bisects the town like the line dividing our brain; Naples makes me nervous, but I feel I must get to know it. The milk-train travels in and out of mountains, in train tunnels we move in and out of daylight, pupils dilating, ears popping, pores sweating, neck sweating, until my body contemplates a switch to gills.

Slightly dazed, I jump off the sweaty train at Pompeii and explore the raw ruins on foot and in the ruins I enter another tunnel, tunnel after tunnel, airports, trains, and now this underground forum. A dark passage leads at an angle into the earth and I follow this tunnel into the lower level of the forum complex, the Teatro, down into shade, hiding from the relentless sun for even a few rare moments.

Gaspé's cool breezes; northern glaciers and Columbia ice-fields; Hudson Bay floes and polar bears — can they be real? Any accumulation of ice or snow seems impossible in this pole-axing heat and dust.

Tamika and Ray-Ray spot me from a distance just as I descend; they are following a stone street from the Villa of Mysteries, big oval stones set in the roadway and Tamika and Ray-Ray hop-scotch stone to stone. They were in the Garden of Fugitives, they are excited, they saw the ghostly plaster forms of bodies and can't get over them, the white shapes of bodies, the haunting postures, the dog that died in the House of Orphans, its con-torted last moments; they saw the haunting plaster casts and they trudge dust and pigeons and follow me into the under-world, the dark tunnel passage cool, shade so lovely, so good to be briefly out of the sun under the forum complex. In the sun the burnt skin of my forehead hurts so much it makes me worry. I think we wandered too long on the mountain, too long in the sun.

The famous volcano buried much of the theatre, though

some of the walls were visible for centuries. When they dug out the forum's lower chambers they found human skeletons and a horse. Torches and candles burnt in these haunted underground halls, animals and men waiting, waiting, sweating, then your turn to fight, time to be pushed out into the harsh sun, live or die.

From the level forum floor we raise our eyes to the rising rows of stone seats heaped above us. Ray-Ray looks around. "I bet this was a very bad view for a lot of them who saw it."

The majority of people would be above, staring down at us. This minority on the bottom of the forum standing where we stand — slaves, foreign exiles, prisoners of war, gladiators, those of the *infam* pushed out into the sun — well, in a few moments most of us standing here would die inside this eerie stone oval.

Trident pitchforks to your skull, Roman stabbing swords, curved Bulgarian swords, chains and nets and shields, starved African lions with their ribs showing and there are two entrances: the living march under one archway and the dead find their way out a second exit. A mob chanting above a low stone wall (*do you feel lucky, punk*) and, at the end, if not lucky, dragged bleeding across the sand by Juno's spooky brother in his mask, dragged into privacy behind the walls by the masked figure, who swings his square hammer into the private curve of your porcelain head.

In the ruins I see a dog running and jumping in the distance. The dog runs over lava and candy wrappers and kings' tombs. Is that the same Jack Russell terrier I saw at the train station with its head in the diesel's wheels? In this day's heat the crazy dog chases pigeons in the grassy ruins of the Grande Palace, the dog galloping by ancient Corinthian pillars lined up in rows, pillars or stumps left to hint of the broad space where emperors and nobles and peacocks roamed gardens and reflecting pools before white pumice fell from the sky over the Temple of Jupiter.

The running dog cares not a whit about royal gardens or hidden history or the future or the heat, the dog cares only for the moment and the nearest pigeon. The dog is running full speed in the heat when I arrive and will be running full speed when I leave. Its pink tongue hangs from his narrow jaws and I hear the creature pant, a distinct clicking sound like a tiny engine about to burst.

"How does a dog find water here?" I ask Tamika. The sandy ground is like a desert. I'm told the buried ruins were discovered by a well-digger seeking water. Pompeii once sat on the sea, but the volcano altered the shore, the river diverted by lava and the sea rolled back. I wish I had a water bowl and spigot handy.

The terrier stops and speaks to me with its beautiful brown eyes: *Yes, I am the same dog you saw at the railroad track. I appreciate your concern, but you can do nothing for me. You are visiting here briefly, a stranger, a foreigner, while this is my life, short as it may be. You are used to one way, I am used to another.*

An Irish boy jumps away nervously as the dog madly rockets past, running down another pigeon he will never catch. The dog turns and runs again, over and over. That woman in Canada, I must change her mind, I must swim with her again in the mountains.

A tiny corpse lies in the thick dust, lies flat as a comb.

"Is that an antique rat?"

"Yes, dear," says the Irish boy's mother. *Antico.*

"Where's me jumper? Can we go now? Where's me jumper? Can I have a fizzy drink?"

"I said no! Don't start up."

The dog runs tirelessly, but the Irish mother is strained. Another dog pulls at a trash bag.

"Not another word about fizzy drinks!"

All the poor frazzled parents, all the offended children.

Does the dog bark at Italian pigeons in Italian? It has no owner. I must tell Eve of the dog; the shore is altered and Eve rather than Natasha is my new confessor. The terrier is a stranger. The terrier is me.

We tromp the same Italian dust that slaves and emperors and gladiators ate. Place this ancient soil in your mouth like a thick piece of pizza pie. Eat the rich past. Dig anywhere in Italy and you find the past, you can't escape your past, your acid flashback.

We stagger in the stone heat, we must leave these sand ruins for a drink, leave this skin that feels so sore from the merciless sun. In 1971 Pink Floyd played on this baked spot of real estate, played their slow psychedelia where so many died in Pompeii's stone amphitheatre, the Spectacula. Gather the Teatro's many dead into festival seating on the granite rows: what would the dead slaves and Goth captives make of Pink Floyd's mountain of amplifiers and gongs and kettle drums and acid-trip soundtrack? I've seen the old film, but I'm not sure that Tamika or Ray-Ray even know of Pink Floyd or the clip echoing forever on YouTube searches for the piper at the gates of dawn.

Down in this Teatro's sunny bowl I will be torn apart for the mob's pleasure, I will not leap the wall to slice open an emperor, I will kill another slave, I will fight a bear, I will fly on points and suffer tragic jet lag.

I'm learning. What I didn't realize about ancient Pompeii was how many got out of town. Most fled the city when the volcano started smoking, but some stayed put. I try to imagine that scene, you thought you'd be okay, then that realization, *too late*, rocks flying up into the heavens and dropping on you from the heavens like the worst meteor storm, parents and children at home crouched under the stairs, women and children huddled in a timbered boathouse by the sea, trying to shelter, and the men outside in the open, all waiting for boats at the pier. And their bodies excavated from stony sleep twenty centuries later.

In the family hotel the staff and family members eat a late lunch after we have been fed and our tables cleared. The mother with dyed blond hair and the tired father with his neck brace — once so handsome, in the old black-and-white photos decorating the lobby and halls, posing with movie stars and singers and soccer players, but now he spends the day in the lobby with a tiny TV set and a neck brace. His heart no longer in the hotel business.

Once dashing socialites, now they are aged parents, Euro Cup rattling a tiny TV and their slim son in his Italian football jersey and their daughter in her handkerchief top and low-rider pants that push out a round roll of fat at her midriff and a pampered little dog with cataracts; it stretches its bat-like torso on the cool tiles.

Big Pico, my favourite waiter, sits with the family and beside him a skinny cook; they all lean together at the same table in mid-afternoon, huge man and thin man leaning toward each other over delicious plates and much wine. This is *their* time, not ours, an intimate inner circle, relaxed and pleasantly tired from waiting on us, from serving the guests breakfast and lunch. They speak quietly.

In every bar and café and small shop the Euro Cup plays on television after television, the streets are deserted when a match is in play, even the uniformed police are inside shops and cafés watching the screen and calling out and groaning with the crowd.

When I try to speak Italian I feel I am acting on a stage, Italy is theatre and you must commit to it, lose yourself in the role. But I cannot — I am too timid. The Euro Cup football players are amazingly theatrical, a breeze touches their cheek and they fall to the bright grass, the players writhe on the grass as if shot. After a missed chance they lift their eyes to heaven in wonderment or hold their faces in huge operatic tragedy. As in hockey, the goalies seem a separate breed, faces more aged than the other players sprinting across giant green screens all over Europe.

"You are cheering for Spain."

"Because I wish them to beat the Germans."

In the open lobby two street dogs saunter inside and lie with us at the television as if come to watch the match. The line between street and lobby is not a clear border.

"You are cheering for the Netherlands?"

"Because they beat the Germans."

When the team is bad the nation grieves, the nation silent, but I don't mind a touch of silence in Italy. I can tell whether they have won or lost by the noise in the street. The Italian team loses again and again (such lovely azure jerseys), but it is the British fans who seem to be vomiting. In the stadium fans make monkey sounds at a black player on the pitch and toss banana peels at the player.

As a child I gathered that the Monkees were too busy singing to put anybody down, but the Italians I meet are catholic in their hatred; Italians hate each other and hate other towns and cities and they hate the Deutschlanders and the rest of

Europe and they hate illegals and gypsies and they hate tourists like me.

But for some stupid reason I want them to like me. I want
Pico to think favourably of me, I want his approval, even though
I will never see him again after this summer sojourn. And I fret
about offending a prostitute on the street. And she is what to
me? And in Rome, those charming young Croatian women
splashing water on the aqua tiles every morning — I worry for
them and want them to worry about me. This seems a design
flaw on my part.

A resplendent young couple walks through the lobby.

"*Matrimonio*," says the owner in his neck brace. It seems
centuries ago that I was of a couple like them, borrowing a suit,
toasting the future with champagne and love.

I saw an English tourist pub in Sorrento with a chalkboard
sidewalk sign: *Come in and meet your future ex-wife.*

The German couple at the hotel complain to me. His name is
Dieter; I know this because he left his wallet open on the table
and walked away to peer at some disturbance in the street. He
finds Italy distracting. With ease I pull out a fifty-euro note, to
show Dieter to be more careful, clearly a good idea, but then
find I don't know how to explain what I've done, and the fifty-
euro note stays in my hand.

"Italians all lie to you," Dieter says, "they promise you something and it doesn't happen, they laze about, nothing on time
or when promised."

Dieter's wife speaks in German, yet I understand every
word. "Twenty euro for a taxi, twenty euro for a drink, twenty
euro for this, twenty euro for that. *Mein Gott*, our money goes
like water!"

"Um, speaking of money."

"I'll never come back here," Dieter says imploringly. "A *horrible* place."

Yet I love the horrible place so. In this tiny hotel I have had the best minestrone of my life, the best pesto and pasta and pizza and pork and the best seafood of my life. I love the food, the strange rooms in intoxicating cities, and these lidless ruins by the blinding sea, I love Italy. It is perhaps a foolish and typical tourist notion, but I think I could live in Italy happily. And Dieter says he will never be back.

The German claims that Italians are lazy, especially southern Italians, *terroni*, but Pico in Pompeii works so hard for us. My hotel room has no clock and I travel light, no watch, no cellphone, no laptop. My room does not reveal if it is five a.m. or nine a.m. So I sneak down to the lobby to spy a clock, and I glimpse Pico bent in the kitchen creating his raw pastry, no one else about at this hour. He is here at dawn, he is here at night: when does he live, when does he sleep? I worry whether he has a life outside this hotel, whether he is lonely, whether he will die from work and heat in his black vest buttoned up and long sleeves buttoned down. Does he live with his mother still? Does she wish he'd marry? His feet are killing him, a crooked gait when hurrying to a table; how can he rest his feet? He is not lazy. I worry about him and he worries about me, looks after me so well.

I think of his pastry as croissants, but they may also be called corniches. Is that from the shape, curved like the horns of a bull? To put the horns on someone, which we did all the time as children or in photos, is a grave insult here, as cuckolds are objects of great derision in Italy. The two fingers behind the head is the cuckoo calling with bad news, ribald laughter at the *cornuto*, Othello's fear of poor Desdemona giving him horns (*I have a pain upon my forehead here*). But now, after Natasha left for another, I have sympathy for cuckolds, I've seen that black cloud from both sides now. I'll give Pico Dieter's fifty-euro note.

After another luscious dinner at the hotel, Pico brings me a simple repast, a naked superb pear, and he brings me a knife and fork. Pico has *sprezzatura*, a natural grace.

"Okay?" Pico asks me.

"*Si, si!*"

Did he read my mind? The single pear is exactly what I need after all these rich dishes, such beautiful texture and sweet taste.

Prego, Pico says so kindly every night, his hand and arm extended, like an actor in a silent film, directing me to my lonely table, welcoming me to the table for one, the only solitary place setting among the hotel's couples and families and singing nuns. I am in my place.

Abby, the woman from the train, said she'd meet me here today at four or she'd call the hotel. When the phone rings at the front desk I strain to listen. No call, no email. The sirens do not call to me from the blue grotto.

But the son at the hotel desk has no English and Abby is Texan. He might not understand her accent, her message for me. Is it her on the phone? Does she remember the Alamo? How I wish I had more Italian, I could tell the son that she will call for me. Next time I will be sure to study harder (and you know I will *not* study harder).

Stray dogs run past and I sit outside the hotel at a wobbly wicker table with a huge cold bottle (*grande, per favore*), waiting for her to call or stroll in the front entrance. Two dogs stop and lie at my feet. Dogs here seem to like me, the strays identify with me, though I suppose Hitler or Pol Pot could make the same claim.

A woman walks past with a leashed dog that lunges at a stray at my feet.

"Julio!" she calls.

She looks at me as if it's my fault — does she think every stray dog is mine? I keep buying big bottles in the lobby and the old man has to rise each time from watching his tiny TV, he does not approve. More beer! Why does the Canadian not drink wine?

Sumerians in the Fertile Crescent invented beer, for which I thank them, but then they disappeared from the Land of the Civilized Lords. Maybe a connection, maybe they liked the brew too much. I suppose I could demand big bottles of marmalade.

See you there Tuesday.

Four.

Four.

Now is the appointed hour, now it is five, now it is nine.

Trying to seduce a young American woman on the train to Naples is somehow more honourable than paying a prostitute in Pompeii. Wherein lies the logic? Abby and I were walking and kissing after the train, strangers on a train, two brains connected in the huge station's glass walls.

Two parts of the brain — the insula (in the cerebral cortex) and the striatum — are players in processing intense pleasure and the development of sexual desire into love. The striatum is related to our leaning to drug addiction, our obsessive desire to see more of that person (or drug), that person paramount in our thoughts, her face like a sunny movie in my head. The cerebral cortex calls the shots on memory and perfume, the charged glance and smell of skin, the strata of clothes strewn, the sound of a cork popping as a Stratocaster plays, or whales breathing and diving in the bay, images that linger, that play in the sea in the head.

South Park is on television in Italian, so I assume the match is done and it didn't go well. The Germans pass my wicker table, still speaking solemnly about the economy: "They can no more balance a budget than balance a piano on the end of their nose, but I will admit they can make coffee!"

I touched Abby's neck and smelled her skin, was allowed a view under her blouse, but I will never quite get under that enticing black bra. Abby decides I must wait, or something happened to her in Naples. How to know? I can't live like this much longer. I thought she'd make me whole somehow, keep the pieces together, she would be my duct tape.

All these people packing the street and shops: how do they do it? They move directly, they know what they want! They function as if they designed themselves and no need for duct tape.

Maybe she is delayed or ill, I worry she has been robbed in Naples or hit by the same model of Pontiac I used to have, and I'll never know. I wait hours at my table, sick with the knowledge of failure, that yet another person is standing me up. It's too many in a row, I'm not designed to take this. As the dispirited boxer said, *No más*. Something has changed in me since Natasha. I have been resilient in the past, tough, even callous, but now I have no defences, a child, an infant to a milky breast, welcome, you have been born into a puzzling world full of slaps and kisses and nipples and crowbars. *No más*.

Do you think there will come a day when I will hang out

with someone calmly and happily as part of a normal day? To just walk and maybe hold hands and look up at the flawless blue sky and perhaps an eagle there in eyesight, a blithe eagle circling on thermals and we agree that really is something or maybe in Sorrento we glimpse the sea through the crumbling Greek Arch, hey let's take a picture, and perhaps a cold drink on the beach, foaming surf and a bar with shady umbrellas where the woman says six euros, special price for you, and the next place way out on the pier, breakers rolling right under us, they charge only four euros for a good beer, *some special price*, and ha ha we laugh because it's funny, the world is funny and sunny, and kiss kiss, and maybe a movie or floodlit green fountains or mottled ruin or a bus on a cliff and it could be love, it could work, it could be a pipe dream or it could be fantastic. But if I ever use the word *closure* or say, *I'm blessed, truly blessed*, then you have permission to kick me.

"What's the story, morning glory?"

"What's up, fool?" Ray-Ray and Tamika stroll toward my wicker table.

"Look what the cat dragged in. Pull up a chair." I buy them anything they want (name your poison), happy to see them, to break my funk, my lowered spirits, happy to have their company at my lonely table in Fortress Europe.

Stucco walls line the road. A yellow sky smeared like oil paint and above that yellow smear perches a mumbling thunderstorm. No rain in weeks and now we drink inside a giant jagged tunnel, light waning after a bright boiling day. As the new weather alters the air's colour, the street moves through many shades of mauve, and finally it rains, canary-coloured plaster going dark in rain, in welcome rain.

Thunder and lightning reverberate over the ruins and the volcano and my moods; our nervous hotel dog opens his jaws and speaks to the sparking sky, loose dogs loping everywhere. In wicker chairs we watch the wild sky and street and rain dogs.

The dogs running free make Tamika jumpy. When we walk to a piazza, dogs trot out of nowhere, surrounding us while we seek a bank machine that will take our cards. Ray-Ray needs to move small payments from one credit card to another to keep the cards alive like premature infants. I remember doing the same when I got out of school and was unemployed, courting my wife, paying the bar tab with plastic and keeping the cash others threw in for their part of the bill.

"Damn! That's not right!" Tamika exclaims, swinging her head on a swivel to track the dogs. "Where are all the dogs coming from? I don't mind them on leashes, but I don't like them running free."

It is perhaps a naive or racist notion, but I had assumed Tamika would be in favour of creatures being free. I'm free, I'm no longer married, and how odd that concept seems.

Ray-Ray stops to talk with every black he sees in Italy. He grabs my arm, asks me, "Where is *Nowhere*?"

"What do you mean?"

"Those guys I just talked to say they live in Nowhere."

"They're homeless? They live on the street?"

"No! A real place, man, they said they live in Nowhere."

"A place called Nowhere."

"It's way up north, man, they said it's a good place, I should come visit."

"It's a country up north?"

"Yeah, man, way up there."

"You mean Norway?"

"Yes, man! Nowhere! It's a good place. I should go up and see Nowhere, I don't dig it here in Italy." Ray-Ray lowers his voice to a confidential tone. "In fact, I think I'll leave tomorrow."

"Give it a chance."

"Man, they like me way more in China. People bow to you! China is smart, they might be communist, but they're business-minded, they know you're there for a reason, and they want you there. If you need something they want to help! And the Chinese love basketball, man, they thought I was NBA, girls wanted to know if I knew Kobe Bryant and Yao Ming and them. They don't like me here in Italy, so why should I give it a chance? Italy is closed, man, just a way different mentality, folks here don't have a heart the size of a pea."

Ray-Ray has disappeared a number of times when our group is on the Metro (he had lost his pass) or in the halls of a museum, falls behind the group and vanishes. He says he ran into some great people from Nigeria who had a barbershop in Rome; in fact, they owned the whole block, all Nigerians. He likes that idea. While we gazed at vases and ancient marble he spent the whole day happily hanging around the barbershop, drinking beer and chatting with all who came and went. They could tell Ray-Ray had not spent all his life in Nigeria, his face was smooth and unmarked and not showing hardship. He was in a great mood after, he liked his barbershop hours better than strolling the grand boulevards or standing under dead saints and pillars and great marbles.

In Italy we walk such crowded cities and underground grottoes stuffed with grinning skeletons crowded in bunks and deep hallways like mine shafts and then on trains we see so much empty countryside between the big cities. Millions crammed tight into projects and slums and bulldozers pushing mountains of trash, yet so much wide open country just past the door, just down the road a piece. I suppose the same is true in Canada, the same all around the world.

We don't want *lebensraum*, we shun the orchard above the stream and we love cement curbs and peeling walls. If we are not born inside the city we move there as soon as we can, we follow our bliss, our desire for hustle and excitement and dumpsters and rats in stairwells and staple guns and opiates, to hang out on a concrete corner or line up for a bonehead job and pick each other's pocket and scent doorways with the ammonia of our urine and exist without leafy trees or pink blossoms, our desire to avoid God and nature and to take elevators, to ride machines climbing toward boxes set atop boxes like bone ossuaries set in the sky, our manic desire to stand on each other's head to the soundtrack of machines on the walls and machines past the window circling the sky and machines rumbling the ground under our feet.

Ray-Ray said earlier that he felt sick, maybe he caught something in China or on the plane.

I ask, "How you doing today?" I shouldn't have joked that they probably spit in our food.

"Man, thank you for asking. I could be dying and that dude running this show doesn't care." Ray-Ray says, "I've had it, man, I'm leaving tomorrow." He forgets that he says these words to me every day.

•

Once again to the trains, all the trains in the gloaming and buses beneath olive valleys and aqueducts and trefoil arches in plumes of diesel. Factions of our group always on the move like vapour, up and down, back and forth over roses and skeletons, changing towns and minds, changing trains and tunnels, crowded platforms and subterranean stairs and no seats on the trains and such sweaty carriages under the looming volcano, and cactus and lava fields and burning rock once taken for portals to hell.

A shantytown burns below a freeway (is it a Roma enclave?) and I know I could drip my endless sweat over the class-war conflagration and easily extinguish the flames. I have never sweated like this, I'm sure our collective sweat will pool on the floor of the train until our ankles are deep in sweat, in aqua vitae, the salt water of life.

Naples, the city streets at night — ah, I can still conjure the scent of crazed Vespas in the heaped garbage and brilliantined pickpockets — then to pull ourselves from a mattress at dawn for another woozy train to Pompeii's sun-bright ruin, and a milk-train back again to Naples in sore shoes to climb a narrow thirteenth-century alley of cobbles and scooters and skewback abutments and we dodge the Vespas and wolf down the best food ever laid against my tongue.

The Naples station, where I last saw Abby, makes me feel like a loser, the Naples station a sad axis. I buy a ticket at a machine. All the redolent names, Pompeii, Herculaneum, Sorrento, Amalfi, Positano, and soon we will be back in the bosom of peach-coloured Rome.

We climb on the last train and down the aisle. I take a seat on the right. Ray-Ray takes a seat on the left of the aisle. Ray-Ray tells me he is the second son of second wife, he says this is lower status than the eldest son. This was years back, in Nigeria. I never know what to believe, what is real.

Ray-Ray says to me, "Bet you five euro no one will sit by me."

Ray-Ray chases all the chambermaids and is a bit of a con man, but he is a cream puff at heart and he loves life, loves the world. But he is so tall and black; the Italians fear his looks.

"Will you take my bet?" Ray-Ray asks me. "Five euro."

Sure, why not. Someone will sit by him. The seats around me fill up. The rest of the train fills. The feeling of pure will as the train shunts out of the station, every seat taken except for three empty blue seats around Ray-Ray. I pay him his five euro.

In Rome we traverse train station tunnels and subway stairs and we stumble up into ground-level sunlight and cross the street to a tiny corridor of mirrors that passes for a hotel lobby, mirrors offering so many puzzled burnt versions of me coming through the door.

This narrow hallway seemed lunatic the very first time I entered, funhouse mirrors and a frenzied school group trying to check in, herds of children screaming and climbing heaps of crocodile luggage — Italy seemed crazy, but now to my eyes the mirrored enclosure is endearing, normal.

Monique at the reception desk hasn't moved from her perch and she sends me to my same room, the sunny terrace and fat ceramic urns waiting at the top of the stairs, which pleases me, as if Monique the French woman and Marco the American intern kept the room empty and waiting just for me, even though I hadn't reserved it or asked. And that lovely feeling, at the sink washing dark mountain grapes that float and bump in water pooled in my hands, as if cupping a cold stream, chilling my fingers. Rome! Grapes! See, I am not always complaining, not always morbid.

•

Eve finds me for a drink and chat on my high terrace. Eve comes and goes from city to city, my cousin is contained, I know nothing of the rest of her life, of Switzerland's dark peaks and fireworks by the quicksilver lake, the Jardin Anglais, the weed and eau-de-vie. I'm living near the top of a tree; I stare out at Rome and the green parrot in the tall trees pleases me; trees sway in green hours and I water my flowers again. No sign of the smoking Spanish woman in the atrium, but my orphans and nuns below make me happy.

Eve agrees with me. "It's so beautiful here that it makes me happy; the colours, that sun every morning. But I have trouble with happiness; I'm suspicious of it. My mother always said I was a very serious child. I should eat something. You're always laughing at me, mocking me."

"I am not mocking you." She always thinks the worst of me. I swear on a stack o' bibles that I am more mocked than mocking.

A light dusting of freckles on my cousin's lovely skin, like an animal imprint. I like them. She hates the freckles, uses lemon juice to fade them.

My cousin had two periods in one month. Short cycles, she says, and lots of blood. One day I saw her wince from a cramp and gave her some of my painkillers. She washes her sheets in her shower and dries them on my terrace, which has far more room and sun.

"You must wash blood quickly before it sets. Do you ever think about what it's like to have a period, to have blood flow from you? What if your penis was gushing blood? Do you ever think about what it's like for women?"

"I certainly will think about it now."

She says it so casually, but now I can't lose an image of my cock gushing blood. I give her raisins for iron, give her a bottle of stout, which also has iron.

"Did you know," she says, "that the beer bottle was invented in 1850?"

"I did not know that."

"What did frat boys do before 1850? Is the chemist's open still? I am out of womanly aids."

We walk streets to the river and river walls; at the top of a dizzyingly high river wall, far above the Tiber, a couple reclines lazily on a bench dappled by plane trees, olive-coloured trees that look tortured, the skin flensed or peeling.

"The Beautiful Scooter Couple," whispers Eve, as if pointing out a doe and fawn that might bolt before we can steal their picture, as if pointing out minor Carnaby Street gods. The Beautiful Scooter Couple's jaunty red Vespa leans on its kickstand while tiny Italian cars speed past, gleaming and frantic.

The young woman gazes at a book while her boyfriend snoozes, his head resting lightly in her lap as she reads, a fashionably sleepy couple lounging at the top of a perilous wall, a steep embankment hewn of stone blocks, *mattoni*, and the sunny river far below.

I envy this fabulous boy and girl, calmly part of their world, part of the bench and wall and shade trees — trunks muscled, priapic, the odd skin of the trees mottled like military camouflage — the boy and girl so relaxed with each other while just inches away crazed Roman traffic assembles itself and tears away again and the Tiber flows under the high stone wall, our Italian couple perched at the edge of a precipice in such peace. They have such easy ownership of themselves!

•

The Tiber below the precipice is a discouraging yellow-green, but fish are alive in the rilled murk. Melville called the Tiber a ditch, Hawthorne saw pease-soup, and David Garrick termed it a scurvy draught, but I have affection for the purling river.

Breezes push the surface of the Tiber upstream in silent V shapes, as if the muscled river wants to swim overtop its own current.

Eve hums almost inaudibly, "Let's go down…Funkytown."

From the heights we stare down. In a bridge's shade stand shirtless men fishing an ancient river. Eve studies the men's shoulders and sun-lined features, Eve says, "Caesar, Nero, Caligula, or Christ, the fisher of men, any Pope, any time, you'd see the same faces down here by the water."

The shirtless men fish with red bait waiting on wax paper like vivid hamburger or crushed meat, some kind of blood language to the fish. Despite having been warned of robberies and thieves, I enjoy exploring the paths that hug the shore right at water level.

Thanks so much for putting that song in my head: *Funkytown!*

At the bench atop the cliff the scooter boy naps in the girl's lovely lap, and then the boyfriend wakes and opens his eyes, looks about slowly, *where am I*, sleepy as a cat. Bemused at his befuddled expression she lowers her book. He says something in her ear and she lifts her face and laughs and as she laughs she pulls his arm tighter to her, a heartbreaking move to some of those watching, surely she must know that.

They rise up, rise and stroll to their red Vespa, their scooter named after a wasp. The scooter and front wheel look so delicate.

Her boyfriend puts on his helmet, but first she opens a tiny juice-box for her sleepy spaceman, oh, she taps the straw oh so lightly against the juice-box, she is so tender, convincing the tiny straw it must please move just inside where the juice waits for us, and she pierces the membrane so lightly and lifts the juice to his mouth, a love letter to the pink tongue waiting in the opening of his black helmet. His face is not visible, a hidden knight; I watch her, just her waiting by the scooter.

"You're staring," says Eve.

Oh.

De mortuis nil nisi bonum; of the dead say nothing but good. In a few weeks the Beautiful Scooter Couple will die on the Amalfi coast's narrow highway, a tunnel curve, their scooter bouncing like a toy off the front of a bus I ride, the couple above another kind of cliff on the coast, a sea-cliff that leans like a naval prow over the curling surf and cobalt water.

But this moment we are deep in the heart of Rome's kingdom of private walls, where the boyfriend drinks the proffered fruit juice, her billet-doux, her juice in his throat and his stomach and then the young woman brings her long legs to the seat behind him and her arms and her legs cling like a twin to his body and the noise of the tiny engine as they vanish into Rome's stunning riptides of traffic.

This Roman girlfriend gives me pause, her image lingers in my head, her tender hands cupping the juice-box. Has anyone ever been so tender and careful with me?

One person. Natasha said we were twins, but then my twin turned away in a far city. That lightning moment of liberal loathing and those malicious months that follow, your body delivering some constant terrible product (*call now for your free trial!*).

A message came from Natasha a few weeks before she turned away from me:

> *Hi charming boy, miss you, very nice that you called while I was on my bike in the country; I can't wait to see you, get here as soon as you can. You are needed regarding pressing country matters. I will be your own personal therapist very soon; we can lie down on the blue quilt and talk about your troubling dreams. Love, your Natasha*
>
> *P.S. I'm listening to* Veedon Fleece; *you lent it to me, remember?*

I remember too much. That's the problem. Sun through Venetian blinds on an easy chair, her tube amp and guitar, metal gleaming in the light, every detail delineated of the amp's grey herringbone grill and her voice soft: *When I lost my baby.*

But I won't lose my mind, won't follow Natasha, thinking I can bring her back, I refuse to be some mawkish Orpheus descending a mall escalator into the hipster underworld.

I like the walkways along the river, though the sidewalks disappear in the spring floods. At the café at night Eve orders a dish called "strangled priests," she observes that I am like her mother, putting butter on everything. It is odd to consider how much butter I have swallowed in my life, how many gallons, barrels, trucks, ocean-going tankers.

Eve tells us of the time she entered a tiny taverna deep in the south of Italy, asked a man for directions, and an ancient woman spit on my cousin's bare arm.

"She spit on you for real?" asks Ray-Ray.

Eve says amiably, "I was wearing a top that showed too much skin."

Usually she carried two shawls: one for her shoulders and one for her head, in case she was going into a church or formal event, but she didn't think she needed a shawl in this shop.

"Man, no one spit on me in China," says Ray-Ray. "Seriously."

Perhaps that is why she prefers the north of Italy. She is unsure of the south; likes the Alps, but says her favourite place in the world is Venice, with its burnt opera house and blackened squid in seasick palaces. Not dear dirty Naples or Sicily's dry hills.

On the terrace I stand and survey my kingdoms, my Holy Roman Empires, another Pope I am, a new King of Rome!

We eat and drink and walk and I realize I missed the streets and lovely murky rivers to the sea, what is borne by the chartered river past the red palazzos, the peach-coloured walls and cheetah shadows and forlorn Italian faces and frank sexual fashions. And I missed my cousin. I tell Eve of the angry prostitute in Pompeii and of Abby's no-show.

She says, You are such a fool with women, but she listens and laughs at my tales.

Stand on a patio chair on my terrace and look toward the river; there is a glass and brass cupola and a huddle of polished white statues in situ on one high corner of a building jutting out like a ship above the Vatican north wall. I am a spy in a tower: who are these odd statues on a lofty ledge to the east of me?

My statues are nowhere near St. Peter's high violet Basilica, my statues stand on an isolated corner in some plaintive ex-Catholic exile, their perch high with birds and helicopters, set on a corner far from the centres of power. Who are they? Perhaps the statues are a choir of strangled Popes or pretenders or disbarred lawyers or dubious patron saints or usurers hanging cozeners, bare legs tiptoeing their own cliff edge.

Here is the odd thing: I search all avenues under the wall, but I can never spot this mysterious group from below on the street. From my door I turn left and follow the vast wall, which should lead me speedily to them, but there is no sight of their faces above. My statues only exist when I look at them from my rooftop terrace, the statues are not visible at ground level. Am I the only one who sees them? Look, their milk eyes turned to the city, but if I run down the stairs they no longer exist.

I am fascinated by this lonely lovely group of statues. They look thuggish, hip, look like they played their first show at CBGB in the Bowery in 1975. Why can I not find them when I'm walking on the street? Is there an app? Should I sneak inside the Vatican walls to look for the dead white saints?

The Mexican rock climber in our hotel went over the wall for a lark and was caught immediately by the Pope's Swiss Guard; hard to take them seriously in their court jester garb, but they are extremely serious, they have clout. They threatened to kick Father Silas and his entire art group out of the country and as penance Father Silas had to rush the rock climber to the airport and push him onto the next flight to Mexico; within hours of dropping like a spider down the Vatican walls the climber disappeared from Italy and he almost took the rest of the group with him.

My cousin and others in the group make a day trip to the beach at Ostia. Such heat, not used to it, air wavering in heat, like fumes dancing over a nozzle at a gas pump. My cousin's sunburnt shoulders are so red and tender, and in the evening we are altered, groggy, as if felled by sunstroke, *coup de soleil*.

I have a round plastic container from the discount store, soothing cold cream, *crema corpo*, for her tender shoulders. She opens her blouse in my room. It's better if I don't know such things, if I am not allowed to see light on her.

In the amazing ruins we eat figs and apples and *zampone*, stuffed pig trotters, in the amazing ruins of temples, of marriage. There stands my cousin and her legs and lingering glances. Do not go near there, do not follow her frock in the frescoes as wild dogs run past, *mondo cane*.

Man is his dizzy desire and I desire knowledge of her bare shoulders, that curved planet, that new home. Her neck part of a naked crescent, a lovely curve from naked earlobe to naked shoulder. Why do I love her neck so, that nexus of delicate ear and fine hair and shampoo scent, the shoulders, the skin, the jaw and cheek, the shadows and perfume; it has everything, right there. I can hide my face there; what a world exists just there!

She asks for lotion for her skin. I approach my cousin with a round container of lotion from an Italian shop, approach a planet, once distant, now in view in Rome, a room with a view. Her shoulders glow in the spacecraft window, closer, closer to touch, a new looming planet, the lightest touch, my fingers like landing craft and her intake of breath.

Crema corpo, rovitalizanta aloe vera. Rubbing her tender shoulders and her neck, her back, lightly down her spine to her round hips. I worry she'll get mad, but I can feel her body move nicely to my touch. She stretches her neck and shoulders, murmuring pleasant sounds, moves into my pressure as a cat will.

I will not lie with her, but I keep rubbing more lotion, her shoulders and back and lower and lower down her back, on the sides of her hips and brief forays near her belly and a bit lower below her navel, teasing, testing, lower and lower, circling closer and closer, so close, but never all the way.

My cousin says, "You have such a calming effect on me."

"Me?" My mind is always racing and my life is chaos.

"You seem very calm." The East German woman travelling in the west of Ireland said the same thing to me, used a German word for calm.

My hands wander, my mind wanders, catacombs and tunnels and travel, planes, airports and tunnels, my mind inside her, the lines where her strap was in the sun, the lines and borders, the line and colour of her face, the lineament of her eye and cheekbone skin. I think of the old woman in the south of this country spitting on Eve's skin. Country matters.

My cousin gasps when my fingers stray and find where she is wet, my fingers connect with her brain, a direct tendril, another hidden passageway, her breath quiet as the mountain town that makes you sing.

My hand wrecked a marriage, wrecked unions, and I killed the Beautiful Scooter Couple, and I listen to the Fleshtones, their best album, *Roman Gods*. At night when I get under the covers my cousin seems awake, but she mutters a language I can't understand.

What did you say?

She kicks my shin or calf. Is she being impish? She pulls at my hair. How to interpret this? She goes back to sleep, breathing rhythmically.

The next day she laughs with joy at my account. I kicked you? I spoke gibberish? She recalls none of it. She leaves my room like a sleepwalker. Soon we will all leave Rome. We move, we sin, we confess, we fly to and fro, we are on earth, then we are in the heavens, then we are not, we are on earth, then we are flung through the heavens, then we are not in the heavens.

And she loves me, then she loves me not, she becomes another woman who says in a doorway or in an airport, says I'd hate to lose touch with you, you know I love you in so many ways. Another one who says, It's been wonderful, as did Natasha, Natasha my buried past, another quiet buried city.

"Don't be depressed," my cousin says, "I know you'll be depressed." Or did Natasha in Canada say that? All these people living in your past as if in a nearby apartment building and waiting for you to get there. The anatomy of desire and the anatomy of loss — I have them mixed up in my depressed, sunburnt head.

My cousin looks pale in the train window. My cousin is in my room, no, she is gone for good this time, she is walking a narrow lane miles away, she is coming downhill in another country, she walks a line between whitewashed homes that have been there forever, a lane curving this way and that and quiet as a suture. She leaves my room, leaves the station, leaves the airport and somewhere a waitress carries a big curved glass, walking a beeline just for me.

In Pompeii last week the hunched train lurched forward and the steel wheels did not slice off the dog's head. Perhaps like the dog I'll persist, survive. Perhaps the terrier did hear and heed me, perhaps the terrier knows many languages, will travel to Russia and China, will find our chambermaids in the white stone of Croatia. The sunny peak and the valley depth so close together. The Scooter Couple is so beautiful, yet they die high above the charming sea, the shallow coast, they fall from the ledge, the ledger.

•

Late in a trip: that urge to simply throw away your luggage. In my last days in Rome I grow obsessed by my group of statues peopling a ledge, this shadow empire. I stare out from my terrace and I pace back and forth on blisters under the high walls of the Vatican; before I leave Rome I must find where these milk-eyed figures live above us, these stone gods that only my eyes see.

I borrow binoculars from Marco the American intern and wonder if Marco could be our hotel thief. Marco knows the halls and exits, knows all the rooms and hours, has all the keys on their brass hooks, and Marco will vanish across the ocean at summer's end.

As I focus the binocs on the statues they turn their heads to look toward me and lean to speak with each other, as if posing for an album cover, say early Blues Magoos or Velvet Underground. One statue wears Bob Dylan sunglasses, one resembles Lou Reed, another pats his perfectly curled hair. They whisper to each other and one statue turns his hips, wags a pale erection at me, his Roman good luck charm, a large statue gripping his generous white phallus with two hands far above milling streets crowded with tourists all dressed in Tilley and tombstone motley.

We meet in the street when it is dark and my new gang of ghostly statues brings me along on an illicit mission. The statues are not strangled Popes, they are not exiled saints, their ambitions are far simpler: they are lard thieves on the hunt, they steal used grease, fryer oil. The statue with Lou Reed ringlets is the ringleader. We gather in the alley behind a famous restaurant; money to be had in rancid lard and biodiesel, the price in our favour, the price climbs daily and they know someone who knows someone who moves grease, who will take this filth from our hands.

Cats rub our legs in the long alley. Wild cats roam Rome's ancient sunken ruins while dogs run free in Pompeii's train station, and this speaks to something about each city: Rome is feline and Pompeii is canine.

My cousin's voice, my cousin's song while our kayaks cut along smartly and her voice carried over the water. Dig in the paddle's blade and the kayak responds. At the shore she swam into jellyfish, Eve recoiling violently to escape, but she rose from the sea with the touch of jellyfish stings becoming vivid red scratches, small red whiplashes lacing her right shoulder and breast, a kind of venom in the stingers, strange asps touching her breast. In our room she dabbed toothpaste on the burns to soothe them, Eve afraid to go in the sea. Was it the long tentacles of a Portuguese man-of-war?

The man who rented us such bright kayaks said, I'm not saying I'm against them or asking to change anything, what I ask is that existing laws be enforced. They are illegal. You do not have to live here, you visit here only as if Italy is a museum, a theme park; you have no idea what it is to live here, how bad it is. It is not a theme park. There are too many foreigners, too many gypsies, too many Arabs and Africans. The northern countries don't care, England and Germany simply send them back to us, but we can't take them all. And our young have such little hope these days, our young must leave, they must leave while these others pour in. How can that be? We must close the borders or lose our way of life, lose our civilization.

Yes of course, I agree. Europe will surely implode, Europe will sink under frivolous debt, everyone must sell their Ferraris, their Audis, Europe will no longer exist and no longer will grocery clerks shout and throw the receipt at me because I don't have exact change.

In Europe he looks at me oddly. I know he's right, I know mine is a foreigner's version of this country, but it's the only version I have.

In the Hotel Europa Ray-Ray leans drunkenly at the bar, Ray-Ray says, "Oh I *love* women," as if it's the saddest sentence in the world.

Europe leans at a bar and my cousin passes on Rollerblades in the rain, her striking face in a crowd, hair wet, arms out for balance, legs looking longer for being up on the tiny wheels. No pads on her bare skin and I worry. She is learning something, a brain harnessed to flesh, or is it flesh harnessed to brain? Both brain and body can be lovely prisons.

Every day we drank frothy juice made from blood oranges, such a favourite since the group has been in Rome, but for two of us the vivid juice speaks also of the knife party (*killer party, man*).

At night I listen to Polly Jean Harvey and her low voice and words seems fraught, loaded, travelling to remembered places, certain shared shrines and rivers, and can someone else sense these places are in your eye again?

At night I see an older Italian woman walking two Jack Russell terriers and I must stop to talk.

Good dog, I say, petting one under the neck.

No, she says, *not* a good dog. They are unusually friendly for Jack Russells and they lick my hands. The Italian PM says his hands are clean, *mani pulite*.

In the alley of grease we have our duties. If anyone troubles us, my role is to be confused, a lost tourist who speaks English only (seems easy), though the statues insist that ours are only venal sins and the police have their hands full with murders and the mob and anarchists and Ultras and *bunga bunga* parties.

The Italian PM must pay his estranged wife a hundred thousand euro a day; how can he have that much and we don't? The grease in our alley reeks. Lewd Priapus is with us, but he is not doing well, is not popular, his huge phallus gets in the way of lugging the sloppy plastic drums.

"Clearly he is of little use in enterprises such as these."

Pliny the Elder died rescuing people from the volcano and here I am with greasy hands stealing casks of lard, looking for scraps others might leave us. Pliny was noble, sailed a fast cutter to find his friends. *Fortune goes to the brave!* he bellowed into the wind. Now there was a man! I must make sharp changes in my life, be like Pliny.

No, you are wrong, insists Priapus beside me in the alley. No, I knew Pliny well and he had grown quite corpulent, his weight and his knees troubling him, he died sitting down and his friends abandoned him in the pumice. He was no real admiral, he was given the naval command in Misenum as a patronage appointment, as a friend of the emperor Vespasian.

But Pliny sailed across the bay to rescue his good friends!

Yes, he did, Pliny was brave, but the wind pinned his cutter to the beach so he was trapped and there was no rescue; they waited and feasted and drank flagons and slept and snored loudly until the volcano drove them from the dwelling.

White pumice fell the first day, and showers of hot cinders and rocks. The doors were blocked yards deep, as if by a blizzard, they had to force their way out, with pillows tied to their heads as helmets. Roof tiles cracked in the heat, villas taking to flame, you can't know what it was like. On the burning ground Pliny collapsed and he asked a slave to kill him.

No, that can't be true, I insist.

Yes, yes, Pliny said he couldn't breathe, he sat down and

couldn't stand up and the party was afraid of suffocation, of being smothered in layers of lava and ash, fire and stones raining on their heads, they thought it the end of the world, they walked away and left Pliny out there in the cinders, laid him on one of his own sails for a last bed. They are as bad as we are, sinners all of us. Don't be disappointed.

I'll try to not be disappointed. My cousin leaves me over and over, on a bicycle, in a kayak, but she has come back over and over, calm as Janus, divided as Janus. We made a bed of a sail, a bed of the grass and earth, pillows under her, the same pillow tied to Pliny's head. Think of life as the fun between heart attacks. I see another firefly hover, a tiny lit bulb in the air, a tiny lit bulb near my brain, and I feel charmed, an omen. The past was so good and I have such faith in the future. I love the future just because it is so nicely vague; the future's so vague I have to wear shades.

The pale statues buy knock-off sunglasses from North African street pedlars. Priapus says, "Keep an eye out for that crazy little bear. He's scratched up all the trees and last week the little bugger scarfed my burrito."

I can't stop thinking of Pliny's undignified death on the burning plain. A tall American man glares at our procession of talkative statues lugging drums of grease past the Vatican.

"Now what in Sam hell?"

He turns to his wife. "When we get back home, at church?" His Dockers hold a beautiful crease, he looks like he once flew jets and commanded aircraft carriers.

"Yes, honey?" says his spouse.

"I'm not giving another damn cent."

His wife stands frozen, her eyes linger on Priapus's dangling gifts. Can this elephant trunk be real? He could pick up peanuts with it.

Near the wife's feet a swarthy man lies face down as if the sidewalk is a movie screen to be studied; the swarthy man refuses to look up at the crowds milling and wheeling by the Vatican walls, but his hand is stretched out for alms.

Dark lumps push out from his scalp: are they a true disease? The lumps resemble small wooden knobs attached to his head, like stained knobs fashioned from smooth dark-grained wood. In Rome we are learning about craft, art. Can I have confidence, can I believe in his affliction of the head? Can I have faith?

The Bible makes some obscure point about a camel and the eye of a needle, Jesus kicked over the salvers and tables of the money-changers. A woman knocks the Pope down in front of St. Peter's, a group of radical women lift their tops in front of St. Peter's, they show their naked breasts as a protest about breasts, breasts protesting about breasts, another group of women shouts, *Manten tus rosarios fuera de mis ovarios*, keep your rosaries off our ovaries.

A man bloodies the PM while shaking hands, and we all line up for gelato the colour of tulip petals. I may join Mr. Berlusconi's People of Liberty Party. Faith or belief is too tender a thing for me, I must trust it to a larger organization. It's a non-stop party, I gather; the politician leans to offshore accounts and underage models, complains his petulant wife.

A mayor of a seaside town south of Rome is murdered for trying to stop illegal developments on the seashore; there are men with guns and suitcases of money and they want more suitcases of money and they want to build more apartments on the seashore.

Is the man prone on the sidewalk a gypsy? A Turk? Croatian? Albanian? He might also like suitcases of money. We tiptoe around his extended arm wondering whether the doorknob lumps on his head are real or a con job to elicit sympathy and more coins. Others tell me this mottled man has been doing this for years, they always see this cousin of Lazarus the leper, his prone body part of the sidewalk scenery. Doves gather around us like my doubts. Like religion, like relations, how to know what is real?

Before she left, my cousin lay pale as a statue under my hand, my white body creme over her back, and this Lazarus lying on the sidewalk on his face dark as a collier, one arm angled out to beg, waiting for the dogs to lick his sores. Is he one of the People of Liberty? Is Lazarus invited to the *bunga bunga* parties in Milan to eat what falls from the table?

We must move on to our reward, our cash money, we move our drums of grease across the burning pumice. And the statues have a gig later tonight playing Fleshtones covers and some R&B in the cellar near Via Cola di Rienzo; we get one free drink; I'll sit in on harmonica, try out a Bullet mic with my new silver chromatic, the one the Pope failed to give me.

The street by the cellar is named after Cola di Rienzo, a rebel and Roman tribune who, like Mussolini, wanted to rule Rome and unify Italy as one kingdom. One Pope had him imprisoned, but he was freed by the next Pope. One mob loved him and one mob burnt his palace and chased him. Cola ran in disguise, but they caught him and cut him apart. So many knives and we have such thin skin. Now people shop for purses and shoes and walk little dogs on his street, on Via Cola di Rienzo.

The other statues are resentful of Priapus, the way he loves to show off his epic gland.

"Last time we bring him along," mutters one statue.

"He's going to ruin my fifty-dollar buzz," adds another.

"I get tired of looking at that donkey dick."

"What a douche."

"Yeah guys, you know, I think I'm gonna jet. Peace out."

We resent Priapus, yet we have a strange pride in just knowing him. You should see this thing! We even tell our wives and girlfriends about his gifts, which might be dangerous if they become curious to know more, to become intimately acquainted with such a formidable phallus.

The swarthy Lazarus lies begging face down on a wide sidewalk below the Vatican walls, tourists forced to step around his one outstretched arm and body. They cross the street to join a lineup at the bustling gelato shop. Well, which flavour do you choose?

At night our mouths fill with dough and oil and wine in a republic of noisy hours. I consume Italy and Italy consumes me, devours me like a woman, I love it, love the wild sea and crazy cliffs and hilltop vistas and then the smudged slums on the horizon like magic, spires vibrating over the rails like a charcoal etching and we step off the train into the tremors and treasures of each Italian city.

The skinny hotel thief must have tagged me; in the mirror I found blood and a scratch on my head and by the morning I had a very minor shiner. Was he wearing a ring? The scratch angled from the corner of my left eye and up and over my forehead.

I'm a night owl, I saw a figure drop onto my terrace; I am territorial; moving without thought I tackled him. He fell easily, surprised by me, but he rolled to his feet like a cat and in that motion may have hit out with a quick fist, though I have no memory of a blow.

Then the thin hotel thief disappeared, a wraith running hand and foot up the wobbly lattice of flowers and across the roof to leap the gap to the next roof. I did not follow the thief and I was wrong about Marco the American intern and Elena the smoking Spanish woman; I wondered if they were guilty and clearly I am no Sherlock Holmes. But I am the only one to know the thief Barabbas; I pushed his solid chest, brushed his shirt, we touched each other, intimate, connected as if by a rope, even though he flew home over the Roman roof.

I will fly home from Europe eventually, I think, but I've lost my sense of home. I can't sleep after the fight with the thief, I am awake all night, my head an adding machine fuelled by adrenalin. *Nostos*, to return home to be killed in the clawfoot bath, a knife in the leg. I miss my family, my children, that concrete manifestation of a home. Who murdered all the Popes? What makes a home? Drops of my own blood lie on the terrace tiles. Can you change your spots if you don't really want to change? Groups of us in an eternal city avoiding eternal questions.

Like my aunt, Angelo the hotel owner warns me to stay away from pickpockets and gypsies; Angelo won't serve them in any of his businesses.

"How does one tell they are gypsies?" I ask.

"That's easy. They *look* like gypsies. They all have TB and they spit."

My aunt says, "True Italians have nice straight legs, but the gypsies and Albanians have crooked legs, from the knee down their legs curve out like a chair. I can tell who is who by looking at their knees and calves. And the Albanians are especially arrogant, while Italians are modest."

I climb the stairs to my room to pack my bags. I am forced to abandon Rome and my campaign to be Pope has come to nothing. I blame Tom Hanks; Tom Hanks really dropped the ball. I hope the next Pope will be better than this German one. The slaves escape from Egypt and aspire to middle management, to the soul's erosion in the service sector; did I leave a CD in the hotel room? I must find Irena the chambermaid and give her a good tip, a gift for her work. She is Croatian; I assume she is not a gypsy. Rome has been sacked before and the locals worry it is happening again. The woman from Iraq has vanished, visited by her uncle and then she is not seen in the neighbourhood again.

Out on my terrace I hear splashing sounds and gleeful voices below; I peer over the edge. In this insane heat someone has given my orphans a wading pool! This makes me very happy. They will never know that I care, that I watch from far above like a powerless God, that I look out and I am pleased for them and their little wading pool and their oranges.

And now my latest spam email seems apropos. *Dearest My Friend: This is to inform you that in my department we have the sum of 3.5 Million euro ready to transfer to you as you prover to me your humbleness and ready to use the money to help the Orphans in the world. This business is secret.*

Our secret. We are all playful orphans seeking to splash each other. Our needs are simple. Now I need to call a taxi. This final steadfast servant arrives outside the hotel door, the most silent man in Italy, perhaps the only silent man in Italy, and to this driver I gladly hand over my gold and last coins and folded bills of colour, the last of my amusing euros, and the quiet Italian steers me to the portals of an airport named after the genius Leonardo da Vinci, west of Rome (in my head the suicide Vic Chesnutt sings in his sad voice, he was looking, but he didn't find his hospital island).

I'm not happy to leave Italy, but I am happy I came, I saw, I want to come back ASAP, *vorrei un biglietto di ritorno. Ritorno*: that sounds so nice, return to the southern light, the light dusting of freckles on my cousin's lovely skin. Red wine knocked over on a linen tablecloth, blood spilt on the sheets; in memory Eve's world is so vivid. Eve ordered strangled priests, Eve pulled my hair and kicked me in bed, muttering a private language. In Naples or Pompeii, what were they saying, who were they kicking when the volcano buried them? The sea glistering below the volcano, like when skiing, my poor eyes bloodshot from the excess of light and beauty.

In his fiery kingdom Pliny the Elder couldn't walk and was buried in ash, they came back to find his body in the cremated world, the buried world, and now the Beautiful Scooter Couple dies on the narrow Amalfi coast road, the road so narrow, a wall to one side and empty sea air on the other side.

A squadron of cyclists clad in tight fabric passes our bus when we slow and then we pick up speed and pass the slick cyclists on a hill. With their helmets and goggles and long thin limbs they resemble bent crickets.

And scooter and bus race toward each other on the southern coast. Such stunning views, and the musical bus horn like a pleasing trumpet flourish at each corner and tunnel. These enchanted heights by the endless sea; it is clear why the ancients felt close to the gods here. On the bus three local women sit with bags of groceries from the larger town, lemons on sale everywhere. The women chat and do not bother with the view, while I stare down the deep ravines and scary cliffs, drinking in some kind of image burn.

Vespa means wasp. The red scooter weaves quickly through cars, wind in their face, the scooter streaks through a galaxy of colours and roars inside a brief noisy tunnel and they accelerate to pass a slow car and in the next sunny curve the oncoming bus strays slightly over the line and the red scooter bounces off the bumper of the bus and breaks into pieces, the delicate scooter devolves into wheels and side mirrors and the bright orbs of plastic signal lights.

The boyfriend's helmet stays on his head, but the young woman's helmet flies away and she skids across the road, her legs bare, no helmet, the ruins of her dress and torn skin, and the young woman tumbles past the cliff edge like luggage tossed from a balcony.

A gap in the low wall and she is simply gone from us, she falls past the cliff turning in air, her legs up behind her and spinning down toward the green sea and her green eyes aim up at the clouds. The boy sits on the flat road far above as if alone on a stage, in shock, helmet on like a diver, his suit torn like sausage casing; the injured boy studies his broken leg and he lives to know that with his scooter he has killed his beautiful girlfriend, the girl I stared at in Rome, the young woman who tenderly gave his tongue juice as he stood with his helmet still on his head. An idea blooms now in his head, quiet as the white towel that once fell from her hip.

Many Greeks sailed these seas before Christ did, before

Christ became a fisher of men, pirate kings owned this rich coast and invasion fleets waited, nervous men in rows, bombers filling a sky overhead with silk. So many voices calling, the women jostling with their groceries from town, but the bus driver can't open the bus door, bent by the impact to the front of the bus. The insect cyclists pass us again and the boyfriend crawls toward the edge of his stage and we can't climb off the bus to stop him.

The young man in the torn black suit glances around our narrow arena, limestone wall rising to one side, empty air dropping on the other. The young man stares at us, his audience stuck in our seats, at the bus that hit him, the bus that hit her. He raises himself on one good arm, pushes with his good arm, and like a crow he drops over into space to follow her down.

And at that moment I begin to understand the language of race and age and grief, that you can have everything at once and suddenly nothing at once, like an orange bullet train shrieking past your platform in Dublin, blurred windows there in a streak you can touch and then just disturbed air ringing above the tracks, nothing else, the train vanished, but that echo of reverb still hanging.

Both of them fly into space, such a height, and both fall to the sea, our Icarus in his tapered Italian suit and his pretty girlfriend hanging over the sea's glare and boats with white scar wakes and lean sails. They fall from the Path of the Gods and meet again on the ancient beaches pinned at the base of these spectacular cliffs and SITA men in blue shirts wave small cars around the scarred wreck and a TV helicopter comes to eat the night with its pure light.

•

The beautiful couple falls into new worlds and now our plane rises toward another world, now I fly to the far west in a giant machine, we have liftoff, hundreds of rows of passengers thrust west in the night, air clubbing through the gnashing turbines and giant black wheels spinning as they tuck themselves up into the Boeing undercarriage, tires and turbines and rows of seated travellers strapped into a dome of stars and jet contrails and blinking lights that betray our route in the sky to citizens who might gaze up at us from below.

Our plane's route takes us high under a ghostly cupola, our plane moves inside the jet-blue ceiling of a vast starry chapel, but are we amazed?

Instead of being amazed, most of us choose to close our eyes, to drift into a preliminary form of vibrating sleep.

As we voyage to vibrating slumber in that rocketing world the uniformed cabin crew wheels out their clumsy carts to serve all of us uniform trays of meals and drinks. Hundreds of our anonymous heads, over and over, day after day. The crew despise us (*I would they were clyster-pipes*). They don't know what I saw and know of Italy, they can't know the racket and form held inside my quiet head.

While held like a brain inside our plane's strange roiling motion I remember Pico toiling endlessly to serve us in the family hotel and I remember those workers digging out a cellar by hand and bucket and families unloading crates of lemons and peppers and crusty loaves in the tin-roof market at dawn and O my love, will you and this song by the Decemberists always make me sad?

I remember the young woman Irena washing the aqua tiles of my room with her hair (how I wanted her in my bed, the giant white bed floating in my tiny room, but I knew it would never happen) and in Rome they allow no high-rises and my floor tiles mimic peacock colours of the sea, mirror the collapsing wave's complex codes and sine curve and the sea's secret inhabitants.

Luke the Apostle sits beside me on the plane, he's cool, he asks his seatmates, *Who is better, the one who sits or the one who serves*? Every day we take what they offer to us, the cabin crew, the chambermaid, the baker, the waiter, every day we take what they give us, what they serve, muttering *grazie*, *grazie*, as they bend to our needs, our care, our eternal care.

High above that charmed parish of villas lit by milky Italian moonlight, high above our planet, we simply sit. We do not swoon or high-five. We sit and we hold serviettes to our thin lips, listening to George Jones (*put your sweet lips*) or Radiohead's "Pyramid Song" and at our plane's tiny windows our tiny eyes swivel in the crowded heavens above that turbulent benevolent boot of a peninsula (*a little closer to the clyster-pipes*), and we devour our last spicy repast and we turn our heads to those serving and we wonder and hope, if we ask meek as orphans, might there be a little more.

And then we travel back to sleep and we travel back to the New World with ancient dreams of Rome's glory and our lack of glory and Janus giving you the eye in Trastevere and the black shamrock sprayed on a wall by the river and under the Vatican my naked cousin Eve showering on a rooftop and the Pope blessing a woman's sunlit form.

Rome's rooftops so raggedly beautiful, Italy so beautiful, the lunatic world so beautiful in its appetites and addictions; we must embrace the world purely, wantonly, for we passengers are alive and in motion, we are free, we are not lying at the bottom of a cliff. The skinny little thief hit me once in the face and I can live with that.

For here is the plain truth: no knife is driven in our thigh and femur, no rope ties our body to a boat, we are not suffocated by a volcano, and no hot stones fall on our head.

So why are we so fucking *sleepy*? In the name of heaven, why do we not swoon and scream, why do we orphans in the orchard not high-five over and over, why do we not laugh and dance in the aisles of the plane? Though I can't actually dance, but you know, um, just a suggestion.

Acknowledgements

"The Dark Brain of Prayer": prize-winner in *Prairie Fire* Short Fiction Contest and nominated for a National Magazine Award and Western Magazine Award

"Butterfly on a Mountain": published in *Prism International*'s Love and Sex issue

"Knife Party": prize-winner in *Prairie Fire* Short Fiction Contest

"Hospital Island (Wild Thing)": published in *This Magazine*

"The Petrified Forest": published in *The New Quarterly*

"Pompeii Über Alles": published in *Descant*'s Berlin issue

"Hallway Snowstorm": commissioned by Canada Code as part of Vancouver's Winter Olympiad, published in *Salon*, and online in *Numero Cinq*

"Adam and Eve Saved from Drowning": published in *The New Quarterly* and nominated for a National Magazine Award

"The Troubled English Bride": shortlisted for a CBC Literary Award, honourable mention in *The Malahat Review*'s Open Season contest, and winner of *SubTerrain*'s Lush Triumphant creative non-fiction contest

"Party Barge": published in *The New Quarterly*

"Exempt from the Fang (Aircraft Carrier)": published on the site *Numero Cinq*

"Pompeii Book of the Dead": published in *Descant*'s Hidden City issue